King and Prince and Squire stared until their eyes watered. Slowly, almost reverently, young Alaric lowered his flame-drenched hands toward the surface of the center *stone,* sweeping hand and arm across the top like an adze, shearing away the granite as though it were the softest sand. . . .

—"Swords Against the Marluk"
KATHERINE KURTZ

Cugel the Clever had no sooner set foot on the Plain of Standing Stones than he felt a presence behind him. Whirling about, he discovered an asm of eight fangs almost on his heels. A blurred voice emanated from the broad black fore-head, from between the bristling antennae. . . .

—"The Bagful of Dreams"
JACK VANCE

The boy opened his mouth to laugh, and Brak the barbarian shrieked in nameless horror as that mouth began to grow—began to stretch—becoming a huge, spectral monstrosity with sharp, filed teeth that gleamed wet with spittle. Teeth the size of Brak's own head. . . .

—"Storm in a Bottle"
JOHN JAKES

Tauno of the merfolk watched in amazement as the beautiful girl's will broke. Tears burst forth. "Bring my father my curse!" she screamed, her voice lashing the gray waves. "Tell him . . . tell all of them . . . leave this land! Before the tupilak dooms them. . . ."

—"The Tupilak"
POUL ANDERSON

Saxif D'Aan had ordered his faithless lover to die upon the Wheel of Chaos . . . had watched day after day as her beautiful limbs were broken, her skin ripped away. Finally he took her down to let her die. And her dying words to Saxif D'Aan were, "I love you. I love you. . . ."

—"The Lands Beyond the World"
MICHAEL MOORCOCK

Dell Books by Lin Carter

The Jandar of Callisto Books:

Other novels:

Sword & Sorcery anthologies (Editor)

K. Bryant 76

Flashing Swords! #4

BARBARIANS AND BLACK MAGICIANS

Edited by Lin Carter

A DELL BOOK

Published by
Dell Publishing Co., Inc.
1 Dag Hammarskjold Plaza
New York, New York 10017

Text copyright © 1977 by Lin Carter
Illustrations copyright © 1977 by Rick Bryant

The five stories in this book, *Flashing Swords! #4,*
are originals and were written specifically for this
anthology. Published by arrangement with the authors.

Dell ® TM 681510, Dell Publishing Co., Inc.

ISBN: 0-440-12627-4

Printed in the United States of America
First printing—November 1977

This fourth volume of

FLASHING SWORDS!

is dedicated to our
late colleague, the
chronicler of the saga
of Hurricane John,
NORVELL PAGE.

Contents

OF WARRIORS AND WIZARDS

The Introduction

This book is a collection of new, never-before-published stories of Sword & Sorcery written by five of the finest living masters of the genre.

Herein you will find a new story of Cugel the Clever by Jack Vance, and a new chapter in John Jakes' saga of Brak the barbarian, and a new Deryni story by Katherine Kurtz, a new addition to the epic legend of Michael Moorcock's famed hero Elric of Melniboné, and a new yarn about the merfolk by Poul Anderson.

All of these good people are members of the world's smallest and most exclusive writers' club—S.A.G.A., which is otherwise known as The Swordsmen and Sorcerers' Guild of America, Ltd. It is so small that it has only ten members.

Perhaps I had better explain, here on the first page, just what Sword & Sorcery is, for those of you who may not know. Well, it sure isn't science fiction—although some of us, like Jack Vance and Mike Moorcock, write that sort of story, too; and it isn't the historical swashbuckler, either—although some of us, like John Jakes, have tried our hand at that sort of thing; and it isn't children's-book fantasy—although at least one of us, Poul Anderson, has written in that area, as well.

What it is, quite simply, is the modern reincarnation

of the oldest form of narrative known to world literature: the heroic fantasy. The adventure story of the
indomitable warrior-hero battling supernatural evil, per-
sonified as monster or magician, god or ghost or
goblin, dragon or demon. The sort of thing the Greek
myths and the Norse legends are all about, and
Beowulf and the *Shah Namah* and the *Mabinogion*.
The kind of yarn they wrote in the Middle Ages, in
sagas and epics about Roland and Oliver, or hero tales
and legends about St. George and the Dragon and
Dietrich of Berne, or prose romances about Amadis of
Gaul and Palmerin of England . . . until a smart aleck
called Cervantes lampooned it in a novel called *Don
Quixote,* and made this kind of stuff the laughingstock
of Europe.

In the early decades of this century, a burly, brood-
ing, furiously energetic Texas writer named Robert E.
Howard revived this form of storytelling for a pulp
magazine called *Weird Tales*.

He spun heroic sagas laid in mythical kingdoms at
the world's dawn in cycles of stories about Kull of High
Atlantis, Conan the Barbarian, Bran Mak Morn, and a
dour Puritan adventurer named Solomon Kane. These
yarns were crisp, vivid, told with verve and gusto,
drenched in color and mood, and narrated with
enormous drive and urgency. They were tremendously
popular with the readers of that long-ago time . . . so
popular, that some of them remain in print to this
day, in one form or another. (Conan, for instance, is
currently available in comic-book form; as such, it is
considered by Those Who Know to be the best comic
book around today.)

Howard snuffed out his own life at the cruelly young
age of thirty, but the standard was carried forward

by a new generation of *Weird Tales* writers: Henry Kuttner, in his Elak of Atlantis series, C. L. Moore in her Jirel of Joiry yarns, Clifford Ball, and others.

When *Weird Tales* faded from its height, Norvell Page, with his adventures of Wan Tengri, and Fritz Leiber, with his cycle of Fafhrd and the Gray Mouser, brought Sword & Sorcery into the pages of another magazine, *Unknown Worlds*. When *Unknown* succumbed to the wartime paper-shortage and declining sales, Leiber went over to another magazine called *Fantastic,* where his stories are still appearing to this day.

We who comprise the membership of S.A.G.A. are mostly people who came into the Sacred Genre recently. I was a kid reader of the pulps who idolized such Olympians as Fritz Leiber and L. Sprague de Camp, emulated them in my first fumbling attempts at writing, and matured (more or less) to eventually become one of them. I expect the same is true of Michael Moorcock and John Jakes, who are about my age or a trifle younger.

Today, Sword & Sorcery has become a small but steady subgenre of fantastic literature, with an enthusiastic following all its own which seems to be viable enough to sustain six or a dozen new books in the field every year. A few years back, those of us who prefer this area of writing joined into the association we call S.A.G.A., and in time came up with the bright idea of creating an annual (or almost annual) anthology of all-new stories in our favorite field, in emulation of such collections of all-new science-fiction stories as Damon Knight's reknowned *Orbit* series.

And there you have it.

* * *

Sword & Sorcery seems to "work" best in the novella length, i.e., in stories around ten to fifteen thousand words long. Because of this, and considering the size of our membership, it became necessary to publish twin anthologies, rather than just one each year. Hence, *Flashing Swords!* #1 and #2, which Dell Books published in 1973 and 1974 respectively, were each made up of the works of four different writers. This new set, #3 and #4, each contain five stories, our membership having increased to ten by the addition of two new members, Avram Davidson and Katherine Kurtz, both but recently voted unanimously into S.A.G.A.

All of which is by way of suggesting, none too subtly, that if you enjoy reading this book you should ransack your paperback stands for *Flashing Swords!* #3. It contains a new Lankhmar yarn by Fritz Leiber, the first tale in a new cycle by L. Sprague de Camp, one of Andre Norton's Witch World sagas, a new fantasy by Avram Davidson, and a new story of Amalric the Mangod of Thoorana by your editor.

A word to the wise. And—*Happy Magic!*

—LIN CARTER

Hollis, Long Island, New York

If sailor tales to sailor tunes,
Storm and adventure, heat and cold,
If schooners, islands and maroons,
And Buccaneers and buried Gold,
And all the old romance retold
Exactly in the ancient way,
Can please, as me they pleased of old,
The wiser youngsters of Today—
             So be it, and fall on!

ROBERT LOUIS STEVENSON

THE BAGFUL
OF DREAMS

Jack Vance

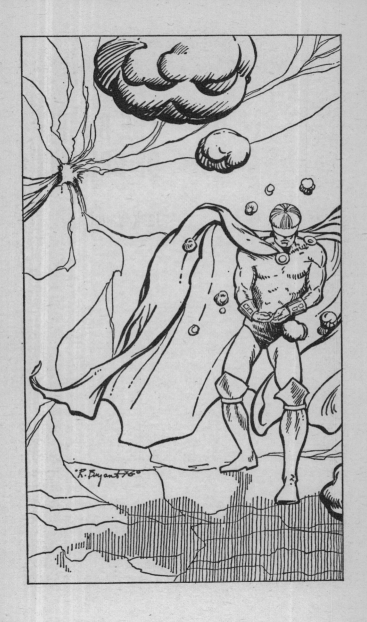

JACK VANCE

Perhaps he is more of a science-fiction writer than he is a writer of Sword & Sorcery—as the armful of Hugo awards he has won for such stories as *The Dragon Masters* and *The Last Castle* would tend to suggest—but if you will look behind the pages of those yarns, or between the lines, or just off the margin, you will see that almost all of them are really fantasies, disguised under a little science-fictional frosting.

Jack does not derive from the Howard tradition, as Jakes and I do. His sources, the writers who shaped and influenced him, are much more lit'ry—Lord Dunsany, I think; probably James Branch Cabell; almost certainly Clark Ashton Smith. Nor does he usually write of warriors as most of the rest of us do. Not for him the brawny barbarian, the swashbuckling savage, or the herculean headbuster. His most famous creation (in the Sacred Genre, at least) is that sly, silver-tongued, ever-resourceful rogue, Cugel, aptly called The Clever.

Cugel first appeared in a novel titled *The Eyes of the Overworld,* and has since appeared in a number of other tales, including one book-length Vancian pastiche called *The Quest of Simbilis,* by the awesomely talented Michael Shea. It seems that Vance had abandoned poor Cugel far from home at the conclusion of *Overworld.* Shea, obviously a devoted Vance buff (as who isn't?), felt this was a shame and begged permission of his creator to rescue Cugel. Vance shrugged and said okay; but then some ideas of his own on how Cugel might fare after *Overworld* seem to have trickled through his gray matter—

Which grew into a new cycle of Cugeliana, like the delicious yarn which follows.

L.C.

THE BAGFUL OF DREAMS

From Troon the road wandered apparently at random among those curious hills known as the Chaim Purpure, sometimes in wan maroon sunlight, as often in the cold black shadow cast by the northern slopes. Cugel, noting the crumbled tombs, the straggling copses of black yew, the inexplicable clefts and wafts of unfamiliar odors, marched at best speed, and presently, without incident, descended upon the Tsombol Marsh. Cugel heaved a sigh of relief, then in the same breath muttered an imprecation against the Tsombol Marsh and the vicissitudes to be expected from a region so bleak and dank.

As before, the road went by an indirect route, swinging around bogs and stagnant ponds, detouring to follow the bed of an ancient highway, sometimes swerving and veering for no obvious purpose whatever. To the further annoyance of Cugel, a cold wind now blew down from the north, bending the reeds, rippling water, flapping the cloak past Cugel's legs. Pulling the long-billed hat over his ears, he hunched his shoulders and walked at a bent-kneed lope, the better to evade the chill.

The wind blew the sky clear of all obscurity; the landscape was presented to the eye as if under a fine lens, with remarkable detail, contrast and clarity; but

Cugel took no satisfaction in the silence and scope of
this ancient peneplain, and when he scanned the dark
blue sky, he noted only a far *pelgrane*, cruising down
the wind. Cugel halted and stood frozen until the
creature had disappeared, then continued even more
briskly than before.

As the afternoon advanced the wind became capri-
cious, blowing first in gusts, then stopping short for
periods of unnatural quiet. During these intervals, Cugel
thought to hear water-wefkins, hiding behind tussocks
and calling to him in the sweet voices of unhappy
maidens: "Cugel, oh Cugel! why do you travel in haste?
Come to my bower and comb my beautiful green hair!"
And "Cugel, oh Cugel! where do you go? Take me with
you, to share the pleasures of your journey!" And
"Cugel, beloved Cugel! The day is dying, the year is at
an end! Come visit me behind the tussock, and we will
console each other's grief!"

Cugel walked only the faster, ever more anxious to
discover shelter for the night; and as the sun trembled
at the edge of Tsombol Marsh he found a small inn,
secluded under five dire oaks. He gratefully took ac-
commodation for the night, and the innkeeper, a tall
man with a pompous abdomen and a round red face
folded into creases of chronic joviality, set out an adequate supper of stewed herbs, glisters, reed-cake, and
thick warm acorn beer. As Cugel ate, the innkeeper
put a question: "I see by your garments that you are a
man of style and dignity; still you cross Tsombol Marsh
on foot: is this not an incongruity?"

"No doubt," said Cugel, "but sometimes I consider
myself the single honorable man in a world of rogues
and tricksters. Under such circumstances it is hard to
accumulate wealth."

The innkeeper pulled thoughtfully at his chin. "Your

difficulties have aroused my sympathy. Tonight I will consider on the matter."

The innkeeper was as good as his word and on the morning, after Cugel had finished his breakfast, he brought forward a large dun-colored beast with powerful hind legs, a tufted tail, and a broad snout, already bridled and saddled for riding. "The least I can do to ease your plight," said the innkeeper, "is to sell you this beast at a nominal figure. Agreed, it lacks elegance, and in fact is a hybrid of dounge and felukhary. Still it moves with an easy stride; it feeds upon inexpensive wastes, and is notorious for its stubborn loyalty."

"All very well," said Cugel. "I appreciate your altruism, but for so ungainly a creature any price whatever is bound to be excessive. Notice the sores at the base of the tail, the eczema along the back, and unless I am mistaken the creature lacks an eye."

"Trifles!" declared the innkeeper. "Do you want a dependable steed to carry you across the Plain of Standing Stones, or an adjunct to your vanity? The beast becomes your property for a mere thirty terces."

Cugel jumped back in shock. "When a fine Cambalese wheriot sells for twenty? My dear fellow, your generosity outreaches my capacity to pay!"

The innkeeper's face expressed only patience and affability. "Here, in the middle of Tsombol Marsh, you will buy not even the smell of a dead wheriot."

"The discussion has become abstract and farfetched," said Cugel. "On a practical level, I insist that your price is outrageous."

For an instant the innkeeper's face lost its genial cast and he spoke in a grumbling voice: "Every person to whom I sell this steed takes the same advantage of my kindliness."

Cugel found the remark somewhat cryptic but never-

theless, detecting irresolution, he pressed his advantage.
"In spite of a dozen misgivings I offer a generous
twelve terces."

"Done!" cried the innkeeper almost before Cugel
had finished speaking. "I repeat, you will discover this
beast to be totally loyal, even beyond your expecta-
tions."

Cugel paid over twelve terces and gingerly mounted
the creature. The landlord gave him a benign farewell. "May you enjoy a safe and comfortable journey!"

Cugel replied in like fashion: "May your enterprises
prosper!" In order to make a brave departure, he tried
to rein the beast around and about in a caracole, but it
merely hunched low to the ground, and padded out
upon the road.

A mile Cugel rode in comfort, and another, and taking all with all, was favorably impressed with his ac-
quisition. "No question but what the beast walks on
soft feet; now let us discover if it will canter at speed."

He shook out the reins; the beast set off down the
road, its gait a unique prancing strut, with tail arched
and head held high, which Cugel thought must surely
make him the object of ridicule. He kicked his heels into
the creature's heaving flanks. "Faster then, at all speed;
let us test your mettle!"

The beast sprang forward with great energy, and
the breeze blew Cugel's cloak flapping behind his shoulders. A massive dire oak stood beside a bend in the
road, an object which the beast seemed to identify
as a landmark. It increased its pace, only to stop suddenly short and elevate its hindquarters, projecting
Cugel into the ditch. When he managed to stagger
back up on the road, he discovered the beast cavorting
across the marsh, in the general direction of the inn.

"A loyal creature indeed!" growled Cugel. "It is unswervingly faithful to the comfort of its barn." He found his black and green hat, clapped it back upon his head and trudged south along the road.

During the late afternoon he came to a village of a dozen mud huts populated by a squat long-armed folk, distinguished by great shocks of whitewashed hair, arranged in original and fanciful styes. Cugel gauged the height of the sun, then examined the terrain ahead, which extended in a dreary succession of tussocks and ponds to the edge of vision. Putting aside all fastidiousness, he approached the largest and most pretentious of the huts.

He found the master of the house sitting on a bench to the side, whitewashing the hair of one of his children into a style of long radiating tufts, like the petals of a white chrysanthemum, while a number of other urchins played nearby in the mud. "Good afternoon," said Cugel. "I am anxious to learn if you can provide me food and lodging for the night, naturally for adequate recompense."

"I will feel privileged to do so," replied the householder. "This is the most commodious hut of Sampsetiska, and I am notorious across the village for my fund of anecdotes. Do you care to inspect the premises?"

"I would be pleased to rest an hour in my chamber before indulging myself in a hot bath."

His host blew out his cheeks, and wiping the whitewash from his hands beckoned Cugel into the hut, where he pointed to a heap of reeds at the side of the room. "There is your bed; recline at your convenience for as long as you wish. As for a bath, the ponds of the swamp are infested with threlkoids and wire-worms, and cannot be recommended."

"In that case," said Cugel, "I will do without. However, I have not eaten since breakfast, and I am willing to take my evening meal as soon as possible."

"My spouse has gone trapping in the swamp," said his host. "It is premature to discuss supper until we learn what she has gleaned from her toil."

In due course the woman returned carrying a wet sack and a wicker basket. She built up a fire and prepared the evening meal, while Erwig the householder brought forth a two-string guitar and all through the twilight entertained Cugel with ballads of the region.

At last the woman called Cugel and Erwig into the hut, where she served bowls of gruel, dishes of fried moss and ganions, lumps of black bread.

After the meal Erwig thrust his spouse and children out into the night. "What we have to say is unsuitable for unsophisticated ears," he explained. "This gentleman is an important traveler and does not wish to measure his every word." Bringing out an earthenware jug, Erwig poured two tots of arrak, one of which he placed before Cugel, then disposed himself for conversation. "Whence came you and where are you bound?"

Cugel tasted the arrak, which scorched the entire interior of his glottal cavity. "I am native to that noble land known as Almery, and I return to this same locality."

"Almery?" mused Erwig. "This is a name beyond my knowing."

"It lies a far distance to the south, with many regions intervening."

Erwig scratched his head in perplexity. "I am accounted a sagacious man; still I cannot divine why you travel so far and so perilously only to return again to the same place."

"In this regard I must blame the malice of my enemies. They have dealt me incalculable harm, and upon my return to Almery I intend to exact a remarkable revenge."

"Nothing is more soothing to the spirit," Erwig agreed. "An immediate obstacle to your plans, however, is the Plain of Standing Stones, by reason of the grues and asms which haunt this particular tract. I might add that pelgrane rove the skies. When you pass beyond the plain and enter the land of Ombalique, you may count yourself a lucky man."

Cugel gave the heavy-bladed knife he had taken from the slaughterhouse at Troon a meaningful twitch. "I am known as Cugel the Clever, and I am not without experience of such creatures. Still I prefer to avoid them. What is the distance to the Plain of Standing Stones, and how long is required to cross?"

"Two miles south the ground rises and the plain begins. The road proceeds in an erratic fashion from sarsen to sarsen for a distance of fifteen miles. A stouthearted wayfarer will cross the plain in four to five hours, assuming that he is not delayed or halted totally by interference from the creatures I have mentioned. The town Cuirnif is then another hour beyond."

"It is said that an inch of foreknowledge is worth ten miles of afterthought—"

"Well spoken!" cried Erwig, swallowing a gulp of arrak.

"—and in this regard, may I inquire your opinion of Cuirnif? What reception may I expect? Are the folk notably eccentric?"

"To some extent," replied Erwig. "They use no whitewash in their hair; and they are slack in their religious observances, making obeisance to Divine Wiulio with the right hand on the abdomen, instead of upon the left buttock, which we here consider a slipshod practice. What is your opinion?"

"The rite should be conducted as you describe," said Cugel. "No other method carries weight."

Erwig refilled Cugel's glass. "I consider this an important endorsement of our views, coming as it does from you, an expert traveler!"

The door opened and Erwig's spouse looked into the hut. "The night is dark, a bitter wind blows from the north, and a black beast prowls at the edge of the marsh."

"Stand among the shadows; Divine Wiulio protects his own. It is unthinkable that you and your brats should annoy our guest."

The woman grudgingly closed the door and returned into the night. Erwig pulled himself forward on his stool and swallowed a quantity of arrak. "The folk of Cuirnif, as I say, are strange enough, but their ruler, Duke Orbal, surpasses them in every category. He devotes himself to the study of marvels and prodigies, and every wandering phantasmagorian, each jack-leg magician with two spells in his head is feted and celebrated and treated to the best of the city."

"A bizarre predilection indeed!" declared Cugel.

Again the door opened and the woman looked into the hut. Erwig put down his glass and frowned over his shoulder. "Well, woman, what is it this time?"

"The beast is now moving among the huts. For all we know it also worships Wiulio."

Erwig attempted argument, but the woman's face became obdurate. "Your guest might as well forego his niceties now as later, since we all, in any event, must sleep on the same heap of reeds." She threw wide the door and commanded her urchins into the hut. Erwig, assured that no further conversation was possible, threw himself upon the reeds, and Cugel followed soon after.

In the morning Cugel breakfasted on ash-cake and herb tea, and prepared to take his departure. Erwig accompanied him to the road. "You have made a favorable impression upon me, and I will assist you across the Plain of Standing Stones. At the first opportunity take up a large pebble the size of your fist and make the trigrammatic sign upon it. If you are attacked, hold high the pebble and cry out: 'Stand aside! I carry a sacred object!' At the first sarsen, deposit the stone and select another from the pile, again make the sign and carry it to the second sarsen, and so across the plain. You still must avoid the notice of pelgrane, as they lack all religious feeling. So then: farewell, and the next time you pass be certain to halt at my hut."

"I suspect that you will never see me again," declared Cugel. "However, if all goes well, a certain Iucounu, known as the Laughing Magician, may in due course come past and I will recommend him to your hospitality."

"It shall be as you wish."

Cugel set forth down the road, which presently angled up to a flat gray plain studded at intervals with twelve-foot pillars of gray stone. Cugel found a large pebble, and placing his right hand on his left buttock made a profound salute to the object. He intoned: "I commend this pebble to the attention of Wiulio! I request that it protect me across this dismal plain!"

He scrutinized the landscape, but aside from the sarsens and the long black shadows laid by the cool red morning sun, he discovered nothing worthy of attention, and thankfully set off along the road.

He had traveled no more than a hundred yards when he felt a presence and whirling about discovered an asm

of eight fangs almost on his heels. Cugel held high the
pebble and cried out: "Away with you! I carry a sacred
object and I do not care to be molested!"

The asm spoke in a soft blurred voice: "Wrong! You
carry an ordinary pebble. I watched and you scamped
the rite. Flee if you wish; I need the exercise."

"Does the wrath of Wiulio mean nothing to you?"
demanded Cugel.

"The question is irrelevant." The asm advanced.
Cugel threw the stone with all his force; it struck the
broad black forehead between the bristling antennae,
and the asm fell flat; before it could rise Cugel had
severed its head.

He started to proceed, then turned back and took up
the stone. "Who knows who guided the throw so ac-
curately? Wiulio deserves the benefit of the doubt."

At the first sarsen, he exchanged stones as the peasant
had recommended and continued across the plain and
so the day went. The sun lurched up to the zenith
in a series of asthenic spasms, rested quietly a period,
then descended westward with exaggerated caution,
like a rheumatic old man groping his way down an
untrustworthy ladder.

Whether or not by virtue of his sacred stones, Cugel
marched unmolested from sarsen to sarsen, though on
several occasions he noted pelgrane sliding across the
sky and flung himself flat to avoid attention. Ahead a
line of low hills appeared and Cugel discerned the
shadow of a steep-sided valley. He increased his pace,
gratified to have crossed the plain in safety, and so perhaps relaxed his vigilance, for high in the sky behind
him sounded a scream of wild triumph.

Cugel fled in a panic and plunged over the edge of
the ravine, where he dodged among rocks and pressed
himself into the shadows. Down swooped the pelgrane,

past and beyond, warbling with joyful excitement: a sound now joined by a human voice raised in outcries and curses.

Cugel stole forward and discovered that, not fifty yards distant, the pelgrane had alighted and now pursued a portly black-haired man in a loose suit of black-and-white diaper. The man took refuge behind an olophar tree, and the pelgrane chased him this way and that, clashing its fangs, snatching with its great clawed hands.

Cugel cautiously crept out upon a little bluff and hid himself in the shrubbery. For all his rotundity, the man showed remarkable deftness in evading the lunges of the pelgrane, although sweat trickled down his plump cheeks and into the short beard which hung below his chin.

The pelgrane, becoming frustrated, began to scream an incoherent invective; it halted to glare through the crotch in the tree and snap with its great maw. On a whimsical impulse Cugel stole down the bank until he reached a point directly above the pelgrane; selecting an appropriate moment, he jumped, to land with both feet on the creature's head, forcing the neck down into the crotch.

"Now," said Cugel to the startled man, "if you will be good enough to fetch a stout cord we will bind this abominable beast securely in place."

"Why show it such mercy?" cried the man. "Did you see how it pursued me? It must be killed and instantly! Move your foot, so that I may hack away its head."

"Not so fast," said Cugel. "For all its faults, it is a valuable specimen to which I have laid claim, and I intent to protect my interests."

"Your claim is not altogether valid," stated the man

after a moment of reflection. "I lured it down within reach and I was just about to stun it when you interfered."

Cugel shrugged. "As you like. I will take my weight off the creature's neck and go my way."

The man in the black-and-white suit made an irritable gesture. "Why go to ridiculous extremes merely to score a rhetorical point? I have a suitable cord over yonder."

The two men dropped a branch over the pelgrane's head and bound it securely in place. The man, who had introduced himself as Iolo the Dream-taker, asked: "Exactly what value do you place upon this creature, and why?"

"It has come to my attention," said Cugel, "that Orbal, Duke of Ombalique, is an amateur of oddities. Surely he would pay well for such a monster, perhaps as much as a hundred terces."

"Your remarks are to the point," Iolo admitted. "Are you sure that the bonds are secure?"

Cugel tested the ropes and in so doing noticed an ornament consisting of a gold chain and blue glass egg attached to the creature's crest. Cugel reached to remove the object but Iolo's hand was there almost as soon. Cugel shouldered Iolo aside and disengaged the amulet, but Iolo instantly caught hold of the chain and the two glared eye to eye.

"I beg you to release your avid grip upon my property," said Cugel in an icy voice.

"Have you no respect for justice?" demanded Iolo. "The object is mine since I saw it first."

"You are talking mischievous nonsense," said Cugel. "If you recall, I removed the trinket from the pelgrane's crest, and you tried to snatch it from my hand."

Iolo stamped his foot in a fury. "I refuse to be

domineered!" And Iolo sought to wrest the object from Cugel's grasp. The two men stumbled and fell against the bank; the blue glass egg fell to the ground and shattered in an explosion of blue smoke to create a hole into the hillside from which a golden-gray tentacle instantly thrust forth to seize Cugel's leg.

Iolo sprang back and watched Cugel's attempts to avoid being drawn into the hole. Cugel called out: "Quick! Fetch a cord and tie the tentacle to yonder stump; otherwise it will drag me into the hill!"

Iolo spoke in a measured voice: "Avarice has brought this fate upon you; I am reluctant to interfere. Additionally, I have but one cord: that binding the pelgrane."

"Kill the pelgrane," panted Cugel. "Put the cord to its more immediate need!"

"All is not so simple," said Iolo. "You have valued this pelgrane at a hundred terces, of which my share is fifty. The rope I assess at ten terces—"

"What!" roared Cugel. "Ten terces for a length of cord worth at most a few coppers?"

"Value is not an immutable quality," Iolo pointed out. "I believe this to be one of the basic doctrines of commerce."

"Very well," said Cugel, gritting his teeth against the tension of the tentacle. "Ten terces for the rope, but I cannot pay fifty for the pelgrane; I carry only forty-five terces."

"So be it," said Iolo. "I will accept as surety the jeweled clip in your hat. Please pay over the forty-five terces."

Cugel, seeing no value in argument, managed to toss his wallet to the ground. Iolo demanded the clip, but Cugel refused to relinquish the jewel until the tentacle had been tied off. With poor grace Iolo hacked the

head off the pelgrane, brought over the rope and secured the tentacle to the stump, thus easing the strain
upon Cugel's leg. "Now then," said Iolo, "the clip if
you please." And he poised his knife significantly near
the rope.

Cugel tossed over the clip. "Now, since you have
gained all my wealth, be so good as to extricate me
from this tentacle."

Iolo ignored the remark and set about making camp
for the night.

Cugel called out plaintively: "Are you bereft of com-
passion? Do you not recall how I rescued you from
the pelgrane?"

"Indeed I do, and I note the consequences of this
act. An anomalous object grips your leg and you have
lost your wealth. There is a lesson to be learned here,
to this effect: never disturb the stasis unless well re-
imbursed in advance."

"True," agreed Cugel. "Still, a serious disequilibrium
now exists which thoughtful men would wish to adjust:
you by prying loose the tentacle, I by extricating my
leg."

"There is something in what you say," remarked Iolo.
"In the morning, when I am rested, I will cast a wisp
and locate the truth."

Cugel expostulated but Iolo turned him a deaf ear
and built up a campfire over which he cooked a stew
of herbs and grasses, which he ate with half a cold
fowl and draughts of wine from a leather bottle, after
which he stoppered the bottle and leaning back against
a tree gave his attention to Cugel. "No doubt you are
on your way to Duke Orbal's great Exposition of Marvels?"

Cugel made a sign in the negative. "I am a traveler,
no more. What is this exposition?"

"Each year Duke Orbal presides over a competition of wonder-workers, the grand prize of which is a thousand terces. This year I intend to win the prize with my Bagful of Dreams."

"Interesting! Your 'Bagful of Dreams' is of course no more than a romantic metaphor?"

"Absolutely not!" declared Iolo in a voice of outraged dignity.

"A kaleidoscopic projection? A set of amusing impersonations? A hallucinatory gas?"

"None of these. I carry a quantity of pure unadulterated dreams, coalesced and crystalized." From his satchel Iolo brought forth a sack of soft gray leather, from which he extracted an object like a snowflake two inches in diameter. He held it up into the firelight where Cugel could admire its fleeting lusters. "With these dreams I will ply Duke Orbal and how can I fail to win over all contestants?"

"Your chances are not inconsequential. How, may I ask, do you obtain these dreams?"

"The process is complicated and secret. Still, I see no reason why I should not describe the general procedures. I live beside Lake Lucanor in the land of Daipassant. On calm nights the surface of the water becomes coated with a dusty skein which reflects the stars as small globules of shine. By using a suitable incantation I am able to lift up impalpable threads composed of pure starlight and water-weft. I weave this thread into nets and then I go forth in search of dreams. I hide in valances, I crouch on roofs, I wander through sleeping houses; I am always ready to net the dreams as they drift by. Each morning I carry these wonderful wisps to my laboratory and there I sort them out and contrive my various minglements. In due course I achieve a crystal of a hundred dreams, and with these confections I hope to enthrall Duke Orbal and win a thousand terces."

"I would offer congratulations were it not for this tentacle gripping my leg," said Cugel.

"Yes, that is a matter we must carefully explore." Iolo fed several logs into the fire, chanted a spell of protection against creatures of the night, and composed himself for sleep.

An hour passed. Cugel tried in vain to ease the grip of the tentacle. He listened to the sounds from the valley and heard the fluting of a night jar. Four black moths fluttered about the fire, then—disturbed perhaps by Iolo's snores—spiraled up one after the other into the gloom and were gone. Cugel reached to the ground for a twig, with which he was able to drag close a long branch, which allowed him to reach another of equal length. Tying the two together with a length of string from his pouch he contrived a pole exactly long enough to reach Iolo's recumbent form. Working with exquisite precision he drew the satchel across the ground, to within reach of his fingers. First he drew forth Iolo's wallet containing two hundred terces which he transferred to his own pouch, then the jeweled clip to his hat, then the soft gray leather bagful of dreams. The satchel contained nothing more of value, save that half of cold fowl which Iolo had reserved for his breakfast and the leather bottle of wine, both of which Cugel put aside for his own use. He returned the satchel to where he had found it, then he separated the branches and tossed them aside. Lacking a better hiding place for the bagful of dreams, Cugel tied the string to the bag and lowered it into the mysterious hole. He ate the fowl and drank the wine, then made himself as comfortable as possible.

In due course the night passed, and the sun swam

up into a plum-colored sky. Iolo roused himself, yawned, belched, blew up the fire and added fuel, after which he gave Cugel a civil good morning. "And how passed the night?"

"As well as could be expected. It is useless, after all, to complain against that which may not be altered."

"Precisely correct!" Iolo went to the satchel for his breakfast and discovered the loss of his property. He leapt erect and stared at Cugel. "My money, my dreams —gone! How do you account for this?"

"Easily. At approximately midnight a robber came out of the woods and pillaged your satchel."

Iolo tore at his black beard. "My precious dreams! Why did you not raise an outcry?"

Cugel scratched his head. "This was not the scope of our understanding; at no time did you give me such instructions, and in all candor I did not care once again to disturb the stasis. Additionally, the robber seemed a kindly man; after taking possession of your belongings, he presented me with half a cold fowl and a bottle of wine, the provenance of which I saw no need to inquire. We held a brief conversation and I learned that like ourselves he is bound for Cuirnif and the Exposition of Marvels."

"Aha! Would you recognize this robber were you to see him again?"

"Without a doubt."

"Well then, let us see as to this tentacle. Perhaps we can pry it loose." Iolo seized the tip of the golden-gray member and bracing himself managed to lift it from Cugel's leg. For twenty minutes he struggled, kicking and thrusting, heaving and prying, and paying no heed to Cugel's roars of pain. Finally the tentacle fell away and Cugel crawled to safety.

With great caution Iolo approached the hole and

peered down into the dark depths. "I see only a glimmer of far lights. The hole is mysterious . . . What is this bit of string fastened to the root which leads into the hole?"

"I tied a rock to the end and attempted to find a bottom to the cavity," Cugel explained. "It amounts to nothing."

Iolo tugged at the string, which first yielded, then resisted, then broke, and Iolo was left looking at the frayed end. "Odd! The string appears to have corroded, as if through contact with some acrid substance. But let us hasten into Cuirnif and there identify the villain who sequestered my valuables."

The two proceeded along a road, past garden plots, fields and vineyards. The peasants working their soil looked up in interest as the two wayfarers passed along the road: the portly round-faced Iolo in his suit of black-and-white diamonds, jowls quivering, beard jerking; and beside him the lean long-legged Cugel, his saturnine visage turned first to this side, then that. Along the way Iolo put ever more searching questions in regard to the robber. Cugel had lost interest in the subject and returned vague, ambiguous, or even contradictory answers, and Iolo's voice became ever sharper.

They entered the town, Cuirnif, crossed the square, and Cugel noted an inn which seemed to offer comfortable accommodations. "Here our paths diverge," he told Iolo. "I plan to take a chamber in the inn yonder."

"The Five Owls? It is the dearest inn of Cuirnif; how will you pay the score?"

Cugel made a confident gesture. "Is not a thousand terces the grand prize at the Exposition of Marvels?"

"Indeed, but what marvel do you propose to display? I warn you, the Duke has no patience with charlatans."

"Events will order themselves," said Cugel. "Meanwhile, I wish you comfortable roofs and the finest of dreams for your net." He performed a courteous salute and took his leave of Iolo.

At the Five Owls Cugel was assigned a pleasant chamber suitably furnished, where he refreshed himself and ordered his attire. Then, descending to the common room, he commanded the best meal the house could afford, together with a decanter of amber sack. Upon completion of his meal he summoned the innkeeper and commended the quality of his table. "In fact, all taken with all, Cuirnif must be considered a place favored by the elements. The prospect is pleasant, the air is bracing, and Duke Orbal appears to be an indulgent ruler."

"Aha then! You have met Duke Orbal?"

"I noticed him across the square, no more. He seems mild and equable."

The innkeeper nodded somewhat noncommittally. "As you say, Duke Orbal is not easily exasperated, until he encounters refractory conduct, whereupon his mildness deserts him. Glance at the crest of the hill; what do you see?"

"Four tubes, or stand-pipes, approximately thirty yards tall and something less than one yard in diameter."

"Your eye is accurate. Into these tubes are dropped insubordinate members of society, without regard for who stands below or who may be coming after. Hence, while you may converse with Duke Orbal or even venture a modest pleasantry or two, never ignore his commands."

Cugel made an airy gesture. "Such strictures will hardly apply to me, a stranger in town."

The innkeeper gave a skeptical grunt. "I assume

that you come to witness the Exposition of Marvels?"

"Even better! I intend to claim the grand prize. In this regard, can you recommend a dependable hostler?"

"Certainly." The innkeeper provided explicit directions.

"I also wish to hire a gang of strong and willing workers," said Cugel. "Where may these be recruited?"

The innkeeper pointed across the street to a rather dingy tavern. "In the yard of The Blue Cuckoo all the riffraff in town take counsel together. Here you will find workers sufficient to your purposes."

"While I visit the hostler, please be good enough to send a pot-boy across to hire twelve of these sturdy fellows."

"As you wish."

At the hostler's Cugel rented a large six-wheeled wagon and a team of draught animals. Returning with the wagon to the Five Owls, he found waiting a work force of twelve miscellaneous types, including a man not only senile and racked with ague, but also lacking a leg. Another, in the throes of intoxication, fought away imaginary insects. Cugel discharged these two on the spot. Another in the group was Iolo the Dreamtaker, who scrutinized Cugel with the liveliest suspicion.

Cugel asked: "My good friend Iolo, what do you do in such sordid company?"

"I take employment in order to buy sustenance," said Iolo with dignity. "May I ask how you obtained funds to embark on such an ambitious program? Also, I notice that you wear in your hat that jeweled clip which only yesterday was my property!"

"It is the second of a pair," said Cugel. "The robber took the first along with your other valuables."

Iolo curled his lips in scorn. "Do you take me for a

fool? Also, why do you require this wagon and this gang of workers?"

"If you care to earn the very substantial wage I propose to pay, you will soon find out for yourself," said Cugel, with which Iolo was forced to be content.

Cugel drove the wagon and the gang of workers out of Cuirnif along the road to the mysterious hole, where he found all as before. He ordered trenches dug into the hillside; crating was installed, after which that block of soil surrounding and including the hole was dragged up on the bed of the wagon, with the protruding tentacle still tied to the stump. During the middle stages of the project Iolo's manner changed. He began calling orders to the workmen and addressed Cugel with great cordiality. "A noble idea, Cugel! We shall profit greatly!"

Cugel raised his eyebrows. "I hope indeed to win the grand prize. Your wage however will be relatively modest, or even scant, unless you work more briskly."

"What!" stormed Iolo. "Surely you agree that this hole is half my property!"

"I agree to nothing of the sort. Please say no more of the matter, or I will be forced to discharge you."

Grumbling and fuming Iolo returned to work, and in due course Cugel conveyed the block of soil, with the hole and tentacle, back to Cuirnif. Along the way he purchased an old tarpaulin with which he concealed the hole, the better to magnify the impact of his display.

At the site of the exposition Cugel slid his exhibit off the wagon and into the shelter of a pavilion, after which he paid off his men, to the dissatisfaction of those who had cultivated extravagant hopes. Cugel gave short shrift to the complaints. "The pay is adequate, and were it ten times as much, the money would still find its way into the till at the Blue Cuckoo."

"One moment!" cried Iolo in a passion. "You and I must arrive at an understanding!"

Cugel merely jumped up on the wagon and drove it back to the hostelry. Some of the men pursued him a few steps; others threw stones, without effect.

On the following day trumpets and gongs announced the formal opening of the exposition. Duke Orbal arrived at the plaza splendid in a robe of old rose trimmed with white feathers, and a hat of pale blue velvet two feet in diameter, with silver tassels around the brim and a cockade of silver puff. Mounting to a rostrum, Duke Orbal addressed the crowd. "As all know, I am considered a visionary eccentric, what with my enthusiasm for marvels and prodigies, but, after all, when the preoccupation is analyzed, is it all so absurd? Think back across the aeons to the times of the Vapurials, the Green and Purple College, the mighty magicians among whose number we include Amberlin, the second Chidule of Porphyrhyncos, Morreion, Calanctus the Calm, and of course the Great Phandaal. These were the days of power, and they are not likely to return except in nostalgic recollection. Hence this, my Exposition of Marvels.

"I see by my schedule that we have a remarkable and stimulating program, and no doubt I will find difficulty in awarding the grand prize." Duke Orbal glanced at a paper. "We will inspect Zaraflam's 'Nimble Squadrons,' Gazzard's 'Unlikely Musicians,' Xallops and his 'Compendium of Universal Knowledge.' Iolo will offer his 'Bagful of Dreams,' and, finally, Cugel will present for our amazement that to which he gives the tantalizing title: 'Nowhere.' A most provocative program! And now without further ado we will proceed to evaluate Zaraflam's 'Nimble Squadrons.' "

The crowd surged around the first pavilion and Zara-

flam brought forth his 'Nimble Squadrons': a parade
of cockroaches smartly turned out in red, white, and
black uniforms. The sergeants brandished swords, the
foot soldiers carried muskets; the squadrons marched
and countermarched in intricate evolutions. "Halt!"
bawled Zaraflam. The cockroaches stopped short.

"Present arms!" The cockroaches obeyed.

"Fire a salute in honor of Duke Orbal!"

The sergeants raised their swords; the footmen
elevated their muskets. Down came the swords; the
muskets exploded emitting little puffs of white smoke.

"Excellent!" declared Duke Orbal. "Zaraflam, I commend your painstaking accuracy!"

"A thousand thanks, your Grace! Have I won the
grand prize?"

"It is still too early to predict eventualities. Now, to
Gazzard and his 'Unlikely Musicians'!"

The spectators moved on to the second pavilion
from which Gazzard presently appeared, his face woe-
begone. "Your Grace and noble citizens of Cuirnif!
My 'Unlikely Musicians' were fish of the Gelid Sea, and
I was assured of the grand prize when I brought them
to Cuirnif. However, during the night a leak drained
the tank dry and the fish are dead . . . I still wish to
remain in contention for the prize; hence I will simulate
the songs of my former troupe. Please adjudicate the
music on this basis."

Duke Orbal made an austere sign. "Impossible. Gazzard's exhibit is hereby declared invalid. We now move
on to Xallops and his remarkable 'Compendium.' "

Xallops stepped forward from his pavilion. "Your
Grace, ladies and gentlemen of Cuirnif! My entry at
this exposition is truly remarkable; however, unlike
Zaraflam and Gazzard, I can take no personal credit for
its existence. By trade I am a ransacker of ancient

tombs, where the risks are great and rewards few. By great good luck I chanced upon that crypt where ten aeons ago the Sorcerer Zinqzin was laid to rest. From this dungeon I rescued the volume which I now display to your astounded eyes." Xallops whisked away a cloth to reveal a great book bound in black leather. "On command this volume must reveal information of any and every sort; it knows each trivial detail, from the moment the Cosmic dung-beetle propelled the planets into orbit around the Sun to the present date. Ask; you shall be answered!"

"Remarkable!" declared Duke Orbal. "Present before us the Lost Ode of Psyrme!"

"Certainly." The book threw back its covers to reveal a page covered with crabbed and undecipherable characters.

Duke Orbal spoke in a perplexed voice: "This is beyond my comprehension; be so good as to furnish a translation."

"The request is denied," said the book. "Such poetry is too sweet for ordinary ilk."

Duke Orbal glanced haughtily at Xallops, who spoke quickly to the book: "Show us scenes from aeons past."

"With pleasure. Reverting to the Nineteenth Aeon of the Fifty-second Cycle, I display a view across Linx-fade Valley, toward Singhapura's Tower of Frozen Blood."

"Magnificent!" declared Duke Orbal. "I am curious to gaze upon the semblance of Singhapura himself."

"As you wish. Here is a scene on Thrungstone Terrace at the Temple at Yan. Singhapura stands beside the flowering wail-bush. In the chair sits the Empress Noxon, now in her hundred and fortieth year. She has tasted no water in her entire lifetime, and eats only bitter glossom, with occasionally a morsel or two of boiled eel."

"Bah!" said Duke Orbal. "A most hideous old creature! Show us rather a beautiful court lady of the Yellow Age."

The book uttered a petulant syllable in an unknown language. The page turned to reveal a marble promenade running beside a placid river. "Notice the vegetation," said the book, indicating with a luminous arrow a row of golden-pewter trees clipped into globular shapes. "Those are irix, the sap of which may be used as an effective vermifuge. The species is now extinct. Along the concourse you will observe a multitude of persons. Those with black stockings are Alulian slaves, whose ancestors arrived from far Canopus. In the middle distance stands a beautiful woman, indicated by a red dot over her head, although her face is turned toward the river."

"This is hardly satisfactory," grumbled Duke Orbal. "Xallops, can you not control the perversity of your exhibit?"

"I fear not, your Grace."

Duke Orbal gave a sniff of displeasure. "A final question! Who among the folk now residing in Cuirnif presents the greatest threat to the welfare of my realm?"

"I am a repository of information, not an oracle," stated the book. "However, I will remark that among those present stands a certain long-legged vagabond with a crafty expression—"

Cugel leapt forward and pointed across the square. "The robber! I believe that I saw him skulking yonder! There he goes now! Summon the constables! Sound the gong!"

While all turned to look, Cugel, slamming shut the book, dug his knuckles meaningfully into the cover. The book grunted in annoyance.

Duke Orbal turned around with a frown of perplexity. "I saw no one."

"Ah well, perhaps I was mistaken. But yonder waits Iolo with his famous Bagful of Dreams!"

The Duke moved on to Iolo's pavilion, followed by the enthralled onlookers. Duke Orbal said: "Iolo the Dream-taker, your fame has preceded you all the far distance from Daipassant. I hereby tender you an official welcome and assure you that your remarkable demonstrations will receive our most sympathetic attention."

Iolo answered in a sullen voice: "Your Grace, I have sorry news to report. For the whole of one year I prepared for this day, hoping of course to win the grand prize. The blast of midnight winds, the outrage of householders, the terrifying attentions of ghosts, shrees, roof-runners and fermins: all of these have caused me discomfort. I have roamed the dark hours in pursuit of my dreams. I have lurked beside dormers, crawled through attics, hovered over couches; I have suffered frights, vicissitudes; never have I counted the cost if through my enterprise I were able to capture some particularly choice specimen. Each dream trapped in my star-shine net I carefully examined and gauged its worth; for every dream cherished and saved, I have released a dozen, and finally from my store of superlatives I fashioned my wonderful crystals, and these I brought down the long road from Daipassant. Then, only last night, under the most mysterious circumstances, my property was sequestered. My precious goods were rifled by a robber whom only Cugel claims to have seen. I therefore make this urgent representation; and I point out that the dreams, whether near or far, represent marvels of superlative quality, and I feel that a careful description of the items—"

Duke Orbal held up his hand. "I must reiterate the judgment rendered upon the good Gazzard. One of our most stringent rules stipulates that neither imaginary nor purported marvels may qualify for the competition. You are hereby extended official condolences for the misfortune you have suffered; perhaps we will have the opportunity to adjudicate your remarkable dreams on another occasion. We will now pass on to Cugel's pavilion and investigate his provocative 'Nowhere'."

Cugel stepped up on the dais before his exhibit. "Your Grace, I present for your inspection a legitimate marvel: not a straggle of untidy insects, not an insolent and pedantic almanac, but an authentic wonderment." Cugel whisked away the cloth. "Behold!"

The duke made a puzzled sound. "A pile of dirt? A stump? What is that odd-looking member emerging from the hole?"

Cugel spoke in tones of compelling fervor. "Your Grace, I will describe the provenance of this marvel. As I departed the Plain of Standing Stones, a pelgrane swooped from the sky which I attacked and killed. On its helm it wore a qandar-egg, a notable source of diasmatic concentrate. In order to deny another baleful creature this power, which conceivably might be used against the best interests of your Grace and all Ombalique, I hurled the qandar-egg to the ground; it exploded and burst a hole into an unknown and mysterious space."

Iolo ran forward sputtering in indignation, "Come, Cugel, I beg you, be accurate in your tale!" He turned to Duke Orbal. "I grappled the pelgrane; Cugel reached from behind a tree and purloined the qandar-egg, but as he turned to flee, it fell from his hands."

Cugel spoke in a lofty voice: "Pay no heed to Iolo's distortions; I fear that he has ingested too many of his own dreams. Be so good as to inspect this tentacle which pulses with the life of another cosmos! Notice the golden luster of the dorsal surface, the green and lavender of these scales, which are formed of pro-scedel, or some other wonderful substance. And on the underside you will discover three colors of a sort never before seen!"

With a nonplussed expression Duke Orbal pulled at his chin. "This is all very well, but where is the rest of the creature? You present not a marvel, but the frac-tion of a marvel! I can make no judgment on the basis of a tail, or hinderquarters, or proboscis, whatever the member may be. Additionally, you claim that the hole enters a far cosmos; still I see only a hole, resembling nothing so much as the den of a wysen-imp."

Iolo thrust himself forward. "May I venture an opin-ion? As I reflect upon events, I have become convinced that Cugel himself stole my Bagful of Dreams, and also my purse containing well over two hundred terces. He ascribed his deed to a robber whom he characterized—to use his words—as a 'vulgar, vicious person, with a red nose and large nostrils.' Now mark this well: as we entered the precincts of Cuirnif, Cugel positively iden-tified your Grace as the robber!"

"One moment!" cried Cugel in outrage. "As usual Iolo deals inaccurately with the facts! True, we entered Cuirnif in each other's company. Agreed, the appear-ance of the robber was the subject of our conversation. Then, as soon as your Grace appeared, Iolo turned me a bland face and pointed with insulting familiarity in your direction. 'That fellow yonder,' said Iolo, 'examine him well. He has a questionable reputation. Could he be the robber?' I said, 'The gentleman to whom you refer appears noble and dignified, hence—' "

Iolo uttered a jeering laugh. "To the contrary, you spoke only of 'turpitude' and 'masks of hypocrisy.' "

"Your remarks are not at all helpful," said Cugel. "Kindly hold your tongue while I continue my demonstration."

Iolo was not to be subdued so easily. He turned to Duke Orbal and cried in a poignant voice: "Hear me out, if you will! I am convinced that the 'robber' is no more than a figment of this rogue's imagination! He took my dreams and hid them, and where else but in the hole? For evidence I cite that length of string which leads into the hole. For what purpose? Obviously to suspend my Bag of Dreams!"

Duke Orbal inspected Cugel with a frown. "Are these accusations valid? Answer exactly, since all can be verified."

Cugel chose his words with care. "I can only affirm what I myself know. Quite conceivably the robber hid Iolo's dreams in the hole while I was otherwise occupied. For what purpose? Who can say? Again, assume as a hypothesis that Iolo, troubled by the paltriness of his exhibit, tossed aside his dreams in disgust. Is this so incredible? Not at all."

Iolo held up clenched fists to the sky, but before he could respond, Duke Orbal asked in a gentle voice: "Has anyone thought to search the hole for this elusive 'Bag of Dreams'?"

Cugel gave an indifferent shrug. "I have never forbidden Iolo access into the hole. He may enter now and search to his heart's content."

"You claim this hole!" returned Iolo. "It therefore

becomes your duty to protect the public. Please return to me my property!"

For several minutes an animated argument took place, until Duke Orbal intervened. "Both parties have raised persuasive points; however, on the whole, I must find against Cugel. I therefore decree that he make an effort to recover the missing dreams."

Cugel disputed the decision with such vigor that Duke Orbal turned to glance along the skyline of the ridge, whereupon Cugel moderated his position. "The judgment of your Grace of course must prevail, and if I must, I will cast about for Iolo's lost dreams, although his theories are clearly absurd."

Cugel obtained a long pole, to which he attached a grapple. Gingerly thrusting his contrivance through the hole, he raked back and forth, but succeeded only in stimulating the tentacle, which thrashed from side to side.

Iolo suddenly cried out in excitement. "I notice a remarkable fact! The block of earth is at most six feet in breadth, yet Cugel plunges into the hole a pole twelve feet in length! What trickery does he practice now?"

Cugel replied in even tones: "I promised Duke Orbal a marvel and a wonderment, and I believe that I have done so. I can no more explain the matter than Zaraflam can elucidate the mental processes of his cockroaches."

Duke Orbal nodded gravely. "Well said, Cugel! Your exhibit indeed entitles you to serious consideration for the grand prize. Still—and this is an important qualification—you offer us only a tantalizing glimpse: a bottomless hole, a length of tentacle, to the effect that your exhibit seems somewhat makeshift and improvised. Contrast, if you will, the precision of Zaraflam's cockroaches!" He held up his hand as Cugel started to expostulate. "You display a hole: good enough. But how is this hole different from any other? Can I in justice offer a thousand terces on such a vague basis!"

"The matter may be resolved in a manner to satisfy us all," said Cugel. "Let Iolo enter the hole, to assure himself that his dreams are indeed elsewhere. Then, on his return, he will bear witness to the truly marvelous nature of my exhibit."

Iolo made an instant protest. "Cugel claims the exhibit; let him make the exploration!"

Cugel offered a heated rejoinder, to which Iolo responded in kind, until Duke Orbal raised his hand for silence. "I pronounce an official decree to the effect that Cugel must immediately enter his extraordinary aperture in search of Iolo's properties, and likewise make a careful study of the environment, for the benefit of us all."

"Your Grace!" protested Cugel. "This is no simple matter! The tentacle almost fills the hole!"

"I see sufficient room for an agile man to slide past."

"Your Grace, to be candid, I do not care to enter the hole, by reason of extreme fear."

Duke Orbal again glanced up at the tubes which stood in a sinister line along the ridge of the hill. He spoke over his shoulder to a burly man in a maroon and black uniform. "Which of the tubes is most suitable for use at this time?"

"The second tube from the right, your Grace, is only one-quarter occupied."

Cugel declared in a trembling voice: "I fear, but I have conquered my fear! I will seek Iolo's lost dreams!"

"Excellent," said Duke Orbal with a tight-lipped grin. "Please do not delay; my patience wears thin."

Cugel tentatively thrust a leg into the hole, but the motion of the tentacle caused him to snatch it out again. Duke Orbal muttered a few words to his sheriff, who brought up a winch. The tentacle was hauled forth from the hole a good five yards. "Now," Duke Orbal instructed Cugel, "straddle the tentacle, seize it with hands and legs and it will draw you back through the hole."

In desperation Cugel clambered upon the tentacle. The tension of the winch was relaxed and Cugel was pulled into the hole.

The light of Earth veered away from the opening and made no entrance; Cugel was plunged into a condition of near-total darkness, where, however, by some paradoxical condition he was able to sense the scope of his new environment in detail.

He stood on a surface at once flat, yet rough with rises and dips and hummocks like the face of a windy sea. The substance underfoot seemed a black spongy stuff, pitted by small cavities and tunnels in which Cugel sensed the motion of innumerable near-invisible points of light. Where the sponge rose high, the crest curled over like breaking surf, or stood ragged and crusty; in either case, the fringes glowed with a phosphorescence of red, pale blue, and several colors Cugel had never before observed. No horizon could be detected and the laws of perspective were notably distorted; the local concepts of distance, proportion, and size were organized by conventions foreign to Cugel's understanding.

Overhead hung dead numb Nothingness. The single feature of note, a large disk the color of rain floated at the zenith, an object so dim as to be almost invisible. At some indeterminate distance—a mile? ten miles? a hundred yards?—a hummock of some bulk overlooked the entire panorama. On closer inspection Cugel saw this hummock to be a prodigious mound of gelatinous flesh, inside which floated a globular organ apparently analogous to an eye. From the base of this creature a hundred tentacles extended far and wide across the black sponge. One of these tentacles passed near Cugel's feet, through the intracosmic gap, and out upon the soil of Earth.

At this moment Cugel noted Iolo's Bag of Dreams, not three feet distant. The black sponge, bruised by the impact, had welled an acrid liquid which had dissolved a hole in the leather, allowing the star-shaped dreams to spill out upon the sponge. In groping with the pole, Cugel had damaged a growth of brown palps. The resulting exudation had dripped upon the dreams and when Cugel picked up one of the fragile flakes, he saw that its edges glowed with eery fringes of color. The combination of oozes which had permeated the object caused his fingers to itch and tingle.

A score of small luminous nodes swarmed around his head, and a soft voice addressed him by name. "Cugel, dear Cugel—what a pleasure that you have come to visit us! What is your opinion of our pleasant land?"

Cugel sprang about in wonder; how could a denizen of this inaccessible place know his name? Not far distant, upon a crust of back sponge, rested a small creature not unlike the monstrous bulk with the floating eye. The luminous nodes circled his head and the voice sounded in his ears: "You are perplexed, but needlessly. We transfer our thoughts in small quanta; if you look closely you will see them speeding through the fluxion: dainty little animalcules eager to unload their weight of enlightenment. There! Notice! Directly before your eyes hovers an excellent example. It is a thought of your

own regarding which you are dubious; hence it hesi-
tates, and awaits your decision."

"What if I speak?" asked Cugel. "Will this not facilitate affairs?"

"To the contrary! Sound is considered offensive and
everyone deplores the slightest murmur."

"This is all very well," grumbled Cugel, "but—"

"Silence, please! Send forth animalcules only!"

Cugel dispatched a whole host of luminous purports:
"I will do my best. Perhaps you can inform me how far
this land extends?"

"Not with certainty. At times I send forth animalcules to explore the far places; they report an infinite
landscape similar to that which you see."

"Duke Orbal of Ombalique has commanded me to
gather information and he will be interested in your
remarks. Are valuable substances to be found here?"

"To a certain extent. There is proscedel and diphany
and an occasional coruscation of zamanders."

"My first concern, of course, is to collect information for Duke Orbal, and I must also rescue Iolo's Bagful of Dreams; still I would be pleased to acquire a
valuable trinket or two, if only to remind myself of our
pleasant association."

"Understandable! I sympathize with your objectives."

"In that case, how may I obtain a quantity of these
valuable substances?"

"Nothing could be more straightforward. Simply send
off animalcules to gather up your requirements." The
creature emitted a whole host of pale plasms which
darted away in all directions and presently returned with
several dozen small spheres sparkling with a frosty blue
light. "Here are zamanders of the first water," said the
creature. "Accept them with my compliments."

Cugel placed the gems in his pouch. "This is a most

convenient system for accumulating wealth. I also wish to obtain a certain amount of diphany."

"Send forth animalcules! Why exert yourself needlessly?"

"We think along similar lines." Cugel dispatched several hundred animalcules which presently returned with twenty small ingots of the precious metal.

Cugel examined his pouch. "I find that I still have room for a quantity of proscedel. If you will take an indulgent attitude toward my acquisitiveness, I will send out the requisite animalcules."

"I would not dream of interfering in your affairs," asserted the creature.

The animalcules sped forth, and before long returned with sufficient proscedel to fill Cugel's pouch. The creature said thoughtfully, "This is at least half of Uthaw's treasure; however, he appears not to have noticed its absence."

"Uthaw?" inquired Cugel. "Do you refer to yonder monstrous hulk?"

"Yes, that is Uthaw, who is as peremptory as he is irascible."

Uthaw's eye rolled toward Cugel and bulged through the outer membrane. A tide of animalcules arrived pulsing with significance. "I notice that Cugel has stolen my treasure, which I denounce as an abuse of hospitality! In retribution, he must dig twenty-two zamanders from below the Shivering Hills. He must then sift eight pounds of prime proscedel from the Dust of Time. Finally he must scrape eight pounds of diphany bloom from the face of the High Disk."

Cugel sent forth animalcules. "Lord Uthaw, the penalty is harsh but just. A moment while I go to fetch the necessary tools!" He gathered up the Bagful of Dreams and sprang to the aperture. Seizing the tentacle he cried through the hole: "Pull the tentacle, work the winch! I have rescued the Bagful of Dreams!"

The tentacle convulsed and thrashed, effectively blocking the opening. Cugel turned and putting his fingers to his mouth emitted a piercing whistle. Uthaw's eye rolled upward and the tentacle fell limp.

The winch heaved at the tentacle and Cugel was drawn back through the hole. Uthaw, recovering his senses, jerked his tentacle so violently that the rope snapped; the winch was sent flying; and several persons were swept from their feet. Uthaw jerked back his tentacle and the hole immediately closed.

Cugel cast the Bagful of Dreams contemptuously at the feet of Iolo. "There you are, ingrate! Take your vapid hallucinations and let us hear no more of you!"

Cugel turned to Duke Orbal. "I am now able to render a report upon the other cosmos. The ground is composed of a black spongelike substance and flickers with phosphorescence. My research revealed no limits to the extent of the land. A pale disk, barely visible, covers a quarter of the sky. The denizens are, first and foremost, an ill-natured hulk named Uthaw, and others more or less similar. No sound is allowed, and meaning is conveyed by animalcules, which also procure the necessities of life. In essence, these are my discoveries, and now, with utmost respect, I claim the grand prize of one thousand terces."

From behind his back Cugel heard Iolo's mocking laughter. Duke Orbal shook his head. "My dear Cugel, what you suggest is impossible. To what exhibit do you refer? The boxful of dirt yonder? It lacks all pretensions to uniqueness."

Cugel cried out in a passionate voice: "But you saw the hole! With your winch you pulled the tentacle! In accordance with your orders I entered the hole and explored the region!"

"True enough, but hole and tentacle are both vanished. I do not for a moment suggest mendacity, but your report is not easily verified. I can hardly grant a prize to an entity so fugitive as the memory of a hole. I fear that on this occasion I must pass you by. The prize will be awarded to Zaraflam and his remarkable cockroaches."

"A moment, your Grace!" called Iolo anxiously. "I am entered in the competition and at last I am able to display my products! Observe these prime specimens, and here is a particularly choice item, distilled from a hundred dreams captured early in the morning from a bevy of beautiful maidens asleep in a bower of fragrant vines."

"Very well," said Duke Orbal. "I will delay the award until I test the quality of your visions. What is the procedure? Must I compose myself for slumber?"

"Not at all! The ingestion of the dream during waking hours produces not a hallucination, but a mood: a sensibility fresh, new and sweet; an allurement of the faculties, an indescribable exhilaration. Still, why should you not be comfortable as you test my dreams? You there! Fetch a couch! And you, a cushion for his Grace's noble head. You! Be good enough to take his Grace's hat."

Cugel saw no profit in remaining and moved to the outskirts of the throng. Iolo brought forth his dream and for a moment seemed puzzled by the ooze still adhering to the object, but then decided to ignore the matter. Cugel, with eyes possibly sensitized by his visit to the subcosmos, thought to glimpse fringes of acid blue luminosity about the object, but Iolo paid no heed, except to rub his fingers as if after contact with some viscid substance.

Making a series of grand gestures, Iolo approached the great chair where Duke Orbal sat at his ease. "I will arrange the dream for its most convenient ingestion," said Iolo. "I place a quantity into each ear; I insert a trifle up each nostril; I arrange the balance under your Grace's illustrious tongue. Now, if your Grace will relax, in half a minute you will experience the quintessence of a hundred exquisite dreams."

Duke Orbal became rigid. His fingers clenched the arms of the chair; his back arched and his eyes bulged from their sockets. He turned over backward, then rolled, jerked, pranced and bounded about the plaza before the amazed eyes of his subjects.

Iolo called out in a brassy voice: "Where is Cugel? Fetch hither that scoundrel Cugel!"

But already Cugel had departed Cuirnif and was nowhere to be found.

THE TUPILAK

Poul Anderson

POUL ANDERSON

Essentially, Poul is like Jack Vance in that, while the vast majority of his novels and magazines are science fiction, his heart belongs to heroic fantasy. I remain convinced that he would vastly prefer to go buccaneering with a boatful of berserkers than pilot a probe to Procyon, given his druthers.

This has just got to be true! While I yield to no one in my admiration for such hard-science novels as *Tau Zero,* or such marvelous sf adventures as the Dominic Flandry epos, it's obvious to me that Poul really puts his heart into the rare—the all *too* rare—fantasy that appears under his name. Books like his first, *The Broken Sword,* or the unforgettable *Three Hearts and Three Lions,* or the more recent *Hrolf Kraki's Saga* and *A Midsummer Tempest,* seem to me stronger, more sincere, more vividly realized than even the best of his sf.

For *Flashing Swords!,* Poul has been spinning a fascinating yarn about merfolk in the Viking Age which will eventually, I feel sure, make up a book. Here is the second tale in the sequence.

L.C.

THE TUPILAK

1

Now Tauno and Eyjan reached Greenland. While waiting to learn the fate of their little sister who went to live ashore, they had searched the seas near Denmark, making sure the Liri folk had not moved to anyplace thereabouts. It was no surprise. A merman or mermaid, swift and warm-blooded as a seal but without fur or blubber for armor, must make such daily catches to stay alive that the smallest band needed a broad reach for its own; and their father had ruled a realm of some size, as kingdoms went below the waves. Everywhere from North Cape and the Gulf of Finland to the Faeroe Islands and Galway coast, what fishing grounds remained—not yet overrun by humans and their nets or banned by curse of a Christian priest—had long been held by others.

Though friendly enough to the siblings, these dwellers could only suggest seeking westward. There proved to be no help around Iceland either, save hospitality during a winter more stern than Tauno and Eyjan had ever known in their young lives. People who had seen several hundred years go by told them that through the past eight or nine decades cold had been deepening. Pack ice groaned in every fjord which had once been clear, and bergs laired in sea-lanes which Erik the Red had freely sailed three centuries ago.

But this was of no great moment to merfolk, who, indeed, found more life in chill than in warm waters. The King of Liri might well have led his people to unclaimed banks off Greenland. In spring, Tauno and Eyjan sought thither.

They spent that summer on the eastern side, fruitlessly, for their search. What tribes of their father's sort that they met were uncouth barbarians who had heard nothing—for, with scant goods to trade, the swimming race actually crossed the ocean less often than did the sons of Adam. When they came upon a group of Inuit, the halflings joined those in hope of better luck.

Danish merfolk had barely gotten rumors of a foreign human breed moving southward through the great glacier-crowned island. Tauno and Eyjan found them to be hardy, skilled, helpful, open-handed, merrier companions and lustier lovers than most shore-dwellers of Europe, heathens who felt no guilt at welcoming Faerie kind into their midst. But after a few months, their way of life took on a sameness which chafed. Having learned a bit of the language, and the fact that nobody had the longed-for news, brother and sister bade farewell and returned to the sea.

Rounding the southern cape, they met dolphins who did bear a word to stir hearts—word of magic at work further up the west coast. The dolphins could say scarcely more; yonder wasn't their territory, and what they got was mere gossip such as they loved to pass onward. Nor did they care to go look; the whisper went that this was a very dangerous sorcery.

It might simply appear to be so, Tauno and Eyjan decided. For instance, the founding of a New Liri could well frighten creatures who had never seen or dreamed of an underwater city. And, whatever was going on, they had a need to know about it more nearly.

From humans back home to whom they had been close, they were aware of how matters stood ashore in Greenland. The Norse had three settlements. Oldest, largest, and southernmost was the Eastern, the Ostri Bygd. Not far from it lay the Mid Bygd. A goodly ways northward despite its name, was a later Western settlement, the Vestri Bygd. The tales of menace came out of that last.

Tauno and Eyjan swam toward it. The season was now well along into fall.

2

An umiak was traveling with land to starboard, at the middle of a school of kayaks. The merman's children broached half a mile off, coughed the water from their lungs, and poised where they were that they might take stock in safety. Shark, orca, storm, reef, riptide had long since winnowed faintheartedness out of their bloodline, but had also taught caution.

"Deeming by what the dolphins said, the . . . thing . . . hereabouts is a foe to white men," Tauno reminded. "Thus, if the matter isn't just that our kith have had to defend themselves against attack, it must be Inuit work. I'd as soon not get a harpoon in me because I'm taken for a white man."

"Oh, nonsense!" Eyjan answered. "I'd never known folk can be as gentle as those who guested us."

"A different set from these, sister mine. And— I heard stories about murders done once in a while."

"If naught else, they'll see we can't be of common earth. What we must avoid is not assault, but frightening them off. Let's go ahead slowly, wearing our cheeriest faces."

"And ready to dive. Aye, then."

Air-breathing, they slanted to intercept the convoy. They felt the chill of the water, but not in the torn and gnawed way that a mortal would; to them, it slid caressingly past every muscle, stoking warmth up within them, tasting not alone of salt but of countless subtler things, life and deeps and distances. Choppy, it rocked them as they went—whitecaps a thousand shades of blue-black overlaid by a shimmer of green. It whooshed and gurgled; afar on the beaches, it roared. A west wind blew sharp-edged under a silver-gray sky where wrack flew like smoke. Gulls filled heaven with wings and cries. To right the land rose steeply, darkling cliffs, glimpses of autumn-yellowed meadows tucked in sheltered nooks, peaks where snow lay hoar, and beyond those a bleak brightness that told of inland ice.

Their attention was mainly on the boats. Those within must have gone on some such errand as fowling, and be homebound; no Inuit dwelt quite as far south as the Norse. The umiak was a big canoe, leather across a framework of whalebone and driftwood, paddled by a score of women. As many kayaks accompanied it, each bearing its man. All the band were merry; their shouts and laughter blew among the gulls' mewings, the waves' squelpings. Tauno and Eyjan saw one young fellow lay alongside the skin boat and speak to a woman who had to be his mother, nursing her newest baby; for she laid down her paddle, hoisted her jacket, and gave him a quick drink at her breast.

Another spied them. A yell awoke. Swordblade-thin, the kayaks darted toward the swimmers.

"Keep behind me, Eyjan," Tauno said. "Hold your spear under the surface, ready for use." He himself trod water, repeatedly lifting his hands to show they were empty. His thews thrummed.

The first kayak foamed to a stop before him. He inside could well-nigh have been a merman too, or rather a sea-centaur, so much did he and his craft belong together. The hide that decked it was laced around his sealskin-clad waist; he could capsize, right himself, and get never a drop on his boots. A double-ended paddle sent him over the waves like a skimming cormorant. A harpoon lay lightly secured before him; the inflated bladder bobbed around.

For several heartbeats, he and the halflings regarded each other. Tauno tried to peer past his astonishment and gauge him. He was youthful, still more powerfully built than most of his stocky brethren, handsome in a broad-faced, small-eyed, coarsely black-maned fashion. Beneath grease and soot, his features were of an almost ivory hue, and bore the barest trace of whiskers. He recovered fast, and surprised the newcomers by asking in accented Norse, "You castaways? Need help?"

"No, I thank you, but we belong here," Tauno replied. The Danish he knew was close enough to the tongue of the colonists that he awaited no trouble in understanding. He smiled, and rolled around to let the Inuk see him.

He might indeed have been a Norseman, big and thick-muscled, save for beardlessness, amber eyes, and the tinge of green in shoulder-length yellow hair. But no mortal could have rested at ease, naked off Greenland in fall. A headband, a belt to hold a pair of obsidian knives, and a narrow roll of leather strapped to his shoulders beneath a spear whose head was of bone, were his whole clothing.

Eyjan was likewise outfitted. She came as close as a female might to sharing his height and strength; in her they showed as fullness and, ashore, a wildcat's gait.

Her skin was less sun-browned than his, for she had
red locks and gray eyes. She also smiled, and dazzled
the Inuk.

"You . . . are—" A protracted native word followed.
It seemed to mean creatures of magic.

"We are your friends," Tauno said in that language;
it was his turn to speak haltingly. He gave the names
of his sister and himself.

"This person is called Minik," the young man responded. He was emboldened, more than his companions, who hovered nervously further off. "Will you
not come aboard the umiak and rest?"

"No—" protested somebody else.

"They are not Norse," Minik said.

Reluctant, the rest yielded. Such inhospitality was un-
heard of among their race. It could not be due to fear
of wizardry; they did live in a world of spirits which
must forever be appeased, but here were simply two
manlike beings who made no threat and could surely
relate wonders. Something terrible must have happened
between them and the Vestri Bygd. And yet—

Eyjan noticed first. "Tauno!" she exclaimed. "They've
a white woman among them!"

He had been too alert to the harpoons to pay much
heed to the boat he was approaching. Now he saw
that about at its middle, staring dumbfounded as the
rest, knelt one who overtopped them; and above a
thrown-back parka hood, her braids shone gold.

The merman's children climbed over the side, careful not to upset the craft, more careful to squat in the
bows prepared for a leap. The hull was laden and
bloody with a catch of auks. Tauno and Eyjan aimed
their awareness at the single man there, a passenger in
the stern, grizzled, wrinkled, and snag-toothed. He

made signs at them, gasped, yelped, then grew abruptly calm and called out: "These bear no ill for us that I can smell." And to them: "This person is called Panig-pak and is said by some to be an angakok"—a sorcerer, familiar of ghosts and demons, healer, foreseer, and, at need, wreaker of harm upon foes. For all his modesty, customary among his people, and for all the shriveling that age had brought upon him, he had an air of wild-animal pride; Tauno thought of wolf and white bear.

The woman squealed and chattered; a few cackled half terrified laughter; their eyes darted like black beetles above the high, wide cheekbones. There drifted from them a scent of fleshly heat and, not unpleasantly, of smoke and oil and the urine wherein they washed their hair. The men crowded their own craft around. They held themselves a bit more reserved—just a bit.

The Norsewoman alone kept still. She wore the same skin coat and trousers and footgear, she was as greasy as they, but her gaze burned blue. That, her fair and tilt-nosed face, her stature and slenderness, roused longings in Tauno which no Inuk woman could al-together quell. He draped a hand between his thighs to hide those thoughts, and took the word:

"Forgive how lamely somebody talks. We learned among a distant band of the People. With them we hunted, fished, feasted, swapped gifts, and became friends. Here we will not linger. We search for our family, and ask no more from you than whatever knowledge you may have of it."

Wind blew, waves trundled, the boat swayed in shrill cold. But it was as if the blonde girl spoke through silence, in her birth-tongue: "Who are you? What are you? Not true merfolk—I think. Your feet are not webbed and your weight does not unbalance this boat."

"Then you know of our kind?" Eyjan asked gladly.

"Through tales I heard from the old country. Naught else."

Eyjan sighed. "Well, you are right. But see how you bewilder us, even as we bewilder you."

The woman hugged to her an infant that, like most of her fellow paddlers, she had along. Hers was towheaded. "Can we indeed talk freely?" she whispered.

A couple of men protested at this lingo they did not understand. Were things not uncanny enough already? She answered them more handily than the halflings could have done. These swimmers could best use Danish. Was it not wisest to let them, so they could explain swiftly and rightly? Afterward she would make clear what they had told. She appealed to Minik and Panigpak. The angakok's jet eyes probed at the strangers. After a while he agreed.

Minik was her man, Tauno realized. How had that happened?

"I . . . hight Bengta Haakonsdatter," she stammered. A pause, a cloud. "I was Bengta Haakonsdatter. I am Atitak. And my daughter—" she held the one-year-old very close—"she was Hallfrid, but we call her Aloqisaq for Minik's grandmother, who died on a floe soon before we came to him."

"Were you stolen away?" Eyjan asked low-voiced.

"No!" Bengta's free hand snatched over the side, caught Minik's shoulder, and clung fast. He flushed, embarrassed at a show the Inuit did not put on; but he let her hold upon him remain. "Tell me of yourselves," she begged.

Eyjan shrugged. "My brother and I are half human," she said. "Our father is a merman, the king of Liri, which was a realm beneath the waters off a coast of Denmark. Our mother was a mortal woman whom he loved and took to live with him. She bore him seven children; we are the last that are left. A priest laid a ban on Liri. Because of her blood, Tauno and I were not troubled by it; but our kindred can never again live there. They fled. Tauno and I had a task which kept us behind. Now we are in search of them. Have you heard aught of merfolk arriving?"

"No," Bengta mumbled. "Though I may well not have, the way my life has gone of late."

"Ask your comrades, dear. Tell them merfolk are not their enemies by nature. Rather, sea dwellers and air breathers together could do what neither alone is able to."

The singing language went back and forth. Often Panigpak put a question through the Norsewoman to the halflings. The facts emerged piecemeal. No, these Inuit knew naught of any advent. However, they spent most of their time ashore, hunting, and seldom went far to sea—never as far as the white men, who in days gone by had sailed beyond the horizon to fetch lumber (Bengta spoke of a place she called Markland) and were still wont to take their skiffs on recklessly long journeys in summer. (They huddled at home throughout the winter, which was when the Inuit traveled—by dog-hauled sleds, overland or across the ice along the coasts.) Hence they in the Bygd might have ken of happenings on islands of which poor ignorant people in kayaks could say nothing. Were that so, surely Bengta's father would know, he being the mightiest man in the settlement.

Tauno and Eyjan could not miss the horror wherewith the name of Haakon Arnorsson was uttered. His very daughter flinched, and her tones harshened.

Nevertheless—"Well, we had better go see him,"

Eyjan murmured. "Shall we carry a message from you, Bengta?"

The girl's will broke. Tears burst forth. "Bring him my curse!" she screamed. "Tell him . . . all of them . . . leave this land . . . before the tupilak dooms them . . . that our angakok put on them . . . for *his* misdeeds!"

Minik clutched his harpoon. Panigpak crouched deeper, secretive, into his furs. Women and kayaks edged back from the two in the bows. Infants sensed unease and broke into wails. "I think we'd better get out of here," Tauno said at the corner of his mouth. Eyjan nodded. In twin arcs, the merman's children dived over the side of the umiak and vanished beneath restless bitter waters.

3

The talk had revealed where Haakon's garth lay on the great bight which sheltered the Vestri Bygd. The short gray day had turned to dusk when the halflings found it. That gloom hid them while they donned the garb rolled into their packs. It would hardly disguise what they were. Instead of cloth, which dampness would soon have rotted, the stuff was three-ply fish-skin, rainbow-scaled, from Liri. However, those tunics would not offend Christians as badly as nakedness did. Out of waterproof envelopes they took steel knives, though they did not lay aside their rustfree weapons of stone and bone, and they bore their spears in their hands.

Thereafter they walked to the steading. Wind whined sharp-toothed; waves ground together the stones of the beach. Faerie sight brought more out of the murk than a human could see; but the view between hunchbacked hills was everywhere desolate. The settlement was not a town, it was homes scattered across many wild miles: for brief bleak summers made this land a niggard with the grass that, as pasture and hay for livestock, was the only crop the dwellers could count on raising. Stubble, thin beneath their bare feet, told the wayfarers how scant the latest harvest had been. A paddock, fenced by bleached whale ribs, was large, must formerly have kept a fair number of beasts, but now held a few scrawny sheep and a couple of likewise wretched cows. A small inlet ended here, and three boats lay drawn aground. They were six-man skiffs, well built, well suited to this country of countless winding fjords; but beneath the pungent tar that blackened them Tauno descried how old their timbers were.

Ahead loomed the buildings, a house, a barn, and two sheds ringing a dirt courtyard. They were of dry-laid rock, moss-chinked, turf-decked, barely fit for the poorest of fishermen in Denmark. Peat-fire smoke drifted out of a roofhole. Gleams trickled through cracks in warped ancient shutters. Four hounds bounded clamorous from the door. They were big animals, wolf blood in them, and their leanness made them appear twice frightful. But when they caught the scent of the halflings, they tucked down their tails and slunk aside.

The door opened. A tall man stood outlined black between the posts, a spear of his own at the ready. Several more gathered at his back. "Who comes?" he called distrustfully.

"Two of us," Tauno answered from the dark. "Fear not if we look eerie. Our will toward you is good."

A gasp arose as he and Eyjan stepped into the fire-glow, oaths, maybe a hurried prayer. The tall man crossed himself. "In Jesu name, say what you are," he demanded, shaken but undaunted.

"We are not mortals," Eyjan told him. The admission always scared less when it came from her sweetly curved lips. "Yet we can speak the name of Jesu Kristi as well as you, and we mean no harm. We may even help, in return for an easy favor we hope you can grant us."

The man drew a loud breath, squared his shoulders, and trod forth. He was as gaunt as his dogs, and had never been stout; but his hands were large and strong. His face was thin too, in cheeks, straight nose, tightly held mouth, plowshare chin, faded blue eyes, framed by gray hair and cropped gray beard. Beneath a seal-skin coat, he wore a coarse wadmal shirt and woolen breeks. A sword, which he must have belted on when he heard the noise, hung at his waist; to judge from the shape, it had been forged for a Viking. Were they truly that backward here, or could they afford nothing new?

"Will you give me your name too, and name your tribe?" he ordered more than asked. Defiantly: "I am Haakon Arnorsson, and this is my steading Ulfsgaard."

"We knew that," Eyjan said, "since we asked who the chief man is in these parts." In about the same words as she had used to his daughter, she told of the quest up to yesterday—save for merely relating that Liri had become barren, not that the cause of the flight therefrom was an exorcism. Meanwhile the men of the household got courage to shuffle nigh, and the women and children to jam the doorway. Most were younger than Haakon, and stunted by a lifetime of ill feeding; some hobbled on bowed legs or in unmistakable pain from rheumatism and deformed bones. The night made them shiver in their patched garments. A stench welled from the house which the eye-smarting smoke could not altogether blanket, sourness of bathless bodies that must live packed in a narrow space.

"Can you tell us anything?" Eyjan finished. "We will pay . . . not gold, of which we have none here, but more fish and sea-game than I think you'd catch for yourselves."

Haakon brooded. The wind moaned, the folk whispered and made signs in the air, not all of the Cross. At last he flung his head on high and snapped: "Where did you learn of me? From the Skrælings, no?"

"The what?"

"The Skrælings. Our ugly, stumpy heathen, who've been drifting into Greenland from the west these past hundred years." A snarl: "Drifting in together with frosty summers, smitten fields, God's curse on us—that I think their own warlocks brought down!"

Tauno braced muscles and mind. "Aye," he answered aloud. "From a party of them, and from your daughter Bengta, Haakon. Will you trade your knowledge for news of how she is?"

An outcry lifted. Haakon showed teeth in his beard and sucked air in between them. Then he stamped spear-butt on earth and roared, "Enough! Be still, you whelps!" When he had his silence, he said quite quietly, "Come within and we'll talk."

Eyjan plucked Tauno's elbow. "Should we?" she questioned in the mer-language. "Outdoors, we can escape from an onset. Between walls, they can trap us."

"A needful risk," her brother decided. To Haakon: "Do you bid us be your guests? Will you hold us peace-holy while we are beneath your roof?"

Haakon traced the Cross. "By God and St. Olaf I swear that, if you plight your own harmlessness."

"On our honor, we do," they said, the nearest thing
to an oath that Faerie folk knew. They had found that
Christians took it as mockery if soulless beings like them
called on the sacred.

Haakon led them over his threshold. Eyjan well-nigh
gagged at the full stink, and Tauno wrinkled his nose.
The Inuit were not dainty, but the ripeness in their
quarters betokened health and abundance. Here—

A miserly peat fire, in a pit in the clay floor, gave the
sole light until Haakon commanded that a few soap-
stone lamps be filled with blubber and kindled. Thereafter his poverty became clear. The house had but a
single room. People had been readying for sleep;
straw pallets were spread on the benches which lined
the walls, in a shut-bed that must be the master's, and
on the ground for the lowly. The entire number was
about thirty. So must they lie among each other's
snores, after listening to whatever hasty lovemaking
any couple had strength for. An end of the chamber
held a rude kitchen. Smoked meat and stockfish hung
from the rafters, flatbread on poles in between; all
were grimly little when the wind was blowing winter in.

And yet their forebears had not been badly off. There
was a high seat for lord and lady, richly carved though
the paint was gone, that had doubtless come from Nor-
way. Above it gleamed a crucifix of gilt bronze. Well-
wrought cedar chests stood about. However rotted and
smoke-stained, tapestries hung that had once been beautiful. Weapons and tools racked between them remained
good to see. It was all more than these few dwellers
could use. Tauno whispered to Eyjan, "I reckon the
family and retainers used to live in a better house, a
real hall, but moved out when it got too hard to keep
warm for a handful, and built this hovel."

She nodded. "Aye. They'd not have used the lamps

tonight, had we not come. I think they keep the fat against a famine they await." She shivered. "Hu, a lightless Greenland winter! Drowned Averorn was more blithe."

Haakon took the high seat and, with manners else-where long out of date, beckoned his visitors to sit on the bench opposite. He ordered beer brought. It was weak and sour, but came in silver goblets. He explained he was a widower. (From her behavior toward him, they guessed the child was his which bulged the belly of a young slattern.) Three sons and a daughter were alive—he believed; the oldest lad had gotten a berth on a ship bound back to Oslo, and not been heard of for years. The second was married and on a small farm. The third, Jonas, was still here, a wiry pointy-nosed youth with lank pale hair who regarded Tauno in fox wariness and Eyjan in ill-hidden lust. The rest were poor kin and hirelings, who worked for room and board.

"As for my daughter—"

Bodies stirred and mumbled among thick, moving shadows. Eyes gleamed white, fear could be smelled and felt in the smoke. Haakon's voice, which had been firm, barked forth: "What can you tell of her?"

"What can you tell of merfolk?" Tauno retorted.

The Norseman curbed his wits. "Something . . . maybe."

His voice gasped and choked through the dimness. "I doubt that," Eyjan breathed in her brother's ear. "I think he lies."

"I fear you're right," he answered as low. "But let's play his game. We've a mystery here."

Aloud: "We found her at sea, not far hence, amidst Inuit—Skrælings, do you call them? She and her baby looked well." They looked better than anybody here, he thought. Belike Haakon had seen to it that she got ample food while growing, because he wanted her to bear him strong grandsons or because he loved her. "I warn you, though, you'll not like what she told us to tell you. Bear in mind, this was none of our doing. We were on hand for a very brief time, and we don't even understand what she meant by her words."

The father's knuckles stood white around his sword-hilt. Jonas his son, seated on the bench next to him, likewise grasped dagger. "Well?" Haakon snapped.

"I am sorry. She cursed you. She said everybody should depart this country, lest you die of a—a tupilak, whatever that is—a magician of theirs has made to punish a sin of yours."

Jonas sprang to his feet. "Have they taken her soul out of the body they took?" he shrieked through a hubbub.

Did Haakon groan? He gave no other sign of his wound. "Be still!" he required. The uproar waxed. He rose, drew his sword, brandished it and said flatly, "Sit down. Hold your mouths. Whoever does not will soon be one less to feed through the winter."

Quiet fell, save for wind piping around walls and snuffing at the door. Haakon sheathed blade and lowered his spare frame. "I have an offer for you two," he said, word by word. "A fair trade. You've told us you're half human, but can breathe underwater as well as a real merman, and swim almost as well. By your weapons, I ween you can fight there too."

Tauno nodded.

"And you ought not to fear sorcery, being of the Outworld yourselves," Haakon went on.

Eyjan stiffened. Jonas said in haste, "Oh, he doesn't mean *you* are evil."

"No," Haakon agreed. "In truth, I've a bargain to

strike with you." He leaned forward. "See here. There is indeed . . . a flock of what must be mermen . . . around an island to the west. I saw them shortly before, before our woes began. I was out fishing. Sturli and Mikkel were along," he added to the astounded household, "but you remember that the tupilak got them. We were . . . alarmed at what we saw, unsure what Christian men should do, and felt we'd best hold our peace till we could ask a priest. I mean a wise priest, not Sira Sigurd of this parish, who can't read a line and who garbles the mass. I know he does; I've been to church in the Ostri Bygd and heeded what was done and sung. And surely he's failed to pray us free of the tupilak. Folk around here are sliding fast into ignorance, cut off as we mostly have been—" His features writhed. "Aye, sliding into heathendom."

He needed a minute to regain his calm. "Well," he said. "We meant to seek counsel from the bishop at Gardar, and meanwhile keep still about the sight lest we stampede somebody into foolishness or worse. But then the tupilak came, and we—I never had the chance to go." He caught the eyes of his guests. "Of course, I can't swear those beings are yours. But they are late-comers, so it seems reasonable, no? I doubt you could find the island by yourselves. The waters are vast between here and Markland. You'd at least have a long, perilous search, twice perilous because of the tupilak. I can steer by stars and sunstone and take you straight there. But . . . none from the Vestri Bygd can put to sea and live, unless the tupilak be destroyed."

"Tell us," Eyjan urged from the bottom of her throat.

Haakon sat back, tossed off his beer, signaled for more all around, and spoke rapidly:

"Best I begin at the beginning. The beginning, when men first found and settled Greenland. They went fur-

ther on in those days—failed to abide in Vinland,
good though that was said to be, but for a long time
afterward would voyage to Markland and fetch timber
for this treeless country of ours. And each year ships
came from abroad to barter iron and linen and such-
like wares for our skins, furs, eiderdown, whalebone,
walrus ivory, narwhal tusk—"

Tauno could not entirely quench a grin. He had seen
that last sold in Europe as unicorn's horn.

Haakon frowned but continued: "We Greenlanders
were never wealthy, but we flourished, our numbers
waxed, until the land-hungry moved north and started
this third of the settlements. But then the weather
worsened, slowly at first, afterward ever faster—summer cold and harvest hail letting us garner little hay
any more; storms, fogs, and icebergs at sea. Fewer and
fewer ships arrived, because of the danger and because
of upheavals at home. Now years may well go by between two cargoes from outside. Without that which we
must have to live and work, and cannot win from our
home-acres, we grow more poor, more backward, less
able to cope. And . . . the Skrælings are moving in."

"They're peaceful, are they not?" Eyjan asked
softly.

Haakon spat an oath, Jonas onto the floor. "They're
troll-sly," the older growled. "By their witchcraft they
can live where Christians cannot; but it brings God's
anger down on Greenland."

"How can you speak well of a breed so hideous, a
lovely girl like you?" Jonas added. He tried a smile in
her direction.

Haakon's palm chopped the air. "As for my house,"
he said, "the tale is quickly told. For twenty-odd years,
a Skræling pack has camped, hunted, and fished a short
ways north of the Bygd. They would come to trade with

us, and Norsemen would less often visit them. I thought
ill of this, but had no way to forbid it, when they offered
what we needed. Yet they were luring our folk into sin
—foremost our young men, for their women have no
shame, will spread legs for anybody with their husbands'
knowledge and consent . . . and some youths also
sought to learn Skræling tricks of the chase, Skræling
arts like making huts of snow and training dogs to pull
sleds—"

Pain sawed in his tone: "Four years ago, I married
my daughter off to Sven Egilsson. He was a likely
lad, and they—abode happily together, I suppose,
though his holding was meager, cut at the very edge of
the Bygd, closer to Skrælings than to any but one or
two Christian families. They had two children who
lived, a boy and girl, and a carl to help with the work.

"Last summer, want smote us in earnest. Hay harvest failed, we must butcher most of our livestock,
and nevertheless would have starved save for what we
could draw from the sea. A gruesome winter followed.
After a blizzard which raged for days—no, for an un-
guessable part of the sunless night which is winter
here—I could not but lead men north to see how Bengta fared. He found Sven, my grandson Dag, and the
carl dead, under skimpy cairns, for the earth was frozen
too hard to dig a grave in, the unhallowed earth. Bengta
and little Hallfrid were gone. The place was bare of
fuel. Traces—sled tracks, dog droppings—bespoke a
Skræling who had come and taken them.

"Mad with grief and rage, I led my men to the stone
huts where those creatures den in winter. We found
most were away, hunting, gadding about, I know not
what. Bengta too. Those who were left said she had
come of her free will, bringing her live child—come
with a male of theirs, come to his vile couch, though

he already had a mate—We slaughtered them. We spared a single crone to pass word that in spring we'd hunt down the rest like the vermin they are, did they not return our stolen girls."

Shadows closed in as the fire waned. Dank chill gnawed and gnawed. Eyjan asked mutely, into Haakon's labored breathing:

"Did you never think they might have spoken truth? There were no signs of violence on the bodies, were there? I'd say hunger and cold, when supplies gave out, were the murderers, or else an illness such as your sort brings on itself by living in filth. Then Minik— the Inuk, the man—he went yonder, anxious about her, and she took refuge with him. I daresay they'd long been friends."

"Aye," Haakon confessed. "She was ever much taken by the Skrælings, prattled words of theirs as early as she did Norse, hearkened to their tales when they came here, the dear, trusting lass. . . . Well, he could have brought her to me, could he not? I'd have rewarded him. No, he must have borne her off by might. Later —what you heard in the boat shows—that damned old witch-man cast a spell on her. God have mercy! She's as lost and enwebbed as any traveler lured into an elfhill—lost from her kin, lost from her salvation, she and my granddaughter both—unless we can regain them—"

"What happened next?" Tauno asked in a while.

"They abandoned that ground, of course, and shifted to somewhere else in the wilderness. Early this spring, hunters of ours came on one of theirs and fetched him bound to me. I hung him over a slow fire to make him tell where they were, but he would not. So I let him go free—save for an eye, to prove I meant what I said—and tell them that unless they sent me my daughter and granddaughter, and for my justice the nithings who defiled her, no man in the Bygd will rest until every last troll of theirs is slain; for all of us have women to ward.

"A few days afterward, the tupilak came."

"And what is that?" Tauno wondered. His spine prickled.

Haakon grimaced. "When she was a child, Bengta passed on to me a story about a tupilak that she had from the Skrælings. I thought it was a mere boogey tale and might give her nightmares. Then *she* consoled *me* and promised not. Oh, she was the most loving daughter a man could have, until—

"Well. A tupilak is a sea monster made by witchcraft. The warlock builds a frame, stretches a walrus hide across, stuffs the whole with hay and sews it up, adds fangs and claws and—and sings over it. Then it moves, seeks the water, preys on his enemies. This tupilak attacks white men. It staves in a skiff, or capsizes it, or crawls over the side. Spears, arrows, axes, nothing avails against a thing that has no blood, that is not really alive. It eats the crew. . . . What few escaped bear witness.

"This whole summer, we've been forbidden the sea. We cannot fish, seal, fowl, and gather eggs on the rookery islands; we cannot send word to the Ostri Bygd for help. Men set out overland—we've heard naught. Maybe the Skrælings got them, though like as not, they simply lost their way and starved in that gashed and frozen desert. The southerners are used to not hearing from us for long at a time; in any case, they have troubles of their own; and if they did send a boat or two, the tupilak waylaid those.

"We've barely stocks on hand to last out the winter. But next year we die."

"Or you go away," Tauno said into his anguish. "Now I see what Bengta meant. You must leave, seek new homes to southward. I suppose the angakok will call off his beast if you do."

"We'll be go-betweens if you wish," Eyjan offered.

Some of the men cursed, some shouted. Jonas drew his knife. Haakon sat as though carved in flint, and stated: "No. Here are our homes. Our memories, our buried fathers, our freedom. They're not much better off in the south than we are here; they can take us in, but only as hirelings, miserably poor. No, I say. We'll harry the Skrælings instead till they are gone."

Once more he leaned forward, left fist clenched on knee, right hand raised crook-fingered like the talons of a Greenland falcon. "Thus we arrive at my bargain," he told the merman's children. "Let us take the boats out tomorrow. The tupilak will know, and come. While we fight it from the hulls, you attack from beneath. It can be slain—cut to pieces, at least. That story Bengta heard was of how a valiant man got rid of a tupilak. He invented the kayak, you see, to capsize on purpose and reach the thing's underside. Belike that's an old wives' tale in itself. Anyhow, no man of us has skill with those piddleboats. Still, it shows what the Skrælings believe is possible, and they ought to know; right?

"Help free us from our demon, and I'll guide you to your people. Otherwise,"—Haakon smiled stiffly—"I'd not be surprised if the creature took you for Norse, and took you by surprise. You are half of our blood. Be true to your race, and we will be true to you."

Again was a windy hush. Tauno and Eyjan exchanged a look. "No," said the brother.

"What?" burst from Haakon. He tried to jeer: "Are you afraid? When you'd have allies? Then flee these waters at dawn."

"I think you lie to us," Tauno said. "Not about your bloodiness toward the Inuit, nor about their revenge, no —but about those merfolk. It rings false."

"I watched faces," Eyjan put in. "Your own following doesn't swallow that yarn."

Jonas grabbed at his dagger. "Do you call my father a liar?"

"I call him a desperate man," Tauno said. "However —" He pointed to the crucifix above the high seat. "Take that sign of your God between both hands, Haakon Arnorsson. Kiss your God on the lips, and swear by your hope of going to Him after you die, that you have have spoken entire truth to us, your guests. Then we will fare beside you."

Haakon sat. He stared.

Eyjan rose. "Best we go, Tauno," she sighed. "Goodfolk, we're sorry. But why should we risk our lives for nothing, in a quarrel not ours and unjust to boot? I rede you to do what Bengta said, and leave this land of ill weird."

Haakon leaped erect. Anew, his sword blazed forth. "Seize them!" he shouted.

Tauno's knife sprang free. The sword whirred down and struck it from his grasp. Women and children screamed. But from fear of what might happen if the halflings escaped, the men boiled against them.

Two clung to either arm of Tauno, two to either leg. He banged them around. A club hit the back of his head. He roared. The club thudded twice, thrice. Agony and shooting stars flashed across his world. He crumpled. Between shaggy-clad calves he glimpsed Eyjan.

She had her back to the wall. Spears hemmed her in, the sword hovered aloft, Jonas laid steel at her throat. Tauno fell into nothingness.

4

Day broke as a sullen red glimmer through clouds, a steel sheen on the murk and chop of the fjord. Wind blew whetted. Tauno wondered if the wind was always keening around this place. He awoke on the straw where he had been laid out, to see Haakon tower above him as a shadow. "Up!" called the chieftain, and men grumbled about in the house-dark, babies wailed, older children whimpered.

"Are you well?" Eyjan asked from across the room. Like him, she had spent the night on the floor, wrists and ankles bound, neck leashed to a roofpost.

"Stiff," he said. After hours of sleep, his temples no longer throbbed as when first he regained awareness. Blood clotted his hair, though, thirst his mouth, hunger his guts. "You, my sister?"

Her chuckle came hoarse. "Well, that Jonas lout crawled by ere dawn to fumble at me, then dared not untie my legs. I could have made do, but it was a sort of fun to pretend I couldn't." She was using their father's language. "Should I tell the rest?"

"Not unless you want to take him on, and belike more than him. We're soulless—animals—to be used however men see fit—remember?"

Haakon had come near saying as much when he had them secured: "Never would I have laid hand on any human whom I'd declared a guest, not even a Skræling. But you aren't. Does a man break faith when he butchers a sheep he's kept? My sin would be *not* to force you, for the saving of my people." He added: "Tomorrow you'll help us fight the tupilak, Tauno. Eyjan stays behind, hostage. If we win, you both go free. That oath I will give you upon the Cross."

"Can we nonetheless believe a traitor?" she snarled.

His mouth twisted upward. "What choice have you?"

This morning he had men stand around, weapons bared, while he released Tauno. The halfling rose, flexed the cramp out of his limbs, went to Eyjan and kissed her. Jonas shifted from foot to foot. "Well," he said around a mouthful of cheese and hardtack, "well, let's away and get the thing done."

Tauno shook his head. "First, food and water for my sister and me. As much as we need, too."

Haakon frowned. "Best to eat lightly before battle."

"Not for beings like us."

A middle-aged, brown-haired man, who hight Steinkil, guffawed. "Right. Haakon, you know how seals gorge."

The leader shrugged. He must struggle to hold back dismay when he saw what pounds of meat his captives put down. At the end, he snapped, "Now will you come?" and stalked for the door.

"A little span yet," Tauno said.

Haakon wheeled about. "Have you forgotten what you are, here?"

Tauno gave him stare for stare. "Have you forgotten what captaincy is . . . even here?"

Then the Liri prince knelt by his sister, took her in his arms, and murmured into the fresh fragrances of her hair and flesh, "Eyjan, mine is the better luck. If I die, it will be cleanly. You—They're women, brats, and oldsters who'll guard you. Can't you play on their fears, or trick them somehow, and—?"

"I'll try," she answered. "But oh, Tauno, I'll think

of you the whole while! If only we went together this day!"

They looked into each other's eyes as they voiced the Song of Farewells.

"Hard is the heartbeat when loves must take leave,
Dreary the dreeing, sundered in sorrow,
Unless they part lively, unweighted by weeping,
Gallantly going and boldly abiding,
Lightened by laughter, as oftentimes erstwhile.
Help me to hope that I'll see you right soon!
I'll lend you my luck, but back must you bring it——"

He kissed her again, and she him. He got up and went outside.

Eleven able-bodied men and youths came along. They could man two of the three skiffs that Haakon had from of old. Jonas had wanted to send for more from neighboring farms. "If we fail and perish, this house is stripped of strength."

Haakon denied him. "If we fail, everybody will perish. A fleet of boats could not overcome the tupilak. That was tried, you know. Three got away while it was wrecking the rest. Our main hope this time is our merman, and he's single. Also——" For an instant, glory flickered through his starkness. "I bear the name of king's reeve for this shire, not to risk lives but to guard them. Let us win as we are, and we will live in sagas as long as men live in Greenland."

While the boats were launched, Tauno stripped and bathed. He would not get weapons until the onslaught came. Most of the crew dreaded him too much— nearly as much as the monster. Well had they struck him down and bound him, but he stayed eldritch, and maybe no will less unbendable than Haakon's could have made them venture forth in his company.

Silent, they took their seats. Oars creaked in tholes,

splashed in water, which clucked back against planks and made the skiffs pitch. Spindrift spread salt on lips. Meadows of home fell away aft; the fjord broadened, dark and foam-streaked, between sheer cliffs. Against the overcast wheeled a flock of black guillemot. Their cries were lost in the sinister singing of wind. The sun was a dull and heatless wheel, barely above the mountains; it was as if cold radiated from their snows and the glacier beyond.

Each man had an oar, Tauno also. He sat by Haakon in the bows. Before him were Jonas and Steinkil; the remaining pair in this craft were grubby dwarfs whose names he did not know or care about. The second boat paced them, several fathoms to starboard. He leaned into his work, glad of the chance to limber and warm up, dull though the task was. Erelong Haakon said, "Go easier, Tauno. You're outpulling us."

"Strong as a bear, ha?" Steinkil flung over his shoulder. "Well, could be I'd liefer have a bear aboard."

"Tease him not," said Jonas unexpectedly. "Tauno, I . . . I'm sorry. Believe we'll keep troth with you. My father is a man of honor. I try to be."

"As with my sister last night," gibed the halfling.

Haakon missed a stroke. "What's this?"

Jonas cast Tauno a pleading glance. The latter took swift thought and said, "Oh, anybody could see how he hankered." He felt no real anger at the attempted ravishment. Such matters meant little to him or Eyjan; if she'd had fewer partners than he, it was because she was two years younger; she knew the small spell that kept her from conceiving against her wish. He himself would happily tumble Jonas's sister Bengta, should that unlikely chance come—the more so when he and his own sister had had trouble holding back from each other on their long journey, for the sake of their mother who had abhorred that . . . Besides, they could lose naught by his making the youngster look pitifully grateful.

"Mortal sin," Haakon growled. "Put that desire from you, boy. Confess and—make lax Sira Sigurd give you a real penance."

"Blame him not," Steinkil urged. "She's the fairest sight I've ever seen, and brazenly clad."

"A vessel of hell." Haakon's words came ragged. "Beware, beware. We're losing the Faith in our loneliness. I shudder to think where our descendants will end, unless we—When we've finished the tupilak—when we have, I say—I will go after my daughter. What made her do it?" he almost screamed. "Forsake God—her blood, her kind—aye, a house around her, woven clothes on her back, white man's food and drink and tools and ways, everything we've fought through lifetimes to keep—play whore to the wild man who violated her, huddle in a snow hut and devour raw meat—What power of Satan could make her freely do it?"

He saw how they stared from the other skiff, clamped his lips, and rowed.

They had been an hour under weigh, and begun to hear thunder where open sea surfed on headlands, when their enemy found them.

A man in the next boat screamed. Tauno saw foam around a huge brown bulk. It struck yonder hull, which boomed and lurched. "Fend it off!" Haakon bellowed. "Use your spears! Pull, you cravens! Get us over there!"

He and Tauno shipped their oars and crouched on their feet. The halfling reached low, took from the bilge a belt bearing three sheath knives which he had asked for, and buckled it on. Not yet did he go overboard. He watched what they neared, his eyes gone diamond sharp, ears keen to every splash and bang and curse and prayer, nostrils drinking deep of the wind to feed lungs and slugging heart. His will shrank at the sight, until Eyjan's image made him rally.

The tupilak had hooked a flipper, whereon were bear's claws, across a rail. Its weight was less than a live animal's, but the boat was nonetheless canted till men must struggle to keep afoot and aboard. Two shafts were stuck in the wrinkled hide—they wagged in horrible foolishness—and the broken halves of two more from earlier combats. No blood ran thence. At the end of a long, whipping neck, the head of a shark gaped and glassily glared. The limb jerked, the boat rocked, a man fell against the jaws, they sheared. Now blood spurted and bowels trailed. The wind blew away the steam of their warmth.

A rower aft in Haakon's boat yammered his terror. Steinkil leaned to cuff him, then doggedly returned to his oar. They closed from behind. Haakon braced his legs wide and hacked with a will. Tauno knew he sought to tear the walrus skin, let out the stuffing of hay and rotten corpses—

The flukes of a killer whale lashed back, up from roiled water, down on the bow. Wood splintered. Haakon tumbled. Tauno dived.

He needed a split minute to empty his lungs, let in the brine, and change his body over to undersea breathing. The icy green currents around him dimmed and shortened vision—he saw churned chaos above and ahead—battle clamor washed dully past his ears. The currents were tainted by the iron smell and taste of human gore. A dead man sank past, slowly twirling on his way to the eels.

"We'll keep the thing busy as long as we can, while you hit from below," Haakon had said. "That won't be very long."

Ready, Tauno gripped a blade between his teeth and surged forward. Attacking, he lost both fear and self. There was no Tauno, no tupilak, no band of men; there was a fight.

The hulls were shadows, breaking and re-forming, on the splintery bright ceiling of his green world. Clearer was the tupilak, the curve of its paunch . . . he saw how thongs stitched it together, he caught an ooze of mildew and moldered flesh. Claws scythed on the rear flippers. Tauno swooped inward.

The knife was in his hand. His legs drove him past as he cut. A long gap in the seam followed the blade. He swung beyond reach of a foot that swatted at him.

Arcing back in a stream of bubbles, he saw some bones of sailors drop out. Mindless, the tupilak raged yet against the Norse. He glimpsed how the tail battered, and the noise shook him.

In again—hold breath against graveyard foulness, slice away from the seam, grab that corner, heave the flap of skin wide—A slash caught him along the ribs, he lost his knife, he barely kicked free.

The beast sounded. The shark snout turned about in search. Paddles and tail sent the gross form toward him. He thought fleetingly that had those been Inuit in the boats, they'd have known to sink many harpoons in the body, trailing bladders to hamper it. Well, at best the man-eater was slow and awkward. He could swim rings around it. To get close, however, was . . . something that must be done.

The maw flapped hollow about a skeleton that, yes, seemed to be coming apart here and there. But feet and tail still drove, jaws still clashed. Tauno got onto the back, where nothing could reach him. He clamped thighs tight, though barnacles chewed them. He drew a second blade, and worked.

He could not reach clear around that bulk. But when he let go, the tail threshed feebly, half severed. Dizziness passed in dark rags before his eyes. He must withdraw for a short rest.

Did a dim knowledge stir in the tupilak, or was it driven to fulfill the curse? It lumbered back to the boats.

If it sank those, whether or not it outlasted them, would Eyjan's captors ever let her go? He heard the mass ram on strakes, and rose for a look through air.

The second skiff drifted awash, helpless till the four crewmen left could bail out the hull and retrieve their floating oars. The tupilak struck again and again on Haakon's vessel, whose prow was broken and whose planks were being torn free of the ribs. Neck and head reached in after prey. Where was the sheriff? His son Jonas hewed bravely with an ax—likewise, beside him, Steinkil. Two more poked futile spears from either side. As Tauno watched, Steinkil stumbled into the teeth. They shut. Blood geysered. He reeled back, clasping the wrist where his right hand had been.

Haakon stood forth. He must have been knocked out. Crimson smeared his own face and body, the last bright hue under wolf-gray heaven. Somehow he spied Tauno, yards away. "Do you want help, merman?" he shouted.

From under a thwart, he lifted the boat's anchor, wooden-shanked but with ring, stock, and flukes of iron from former days, made fast by a leather cable to what remained of the stempost. Jonas had drawn back when Steinkil was crippled. The other two cowered behind him. Haakon staggered aft. The jagged mouth yawned ready. He brought the anchor on high, crashed it down. A fluke put out the right eye and caught in the socket.

The jaws had him. Somehow he pulled free. "Men, swim!" he cried. "Tauno, take the beast—" He crumpled.

The halfling had strength back, and arrowed forward. Reckless of claws, he ripped. On the edge of sight, he saw Haakon's crew go into the bay. The tupilak did not give chase. Tauno was harming it too much.

It plunged when he did, seeking to seize him. But a Greenland skiff dragged behind. Hardly more could it move than if the sea had frozen around it.

Tauno's knives bit. Each piece that he cut away returned to the death whence the angakok had raised it.

Finally an empty hide floated and a shark's head sank down into darkness. The waves cleansed themselves. When Tauno reached the second boat, air-breathing again, he felt the wind on his brow like an austere benediction.

Though now made useable again, the craft was not for him to board safely. Nine men were already an overload in a hull so weakened and sprung—nine, for by use of flotsam, both Haakon and Steinkil had been brought across. Tauno hung on the rail. The hale stared at him, drained of everything save awe. Steinkil, with his rudely bandaged stump, looked as though he would live. Haakon would not. From breastbone to manhood, he was flayed open. His long frame sprawled in blood and entrails between two thwarts.

Yet he clung to wakefulness. His eyes and Tauno's met, dimming blue on hot amber. The Liri prince could just catch a harsh whisper: "Merman, I thank you. . . . Honor my oath, Jonas. . . . Merman, forgive me my lie about your people."

"You had yours to think of," Tauno said gently.

"And my daughter. . . . She'll speak to you. . . . I've no right to beg . . . but will you find her and—" Haakon strove for breath. "Beseech her—But if she won't, tell her I . . . I never disowned my Bengta . . . and in Purgatory I'll pray for her—"

"Yes," Tauno said low, "Eyjan and I will do that."

Haakon smiled. "Maybe you do have souls, you merfolk."

Soon afterward he died.

5

Faerie senses found spoor that mortals could never. Tauno and Eyjan cast about for a mere brace of days—though they did travel too through most of the enormous late-autumn nights—before they discovered the Inuit's new camp.

That was in a valley, small and snug above a high-walled bight. From the meadow a trail wound down toward the glimpsed gleam of water. A fresh spring bubbled out of turf gone sere but still soft underfoot. Elsewhere reared mountains, gray-blue where snow did not lie. Through an eastward cleft flashed a mysterious green off the inland ice. A haloed westering sun slanted rays through air brilliant, breathless, and arctic.

Dogs bayed when the two big figures in fishskin tunics strode nigh, then caught the scent and quieted; they did not cringe like white men's hounds. Hunters came out bearing harpoons, knives, or bows; they did not bluster. Women stayed at their backs, holding children close; they did not voice fear or hatred.

Everybody seemed to be at home, enjoying the spoils of a chase that had gone well. Over fires, meat of both caribou and hare made savory smoke. More was hung on poles for safety; the larger hides were being scraped

clean; women had begun chewing on the smaller to
supple them. While stone huts were there against winter, as yet families used their conical tents. Passing
by one of these, the newcomers saw a half-completed
piece of work, a carving in ivory of a musk ox. It was
exquisite.

They raised palms and called, "Peace! Remember us
from the umiak. We are your friends."

Weapons sank or fell to earth. Bengta's man took
the word: "We could not see you well. The sun dazzled
us. Somebody is ashamed."

She herself hastened forth to meet the siblings. "You
won't betray us to the Norse, will you?" she pleaded in
that tongue.

"No," Tauno said. "We do bear a message from
them."

"And hard news for you, dear," Eyjan added. She
caught both Bengta's hands. "Your father is dead. The
tupilak got him as he and Tauno fought it. But he is
avenged, the monster is slain, and before he went, he
blessed you."

"O-o-oh—" The girl stood motionless for a space.
Her breath fogged the crackling cold, till it lost itself
in a sky the color of her eyes. Smoke had dulled her
hair, which she wore now in a knot, Inuit fashion. But
she stood straight and healthy, in furs a queen might
covet. "Oh, Father, I never dreamed—" She wept.
Eyjan hugged and comforted her.

Minik had followed the talk. Awkwardly, he patted
her shoulder. "Excuse her," he said in his own speech.
"She is . . . not as well versed in right ways . . . as one
hopes she will become in due course. Arnanguaq, my
first wife, will make food and roll out bedding for
you." He smiled, shy through sorrow on her behalf.

Panigpak the angakok came likewise from the ring

of staring folk. Trouble touched his worn features. "Somebody thinks he heard something about a tupilak," he forced out. However Tauno loomed above him, his gaze and his stance were steady.

"You heard aright," the halfling replied. He and Eyjan had worked out beforehand what to say in the Inuit. Thus he told of the battle in swift strokes of speech.

The people buzzed their horror. Panigpak was worst hit. "I am a fool," he groaned. "I brought that danger on you, who never harmed us."

"Who could have foreseen?" Tauno consoled. "And, hark, there is more.

"When we returned, Jonas Haakonsson sent his carls to bid the men of the Vestri Bygd meet in a Thing. My sister—he listened to her, and spoke as she urged him. The rest listened to me. We frightened them, you understand, although they did suppose we had been sent for their rescue by the Great Nature." That was as close as Inuit could come to "God." He went on: "We soon saw that little but the masterfulness of Haakon had kept them where they are. They heeded our warning, what wise sea-dwellers had told us, that this land will grow less and less fit for them until those who remain must starve.

"They voted to depart for the south. The lot of them. First they need to be sure nothing will set on their boats. That is my sister's errand and mine—to get your promise of safe passage come summer. Thereafter the whole north country is yours."

The people yelled, danced, surged about; yet they seemed more excited than joyful, and joyful more because the feud had ended than because the victory was theirs. "I will, I will!" Panigpak sobbed. "Yes, I will send my spirit forth as soon as can be, to bargain with

the spirits of the sea for calm weather and many fish.
And my spirit will likewise ask if they who rule our
deeps know aught of your folk."

"Then, Bengta," Eyjan said low, "you must decide
your own tomorrows, and your child's."

Haakon's daughter drew free. Tears had made run-
nels through the soot on her face; the skin shone haw-
thorn blossom fair. But she wept no more, her head
was aloft, her Norse rang: "That I did last year, when
I chose Minik for us twain."

The visitors gave her an astonished regard. Silence
dropped over the Inuit. She clenched her fists and met
their gaze.

"Yes," she said. "Did you think he took me away
out of lust? Never would he force a woman, or deceive
her; he knows not how to. And we were playmates once.
He would have brought Hallfrid and me to my father.
I begged him otherwise, and in kindness he yielded.
Kindness. He had a good and able wife—who has also
made me welcome. Few Inuit want two, when at need
they can borrow; I think you of Faerie can see how
clean a help that is between friends. I? I knew not an
art of the many an Inuk woman must know. I could
only swear I would try to learn. Give me time, and I
hope to be no longer a burden on him."

"So you love him?" Eyjan murmured.

"Not as I loved Sven," Bengta said. "But for what
Minik is, yes, I do."

It was not clear how well her husband had followed
her waterfall of words. He did flush and, in an abashed
way, look pleased.

"My hope is in him, and Hallfrid's," she said.
"Where else is any? I talked to these folk through my
whole life, every hour I could. I too, like you, became
aware of the Fimbul Winter on its way; for they told

how, year by year, they watched the glaciers grow and
the sea lie ever earlier frozen, ever later thawed. When
at last I sat in an ill-made house, fireless, between three
corpses, my baby weakly mewing in my arms for hunger, I was sure of our doom. We in the Vestri Bygd
could hang onto our misery till it strangled us; or we
could go down to the Mid and Ostri Bygds—if those
hold out—and be paupers. Whereas the Inuit . . . look
around you. They've done what the Norse will always
be too stubborn for, they've learned how to live in this
country that, after all, is my home—live well.

"If you were me, Eyjan, would you not have snatched
at a chance to join them?"

"Of course," the other girl answered. "But I am not
Christian."

"What's the Church to me?" Bengta cried. "The
maunderings of an ignorant dodderer. I'll take my
hazard of hell-flames, I who have been through hell's
ice."

Her pride melted. Suddenly she covered her eyes
and gasped, "But that I wrought my father's death . . .
I will be long in atoning for."

"Why do you say so?" Eyjan asked. "When you ran
away, he harried innocent and helpless people. I doubt
you ever guessed that stern man bore so wild a love for
you. When the deed was done, should not their kith
seek revenge, and an end to the threat?"

"The tupilak was mine!" Bengta shrieked. "I thought
of it, when they wanted to send me back for the sake of
peace. I wore down Panigpak till he made it. Mine!"

She sank to her knees. "I told him and everybody—
whatever they did, quarrels and killings must worsen
with worsening years—as long as the Norse remained—
whereas if we drove them out, though it cost lives of
theirs—it would be a mercy to them also—and I be-

lieved this. Holy Mary, Mother of God, witness I believed it!"

Eyjan raised her and embraced her again. Tauno said slowly, "I see. You wanted your kin, the darlings of your youth, you wanted them out before too late. But the angakok would have recalled and dismantled his creature next spring, whatever happened, would he not?"

"Y-y-yes," she stammered on Eyjan's breast. "Then it slew my father."

"We told you, he blessed you ere he died," Tauno said. He ran fingers through his locks. "And yet . . . strange . . . how strange . . . the tupilak sent not in hate but in love."

Presently Atitak, Minik's second wife, was calm enough to help prepare a feast. That night the northlights came forth in such splendor that they covered half of heaven.

STORM IN
A BOTTLE

John Jakes

JOHN JAKES

Now, John differs from Jack or Poul in several interesting ways. While they live on the coast of California, he grimly sticks to his home territory in and around Dayton, Ohio. While Vance was a merchant seaman and Anderson an engineering student, before the both of them turned to the typewriter, John was an adman before retiring to divide his attention between writing fiction and plays.

He differs from them, too, in that the single overwhelming influence which shaped him as a writer was the redoubtable figure of Robert E. Howard. Jakes makes no bones about Brak's direct, lineal descent from the likes of Conan the Cimmerian. Nor is there any particular reason why he should, so long as he continues to spin such beguiling fantasies as the one which follows next.

L.C.

STORM IN A BOTTLE

The train of seven two-wheeled carts creaked around another corner, and the big, yellow-haired barbarian still standing stubbornly upright in the fourth vehicle let out a growl of surprise.

His scarred hands reached automatically for the cart's side-rail, closed. Veins stood out; a long, clotted sword wound down his left forearm began to ooze scarlet again.

One of the small, pelt-clad men crowded into the same cart grumbled when the bigger man accidentally stepped on his foot. In response, the barbarian moved his wrists closer together. The hateful chain-links hanging between iron wrist-cuffs momentarily formed a sort of noose. The barbarian's eyes left no doubt about whose neck the iron noose would fit.

The little, foul-smelling complainer glanced away, looking for sympathy from his companions in the creaking vehicle. The barbarian paid no more attention. Standing tall, he was the only prisoner in all seven carts who did not wear scabrous-looking fur clothing, and whose body was not matted with dark, wiry hair.

For a moment the barbarian forgot his seething rage at being captured, subdued, chained out on the arid plateau two days ago. He was diverted by the sight revealed when the caravan rounded the corner, passing from stifling shadow to the full glare of the sun.

The big man saw a broad avenue, imposingly paved, heat-hazed. The avenue stretched into the distance past shops, public marts, fountained cul-de-sacs where no water ran. At the avenue's far end rose massive buildings of yellow stone, larger and higher than any other structures in the walled city.

The barbarian took note of artfully-sculpted idols lining both sides of the avenue at one-square intervals. All the statues were identical; all were of the same transparent crystal. The image was that of a seated human figure with the head of a long-snouted animal. The creature's open jaws held a thin disc. From the ferocity of the expression, it was clear that the half-beast was about to crunch the disc between its fangs. The image was repeated endlessly, pedestal after crystal-topped pedestal, up the sweltering avenue beneath the cloudless noon sky.

Soldiers of the lord to whose slaving party Brak the barbarian had fallen prey jogged their mounts along the line of seven carts, occasionally cracking short whips. But listlessly. Their dust-covered faces and dust-dulled armor were evidence of the long trek in across the wasteland with the prisoners. On the left wrist of each soldier, from the mounted leader and his subcommanders to the two dozen accompanying foot, a simple bronze bracelet shot off red-gold glints.

Men and women of the city watched the little caravan from positions beneath awnings and on balconies. Some of the watchers wore elegant robes, others more common cloth.

A boy with one leg missing hobbled forward on a crutch and lobbed a stone at the cart in which Brak rode. The big barbarian stiffened, then realized the stone was not for him, but for the pack of bent, sullen-eyed little men crouched at his calves like stunted trees surrounding one that had grown straight.

The rock struck a man near Brak. He yelped, jumped up, began to clash his chain and screech at the watchers. His guttural speech was incomprehensible, but not his fury.

Instantly, three mounted officers converged on the cart, began to arc their whips onto the backs of the prisoners. The little men cringed and shrieked. The tip of one lash flicked Brak's face. With a deep-chested yell, he caught the whip's end and yanked, all his humiliation and self-disgust surfacing as he hauled the surprised officer out of his saddle.

The officer swore, scrabbling in the street on hands and knees. He struggled to free his short-sword. But his fellow officers repaid the barbarian's outburst for him. They pressed their mounts in closer to the cart, whose driver had brought it to an abrupt halt and leaped down out of range of Brak's flailing chains. In a moment, the stifling air resounded with the methodical cracking of whips.

Brak made abortive grabs at one or two. Futile. He closed his eyes and gripped the cart rail, trying not to shudder at each new welt laid atop the others criss-crossing his back. He would show them he was not like these dog-men whimpering at his feet. Above all, he would not cry out.

And somehow, he would escape the accursed chains dangling between his wrists like the weight of the world—

"Enough."

The voice Brak had heard before sliced through the cracking of the whips, and another sound—the mur-murings of the city people as they surged forward to stare at the strange, savage figure of the hulk-shouldered man who wore a lion-hide around his middle and his hair in a long yellow braid down his back.

Brak took another lash as the commander shouted again, *"Enough!"*

The whips laid off. Brak opened his eyes to stare into the thin, leather-cheeked face of the young and dusty veteran to whom he had been presented—beaten to his knees—after his capture.

The commander sidled his mount nearer, shook his head wearily:

"You will cast your life away, then? I told you there was a chance for you, outlander—"

"A chance to wear your chains," Brak said, and spat.

The spittle struck the commander's breastplate, barely dampening the yellow dust. The commander straightened in his saddle, fingers closing tighter around the butt of his whip.

Then, as if from weariness, or fear, or both, he slumped, letting the insult pass.

"You have the strength to keep fighting back but I haven't the strength to keep fighting you," the commander sighed. "We'll let someone else drub you into line. Just be thankful you're not like the rest of the filth we caught. Then you wouldn't even have the opportunity of manful service. You'd be put three floors underground, turning the grind-wheels for the rest of your life."

"I have no part of this fight between you and your lice-ridden enemies!" Brak snarled, gesturing at the glare-eyed little men crouched around him. His chains clinked. "I was a traveler harming no one. I was set upon—!"

The commander shrugged. "We've gone over it before. I'll not debate. While the foes of Lord Magnus yap around his heels—" cruelly, he kicked one of the little men through the uprights of the cart side, "—our fighting companies need every recruit." He held up his left arm. The bronze bracelet flashed. "I've explained your choice. Wear one of these—or a grave-cloth."

He cracked his whip, shouting to the head of the caravan:

"Move on, damn you! We've had fourteen days of this sun!"

"And so have we, and more!" a woman cried from the crowd. "If the Children of the Smoke can't bring the Worldbreaker down with spears, they'll bring him down with magic."

The commander glanced down at the crone. "No rain, then?"

"Does it look like we've been cleansed with rain? Refreshed?" someone else yelled. "The Children of the Smoke have bewitched the sky!"

"*Ah!*" The commander gestured angrily. "They have no wizards—"

"Then why does the plain of Magnus burn?" another voice jeered. "Why do the reservoirs go dry? Tell us that, captain!"

Others joined the clamor. Brak thought a riot might erupt on the spot. Nearly a hundred people started shoving and jostling the cart. But the soldiers drove them back with cuts of their whips and jabs of their short-swords.

Wearily, Brak reflected that it all had the quality of a nightmare. The heat haze blurred everything, including the snowy ramparts of the Mountains of Smoke far eastward. Those mountains supposedly guarded the ap-

proaches to the world's rim, and hid the homes of
whatever gods ruled these so-called civilized lands.

During the sweltering ride across the plateau to the
city, Brak had seen once-fertile fields that were parched,
their crops stunted. He had listened to grumbling con-
versations of the soldiers in the heat of evening and
learned that his fellow prisoners, all sharp teeth and
matted hair and hateful eyes, belonged to a large no-
madic tribe from the foothills of those distant mountains. Every few years, the tribe tried to gain more
lands belonging to the lord who ruled the plateau. It
had been Brak's misfortune to be captured and cast
among the enemy while he was continuing his long
journey southward to golden Khurdisan, where he was
bound to seek his fortune—

Some inquisitive soul in the crowd pointed at Brak.
"Who is he? Where's he from?"

"He says the wild steppes of the north," a soldier
answered.

"Kill him—his presence is another bad omen!" the
cry rang back.

"No worse than no rain for a three-month," snarled
the soldier, riding on.

The cart driver resumed his place and the caravan
again moved down the dusty avenue between the crystal
images of the man-beast with the disc in its mouth. Brak
mastered his fury as best he could, though the new and
old whip-wounds, a webwork on his muscled back,
made it difficult. So did the scowls of the soldiers, the
taunts of the crowd—

The soldiers had slain his pony in the capture. Broken
his broadsword. And chained him. Again he looked
yearningly east, toward the cool blue spires rising above
the rooftops and the city wall. The Mountains of Smoke,

white-crowned. Beyond that barrier, he'd been told, lay down-sloping passes that led into the south—

But he would never see them unless he escaped his chains. Kept his temper—and his life.

He clenched his upper teeth on his lower lip, tasting his own briny sweat, and squinted into the hellish glare of noonday, and saw certain curious things he had not seen before.

2

Most of the citizens abroad in this obviously prosperous city looked wan, frightened. Brak noted another curiosity as the cart rolled past one of the crystal statues. The disc in the mouth of the beast-headed figure had a horizontal crack across its center. He thought this a flaw until he perceived that the discs of several more statues were similarly designed.

He signaled a soldier. The man rode in, but not too close. Brak asked:

"Why is the round thing in the statue's mouth shown broken?"

"Because that is the god-image of Lord Magnus, idiot. Once he held all of creation in his possession—to break or preserve as he saw fit. Now he's an old man. And his wizard, Ool, has no spells against whatever damned magic is being worked on this land."

Brak wiped his sweat-running neck. "You mean no rain."

The soldier nodded. "Without it, the reservoirs go empty. The crops perish. It's never happened before. Not in a hundred years, or a hundred again. This was a green and pleasant land before the parching of the skies."

Brak jerked a hand to indicate the bent, hairy heads around his knees. "And the sorcerers of your enemies worked the enchantment?"

"They have no sorcerers!" the soldier rasped back. "Nothing but old medicine women who birth babies."

Or they had no sorcerers until now, Brak thought. But he kept the retort to himself—because the more closely he looked, the more clearly he could discern the tiredness and terror lurking in the eyes of military man and civilian alike.

Once more he stared down at his chained wrists while the carts lurched nearer the jumble of yellow buildings at the avenue's end. He understood one more thing now. In addition to a tribe of enemies and a magical blight that was decimating city and countryside alike, the kingdom was also burdened with a lord who thought mightily of himself. Enough, anyway, to build endless replicas of a savage image of himself, and plant in its jaws a representation of the World—

That was what it looked like, eh? Brak had never seen it depicted before.

All the emerging circumstances only heightened his determination to escape. But he would take his time, be cunning and careful—

If he survived this particular ride. He didn't care for the expressions of the men and women lining the avenue. They continued to murmur and point at him. He was an omen, and not a favorable one—

Under those hostile glares, a total weariness descended on him suddenly. Maybe this *was* the end after all. Maybe he was fated to die chained and helpless in a country whose strutting lord appeared close to defeat. Worldbreaker indeed! In all the land he'd traversed thus far, Brak had never heard the name.

Another jarring memory reinforced his new pessimism. What about the toll he had exacted for his capture? How would they settle with him for that?

Head lowered, he was staring at the dusty paving-stones rolling by when the shadow of the horse of an attending soldier suddenly vanished.

Shrieks, oaths from both sides of the avenue—

Sudden chittering barks of pleasure from the little prisoners in the carts—

And Brak jerked his head up to gasp while horror shivered his sweaty spine.

In the center of the sky, the sun was disappearing.

A smear of gray widened, dulling the light. Tendrils of the strange cloud reached toward all points on the horizon at once—and what had been noon became stifling twilight almost instantly.

The cart horses reacted to the uproar, neighed, pawed the air. One driver jumped down and fled into an alley, not looking back—

There was no wind, no roar of storm. Only that awesome gray cloud spreading and spreading from the apex of heaven. The commotion along the boulevard turned to hysterical tumult.

Darkening, the cloud seemed to race past the city's walls toward the mountains and the wasted plain in the other direction. A young woman fell to her knees, rent the garments over her breasts, shrieked—

Brak whirled. On his left, he saw a chilling sight: the gigantic statue of the lord with creation in his mouth began to fill with some dark red substance, translucent, *like blood*—

And the redness was rising in every statue along the avenue.

Kicking his horse, the harried young commander raced up and down the line, lashing his whip to keep the crowd back:

"There's no danger. No danger! It's only another of the enemy's magical apparitions—"

But the crystal images kept darkening, like the sky. The red climbed from the waist toward the head. Noon turned to night. All around Brak, the Children of the Smoke still barked and chittered—though many of them now looked fully as frightened as the citizens of the city.

The whipping and the oaths of the soldiers proved futile. The maddened crowds began to surge forward again. Suddenly Brak realized their objective. Another accusing hand pointed his way:

"You brought a polluted pagan through the gates. *That's the reason for all this—!*"

"Stand back, he's a military prisoner!" the commander yelled, just before being buffetted from his horse. The mob surged around the cart, all hateful eyes, clawing hands. Brak felt the left wheel lift.

The Children of the Smoke began to gibber and slaver as the cart tilted. Brak knew what would happen. Tumbled into that mob, he'd be torn apart—

As the cart tilted even more sharply, he jumped wide, heedless of where he landed. Both feet came down on a fat man's shoulder. As Brak continued his fall, hands tore at him. But his weight crashed him through to the pavement.

For a moment he was ringed by dirty feet, the hems of dusty robes. Then he glanced up from hands and knees and saw a ring of almost insane faces. Old, young, male, female—and above them, a sky turned nearly to ebony—

Peripherally, he saw one of the crystal statues. By now it was red to the tips of the beast-head's ears.

"Sacrifice the pagan to drive out the darkness!" a man screamed, lunging.

Brak had no weapon save the length of chain hanging between his hands. He fought to his feet, pressed his wrists together, began to swing them in a circle, whipping them around, faster and faster. The chain opened a man's cheek. Blood gushed. A knife raked Brak's shoulder. He darted away, keeping the chain swinging.

Another man ventured too close. The end of the chain pulped one eyeball. The man dropped, howling—

And then, it seemed, the splendid boulevard of Lord Magnus the Worldbreaker became utter bedlam.

The mob poured at Brak from all directions, a blur of distorted faces, yapping mouths, glazed eyes that promised murder. So this was to be the end, was it? Dying a victim of some accursed magic in which he had no hand, but for which he was being blamed and punished—

The crystal statues had filled completely, scarlet from pedestal to snout-tip. Even the cracked discs of creation were suffused with the evil-looking red. The arch of heaven was dark gray from end to end. Brak abandoned all his former resolve to preserve his life so that he might escape. Now he only wanted to sell his life expensively. If these deranged fools would kill him, they would not do so easily—

Whir and *crack,* the chain whirled. A forearm snapped; a scalp dripped gore. Brak kicked, snarled, spat, worked the chain until he could barely see, so thick was the sweat clogging on his eyelids. Although the sky had blackened, the air had not cooled. He fought in some dim, steaming inferno—

A hand grabbed his ankle. He stamped down, hard. His attacker shrieked, held up ruined, boneless fingers. Whir and *crack,* the chain sliced the air—and suddenly his tormenters began to retreat from his savage figure:

from the whip of his long yellow braid; from the flying fur-puff at the end of the lion's tail at his waist; from that brain-spattered chain swinging, *scything*—

A way opened. He lunged through full speed, crashing into one of the statue pedestals. Behind him, the crowd bayed its anger. The crowd was growing larger as more and more citizens poured in from intersecting avenues. In a moment, backed against the pedestal, Brak was surrounded.

He whirled, leaped high, started to clamber upward, his thighs bloody fom the nail-marks of hands that clawed him. He gained the top of the pedestal, teetered there, feeling the cool of the crystal against his back. To gain momentum for flailing the chain down at the enraged faces and the hands straining to reach him, he whipped the iron links back over his left shoulder—

The chain smashed against the statue. A prolonged glassy crackling modulated into a sudden loud thunderclap. Light smote Brak's eyes, blinding.

Noon light—

The illusion-cloud in the heavens was gone. Below him, terrorized people dropped to their knees, shielded their eyes—

The chain clinked down across Brak's shoulder. Panting, he curled his toes around the pedestal's edge and squinted across the avenue. There, another statue of Lord Magnus the Worldbreaker was crystal-bright, empty of scarlet.

So was every similar image along the avenue.

"You cursed fools—!" Flaying about with his whip, the commander, on horseback again, rode through the mob. "We tried to tell you it was only a wizard's illusion!"

"From where?" someone screamed.

"From the enemy who will conquer!" another cried.

"And *he* dispelled it," the commander said, reining up just below an exhausted Brak leaning against the image. The commander had a puzzling, almost sad expression on his face. "The chain's blow did it—"

The officer gestured with his whip. Brak craned his buzzing head around, saw a crystalline webbing of cracks running through the bent left knee of the seated figure. Again he felt the clutch of inexplicable dread. The darkness and the rising red had indeed been potent mind-spells. No scarlet ran out from the statue. It was solid.

The commander's smile was feeble. "The end of a short and glorious career," he said. "Now you must be taken to Lord Magnus himself. For the one crime of killing three of my men when you were captured— and the greater crime of profaning an image of the lord."

"*Profaning—!*" Brak screamed, gripping the statue to keep from falling. "The chain broke the statue and the spell and that's an *offense*?"

"Regrettably so. I have no choice but to present you to Lord Magnus for sentence of execution."

In the hot noon silence, while the kneeling, cringing throng peered at Brak through fingers or across the uplifted sleeves of robes, the commander looked sick at heart. For a moment his eyes locked with Brak's, as if begging understanding. Brak was too full of rage. He twisted his head around and spat on the webwork of the smashed crystal. He was done; he knew it. The defilement of the idol brought pleasure.

With another, somehow-sad gesture, the commander raised his whip to signal his stunned men forming up on the rim of the terrorized mob. He pointed to Brak and said:

"Drag him down."

3

In the largest of the immense buildings he'd glimpsed from afar, Brak the barbarian was conducted into an echoing hall and thrust to his knees by the tense commander. The vast, high-windowed chamber was an inferno of early afternoon shadows. The air was oppressive. Brak had great difficulty breathing.

On the journey to the great complex of yellow stone, Brak had several times entertained the idea of trying to break free. But each time, he'd decided to wait. Partly out of self-interest; partly from a sort of morbid curiosity. Before his life was taken away, he wanted to set eyes on this lord who styled himself Worldbreaker.

And there was always a faint, formless hope that if he were clever enough—though in what way, he couldn't yet say—he might save himself. The prospect made it seem sensible for him to check his impulse to fight and run.

"You may raise your head to the lord," whispered the decidedly nervous commander who stood next to the kneeling barbarian. Brak obeyed.

All he saw at first was a step. Then another; and eight more, each revealed as his gaze traveled up to a throne that had once been splendid, but was now all green-tinged bronze.

The lower portion of the throne was a massive chair. Its high, solid back rose upward and jutted out over the throne-seat to form the gigantic head and snout of the lord's image, complete with cracked disc in its jaws. In the shelter of this canopy sat the Worldbreaker.

A small, thick-chested man. So short his plain,

worn soldier's boots barely touched the floor. He wore a military kilt and the familiar bronze bracelet of the army on his left wrist. He looked more like a member of the foot troops than he did a king.

He had a squarish, strong-featured face, much lined. Pure white hair hung to his shoulders. Prepared to be contemptuous, Brak found it hard somehow. The ruler did not adorn himself ostentatiously, though perhaps only because of the heat, which was causing the three or four dozen court officials and military men surrounding the throne's base to shift from foot to foot, mop their sweated cheeks with kerchiefs and sigh frequently.

Two things about Lord Magnus the Worldbreaker impressed Brak deeply—and alarmed him as well. One was the man's grave, pitiless stare. The other was his body. Calves and thighs, forearms and shoulders and trunk were a war-map of the past. Mountain ranges and valleys of scar tissue created a whole geography of battle on the flesh of the ruler. He was, Brak sensed, no commander who had sent his armies ahead to fight. He had led them.

"You may address the lord," said a man who glided into sight from the gloom at one side of the great throne.

"Thanks be to you, oh sexless one," returned the commander, genuflecting. Brak peered at this new personage who had taken a place at the lord's right hand.

The newcomer was a tall, heavily robed man of middle years. He looked overweight. He had an oval, curiously hairless head, opaque eyes, flesh as white as the belly of a new-caught fish. Under the man's basilisk stare, Brak shivered.

The commander spoke to the ruler on the throne:

"With great Ool's leave given, Lord Magnus, I beg to report a most unfortunate occurrence on the avenue—"

Ool, Brak thought. *So this gelded creature is the ruler's wizard?* An odd specimen indeed. While the others in the chamber were obviously suffering from the heat, Ool's pasty white jowls and ivory forehead remained dry. His hands were completely hidden within the voluminous linen of his crossed sleeves.

Lord Magnus gave a tired nod:

"I saw, Captain Xeraph. From the watch-roof I saw the dark heavens and the red-running idols. A footman brought word of the desecration of one of them." The little man's gaze hardened, raking Brak up and down. "This is the pagan slave who worked the damage?"

Suddenly Brak was on his feet. "No, lord. I'm no man's slave. I was set on by your human carrion, caught and trussed up with these—" He rattled his iron chain-links.

Ool whispered, "Be silent, barbarian, or you will be slain where you stand."

"I'll be damned before I'll be silent!" Brak yelled.

The hairless wizard inclined his pale head. Three spearmen started clattering down the throne steps, weapons pointed at Brak's chest. The barbarian braced for the attack.

"Hold."

The single, powerful syllable from Lord Magnus checked the spearmen's descent. They swung, looked upward for further instructions. Ool nodded acquiescence, but unhappily; he nibbled at his underlip and treated Brak to a baleful glare.

"You have a ready tongue for a captive," said Lord Magnus in a toneless voice that might have been threatening, or might not. Brak could not tell; nor read that old, scarred countenance. "And you have no knowledge, evidently, that my image is sacred?"

"But shattering it shattered the spell," Brak retorted, glancing pointedly at the pasty-jowled Ool. The man remained impassive. Brak finished, "No one else seemed able to do that."

"Aye, the darkness rolled back," Magnus agreed. "The darkness which cannot be—" his mouth wrenched, a quick, sour imitation of a smile, "—since our mortal enemies have no enchanters to work such spells. None at all! Therefore we cannot be plagued. What happened is impossible—*everything* is impossible!" he shouted, slamming a horn-hard palm on the throne's curved arm.

At that moment Brak sensed just how much rage must be seething under that gnarled old exterior. It was a rage like his own. Although Brak did not care for this lord and never would, he did not precisely hate him, either. It was a puzzling circumstance he did not fully understand.

Lord Magnus went on, "The Children cannot work wizardries against us, therefore all I see is a deception. The water-channels dry and silted—a deception. The people maddened and near to revolt—deception. The noon heavens like midnight—and a chain that breaks the illusion—no, none of it's real. Perhaps not even you, eh, outlander?"

Brak rattled his chains. "Take these off and I'll show you my hands are real. You'll see how real when they close on the throats of your jackals."

The commander, Captain Xeraph, gulped audibly. Gasps and oaths rippled through the crowd clustered near the throne. Swords snicked out of scabbards. Abruptly, Lord Magnus laughed.

The sound was quick, harsh—and stunned everyone, including the big barbarian. With effort, he stared the ruler down. Neither man blinked.

"You seem determined to die quickly," Lord Magnus said.

"It appears I have no choice in the matter, lord." Mocking: "I violated your holy image—"

"And," put in the hairless Ool, his calm tone belying the animosity Brak saw in his eyes, "if our intelligence may be trusted, slew three of Captain Xeraph's best when they took you prisoner."

"Aye," Brak nodded. "Because they had no reason to seize me."

"The fact that you crossed my boundary-marker is reason enough," Lord Magnus advised.

"To you, lord. To a traveler bound to Khurdisan—no."

Magnus lifted one scar-crusted hand, scratched his sweaty chin where a beard stubble already showed white after the day's razoring. "Cease your glowering and grimacing, kindly! Don't you wonder why you're not dead by now? You apparently fail to recognize a chance to survive when it's presented to you."

In the little man's dark eyes, Brak saw nothing he could comprehend. A plot was weaving. But what kind of plot, he could not tell. Still, something in him seized at the half-offered promise. He felt hope for the first time.

The ghoul-white face of Ool the sexless looked stark. *Careful,* Brak thought. *Do not appear over-eager—*

He licked his sweaty lips, said:

"I do not understand the lord's meaning, that's true. But I understand little or nothing of what has befallen me. I tell you again—there was no reason for me to be imprisoned. Or brought to your city in bondage."

"You deny that a man can be slain for killing three soldiers of a land through which he travels?" Magnus asked.

"I was attacked!"

"You deny a man can be punished for desecrating the sacred law of such a land?"

"I never broke your image on purpose. Only accidentally, while trying to save myself from the mob."

"And you broke the darkness too," Magnus mused. Suddenly a finger stabbed out, pointing down. Brak saw that the finger was a toughened stub at the end; lopped off at the first knuckle long ago.

"What is your name, outlander? Where did you journey from? Most important—how did you come by the power that broke the darkness?"

The big barbarian answered, "Lord, I'm called Brak. My home was once the northern steppes. My people cast me out for mocking their gods—"

"Ah, you make a habit of that!" said Magnus, the corners of his mouth twisting again.

"When the rules of such gods defy a man's own good sense, yes. I am bound south for Khurdisan—or I was," he added with a smoldering glance at the uncomfortable Captain Xeraph. "As to why and how I was able to rend the darkness in the sky—" *Careful!* He spaced the next words with deliberate slowness. "—I ask leave not to say."

Ool chuckled, a dry, reedy sound. "In other words, you confirm that you have no real powers."

Staring fiercely at the wizard, Brak replied, "I neither confirm it nor deny it, magician. After I am dead you may make up your own mind."

Again Magnus laughed. He studied Brak closely, said at last:

"But perhaps—as I hinted—there is another way. For

the first time, I am besieged by forces against which my
host and my chariots will not avail. You are a bold
man, barbarian. Strong-looking to boot. You *seem* to
have thaumaturgic skills—whether by training or by
accident, you don't care to reveal. Very well—"

Magnus stood. Brak realized just how short the old
man really was. But his ridged shoulders and scar-
marked belly looked tough as iron.

"You cannot guess the extremes to which we have
gone to overcome this plague of dryness. A plague that
can destroy this kingdom as the pitiful clubs and daggers of the Children of the Smoke never could before.
So despite your crimes, my rude friend—and because
you staved off carnage in the streets—I will strike you
a bargain."

Cold and shrewd, the eyes of the Worldbreaker
pierced down from the sweaty gloom around the
throne.

"You will not die. You will not wear chains—"

Brak's heart almost burst at the sudden, unexpected
reprieve; then he heard the jarring conclusion:

"If you can bring down the rain."

"Bring down the—?"

He wanted to laugh. He couldn't. He was too ap-
palled by the sudden snapping of the trap.

"Open the heavens!" Magnus exclaimed, his voice
genuinely powerful now. "Darken the skies—but this
time, so they flood the land with downpour. Unbind
the spell of the Children of the Smoke—whatever it is,
and from wherever it comes—and you'll neither die
nor wear chains again. That`is my concession and my
promise, Brak barbarian. Whether you have true or
only chance powers, we shall now discover. I warn you,
none has succeeded so far in undoing the plague spell.
My own wizard is helpless—" A lifted hand made Ool

bristle; more softly, Magnus went on, "Though not through any lack of daily effort and industry, I must hasten to add. Now——"

He directed his gaze at the astounded young commander.

"While we test the barbarian, Captain Xeraph, you shall be his guardian and constant companion. Let him not out of your sight for a moment, or your own life is forfeit."

The commander went white. Brak started to protest that he had been lured into a hopeless snare, but Magnus gestured:

"I have already given you a great concession. Keep silent and ask for nothing more."

He turned his back, starting to leave by circling the throne. After a quick glance down the stairs at Brak, the eunuch Ool plucked his lord's forearm. Annoyed, Magnus stopped.

Ool leaned in, whispered. Magnus pondered. Then he wheeled around, said to Brak:

"One further condition—and a wise one, I think. You have two days and two nights to make it rain, no more."

Again Brak sensed the old fighter's desperation; glimpsed it in his eyes just before the Worldbreaker vanished behind the throne, Ool gliding after him, a white specter—

Leaving Brak to reflect dismally that he would have been better off to have been killed outright.

4

"Balls of the gods, will you pick a piece and move it?" shouted Captain Xeraph, jumping up. He stalked through the arch to the little balcony overlooking the

city and, a floor below, a courtyard shared by four
barracks buildings.

Perched on a stool much too small for his bulk,
Brak looked with bleary eyes at the out-of-humor officer pacing back and forth just beyond the arch.
Xeraph was stripped down to his kilt. Both occupants
of the tiny officer's apartment in the yellow stone complex were sticky with perspiration, even though the
sun had simmered out of sight hours ago. But another
light limned the officer's profile as he leaned on the
balcony rail and gazed at the night city.

The rooftops were outlined by red glares from half a
dozen locations. The roaring of mobs and the crashes
of mass destruction carried through the still air. Xeraph's right hand strayed absently to the bracelet on his
left wrist as he stared at the fires with something akin to
longing.

The captain's apartment consisted of two narrow
rooms. Both rooms were sparsely furnished. But the
addition of a pallet for Xeraph's semiprisoner badly
cramped the main room. The master of the quarters
swung suddenly, glaring—another challenge for Brak
to get on with his move.

The huge yellow-haired man picked up the tail of his
lion-clout, used it to wipe sweat from his nose, then
draped it over one muscled thigh so it hung between
his legs. He reached down for the wine jar beside his
bare feet.

He tilted the jug, drank deeply of the dry red wine,
heedless of the way it dripped down his chin onto his
massive chest. Putting the jar aside again, he peered
fuzzily at the playing board set on a low block of stone.

The board featured a pattern of squares in two
colors. On the squares sat oddly-carved wood pieces of

different designs. Half the pieces were lacquered dark green. The others had been left unfinished.

For two hours, Captain Xeraph had been trying to teach him the confusing game. Eating little and drinking much after the disastrous interview with Magnus earlier in the day, Brak had no head for it. Even sober, he had decided, he probably couldn't comprehend it.

But Xeraph was so obviously upset by his enforced confinement with a prisoner that Brak made one more effort. He picked up one of his pieces, the one named— let's see, could he remember?—the fortress.

Xeraph watched him slide the piece to the adjoining square. With a curse, the captain stormed back into the room, snatched up the piece and shook it in Brak's face:

"This is the wizard, you idiot! The wizard cannot move in that pattern. I must have explained it ten times!"

Brak's temper let go. Growling, he lifted a corner of the playing board. Several pieces fell off. With a sweep of his thick arm, he scattered the rest, then flung the board on the floor.

"Take your playthings and throw 'em in the pit!" Brak shouted, his eyes ugly. The hateful chains clinked between his wrists.

For a moment he thought Captain Xeraph would grab his short-sword from the scabbard hanging on a wall peg. Xeraph's neck muscles bunched. But he managed control. He sighed a long, disgusted sigh:

"I shouldn't expect some unlettered foreigner to master a game played by civilized gentlemen. But gods! I'm already sick of tending you—!"

"I didn't ask to be penned up here!" Brak screamed back, and again it seemed as if the two would go for each other's throat. Then, sighing again, Xeraph slumped, as if the heat, the effort of argumentation, were too much.

He sprawled on Brak's pallet while the latter stood glowering and fingering the chain.

"Well, one night's almost done," Xeraph said in a gloomy tone. "One more, and two days, and Magnus will take your head." His eyes sought Brak's. He almost sounded sorrowful: "You have no spells to bring rain, do you?"

Brak's answer was a terse, "Of course not. Why the darkness lifted when I smashed the idol, I don't know. Your lord's a desperate man—he admitted it himself. I have seen men in similar predicaments grow rash and foolish. That's what happened when your lord offered me that ridiculous bargain for my life."

Xeraph clucked his tongue. "The lord's too old—that's what they're all saying. Believe me, Magnus has no lack of courage—"

"His scars prove that."

"—but for once, the odds are too overwhelming. He can't cope with the magic with which the Children have cursed us."

"Nor, apparently, can his own wizard, despite those efforts to which Magnus referred. How does the eunuch try to bring down rain and end the drought?"

The officer shrugged. "To watch Ool do whatever he does—mix potions, wail at the sky—is forbidden to all but a few young boys who attend him. They are specially selected and, I might add, perverted." Xeraph's mouth quirked in distaste. "Every day, Ool rides out in his chariot, that much I know. He goes toward the channel that once brought sweet rainwater from the lower slopes of the Mountains of Smoke." Xeraph gestured eastward. "Somewhere out there, Ool tries to undo the curse—in secret." The captain concluded sarcastically, "Like to discover some of his methods, would you?"

"They sound worthless. On the other hand, since I have no powers of my own, I've thought of the idea. I don't intend to spend the rest of the allotted time pacing this room and drinking myself into oblivion."

That amused Xeraph. "Oh, you think you can improve upon Ool's performance, do you? Acquire magical skills like that?" He snapped his fingers.

Brak scowled. "I doubt it. But there must be an answer somewhere. And if it lies in magic, what better place to begin the search than with Ool?"

"You don't give up easily," Xeraph said, not without admiration. Brak simply stared at the litter of game pieces scattered around his thoroughly dirty feet. Xeraph harrumphed. "Brak, there is no answer! Except this. The rain won't come. And you'll die. Then the rest of us. This time—" Restless, he rose and wandered back to the balcony. "—this time I think the World-breaker himself will be broken. And all of his kingdom in the bargain."

Suddenly Xeraph's voice grew louder: "They're already going mad! Drinking, rioting, setting fires—"

"And you feel you should be out there helping to quell it."

Xeraph spun. "Yes! That duty, I understand. This—" His gesture swept the lamplit chamber resentfully. "It's fool's work."

Speaking out of genuine feeling, Brak said, "Captain, I am sorry the lot fell to you."

"No apologies," Xeraph cut him off. "I obey orders. It's a bad twist of fate's twine, that's all. We've had nothing else for months—why should I expect a change?"

Once more the young officer leaned on the railing, staring in dismay at the sullen scarlet silhouettes of the city's rooftops. His eyes picked up red reflections, simmered with frustration. Hopelessness.

Brak resumed his place on the stool. He picked up a wooden piece which, if his wine-buzzing head served him, represented a male ruler. He asked:

"Has Lord Magnus no trusted advisers to help point the way out of this difficult situation? No generals—?"

"He is the general," Xeraph returned. "He is the government, the chief judge—everything. Before, his shoulders have always been strong enough, his mind quick enough—"

The statement somehow fitted with Brak's appraisal of the tough little warrior. The barbarian studied the piece in his sweat-glistening palm a moment longer.

"The lord hasn't even a wife to counsel him?" he wanted to know.

"He did, many years ago—why go into all this?" Xeraph said irritably.

"I don't know," Brak admitted. "Except that I don't want to be killed."

Xeraph managed an exhausted smile. "That, at least, is something we have in common."

"We were talking of Magnus. He has no sons—?"

Xeraph shook his head. "No issue at all." Briefly, then, he narrated the story of Magnus's consort, a queen whose name he could not even recall because she had died forty years earlier, well before Xeraph himself had been born. But legend said the lord's wife had been exceedingly lovely and desirable.

Lord Magnus had been away on a campaign to harry the Children of the Smoke, who were making one of their abortive advances into his territory. A soldier in the small detachment left behind to garrison the city— "Name unknown, identity unknown," Xeraph commented—entered the apartment of the lord's wife by stealth one night. Presumably drunk, he raped her.

"The lady cried out and the terrified fool cut her throat. There was a great melee in the darkness. The soldier was pursued. Another captain who died only a six-month ago was on duty in the palace at the time, and swore he caught the offender for a moment. Claimed he ran him through with a spear. But the man ultimately escaped in the confusion—to perish of his wound in some back alley, presumably. His corpse was never found. And as I say, his name remains unknown to this day. Magnus was so exercised with grief, he could never take another woman to his side, except for serving girls for single nights of pleasure. Even that stopped five or six years ago," Xeraph finished unhappily.

Brak set the lord-piece aside in favor of the piece he had moved wrongly before: the wizard.

"And this court magician—do you think he serves the Worldbreaker well?"

Xeraph shrugged. "If not well, then faithfully and diligently, at least. You heard the lord say as much. Ool was a wandering shaman, I'm told. He came to court a long time ago, and stayed. Until now, he's always seemed proficient in minor spells and holy rituals But this particular curse has proved too large for his powers—as it has for the lord's. And so we'll be destroyed—"

"Unless it rains."

Captain Xeraph glanced away.

Brak walked to the balcony, looking out into the flame-shot dark. Thinking aloud, he said, "Perhaps I would indeed do well to observe this Ool at work. It's possible I might find inspiration! Discover powers I never knew I had—"

At first Xeraph's expression showed surprise. This was quickly replaced by new annoyance:

"I told you, Brak—observance of the wizard's private mysteries is forbidden. Just as entering his quarters is forbidden."

Brak shook his head. The long yellow braid bobbed gently against his lash-marked back. "When my life is forfeit, nothing's forbidden."

Again Xeraph couldn't contain a half-admiring smile: "Gods, what a determined lout you are. In better times, Lord Magnus could use a hundred like you in his fighting companies."

"I mean to be free of these chains, captain, not serve your lord or any other."

"What about the lord who takes life?" Xeraph retorted. "It's him you'll be serving at sunset the day after tomorrow! Look—why risk more trouble with Ool? You've admitted you have no arcane talents—"

"But I repeat, I won't sit and wait to be executed. If you can think of a better idea than observing the wizard, tell me and I'll do it."

"We'll do it," Xeraph corrected. "Remember, if I lose sight of you—" Matter-of-factly, he stroked an index finger across his sweat-blackened throat. In the distance, another huge crash rent the night. A column of flame and sparks shot heavenward. Somewhere a mob bayed like a beast.

Finally, Brak gave a crisp nod. "Well, then—tomorrow, when I'm rested—and sober—I mean to find this water channel where master Ool tries his futile spells. You can either let me blunder there alone, or you can go with me and fulfill the lord's charge that you keep watch on me."

"You could never pass the city gates without me."

"Don't be too sure, captain."

Slowly Xeraph wiped his palms down his lean thighs. He gave Brak a steady look. Not defying him. Testing:

"But what if I say no to your excursion, my friend?"

"I will go anyway."

"I might stop you."

"You might try," Brak replied softly.

In truth, he felt that the plan was exactly like all other plans afloat in the capital of Magnus the World-breaker: worthless. But he had no other alternative in mind.

He felt like an animal hunted by mounted men and dogs. With certain doom at his heels, he was still unwilling to stop and await death. He preferred motion—even though it was empty of solid hope or solid purpose. At least doing something might temporarily dispel the morbid thoughts of his future—besides, perhaps the scheme wasn't so foolish after all.

The wizard Ool presented curious contradictions. If he had entrenched himself at the court with his magical proficiency in the past, why had his talents suddenly proved wanting? Having experienced firsthand the abilities of both lesser and greater wizards, Brak could understand how Ool might not be competent to overcome the drought spell. Yet it was still odd that none around Lord Magnus raised the question of why Ool failed. They merely accepted it.

Perhaps they were too occupied with the tangible, pressing dangers of an advancing enemy and a populace in near-revolt. Perhaps the outside viewpoint of a stranger was required to see past distractions to simple, essential questions—

Such as the puzzle of Ool. Brak's hard, sweating face confirmed his resolve concerning the matter.

All at once, Captain Xeraph bowed to that, and laughed:

"Damn you for an insolent rogue, Brak—all right, we'll go. At sunrise." He kicked at the fallen play-pieces and added, with a smile that bore no malice, "It can't be any more useless than trying to teach a thick-skulled foreigner this noble game."

Brak smiled a bleak smile in return and reached for the wine jar. Out in the city, more burning buildings began to fall, crashing—

5

The sun ate cruelly at Brak's body, promising painful burns by nightfall. With Captain Xeraph, he was crouched at the foot of a ridge some distance east of the city. The wall, some rooftops and columns of smoke could still be seen through clouds of dust blowing across empty, desiccated fields.

Like Brak, Captain Xeraph had cast aside the coarse cowled cloak each had worn to slip through the city gates shortly after dawn. Xeraph's presence had permitted them to leave with only a brief questioning. The discarded cloaks lay under a stone now, snapping and fluttering at their feet.

Xeraph wore a plain artisan's kilt. Except for his short-sword and the bronze bracelet which could not be removed, there was nothing to mark him as a military man.

He looked fearful as Brak peered toward the jumbled

boulders along the ridge-top. Both men could clearly hear the strange sounds coming from the far side.

Brak knew why Xeraph was upset. What they were about to do was forbidden. Yet as Brak listened, the sounds seemed more odd than alarming; a mystery more than a menace.

He heard the creak of wheels, the rattle of hoofs. Now louder, then fading—exactly like the furious thudding of beaten drumheads. A voice chanted an incomprehensible singsong.

"I am going up to look, captain," Brak said.

Xeraph swallowed. "Very well, we'll—" Abruptly: "No, I'll stay here."

He shoved the point of his sword against Brak's throat. The barbarian edged away quickly but carefully. Xeraph's trembling hand might cause an accident.

"Don't get out of sight, understand?"

Xeraph darted a nervous gance around the sere horizon. Further east stood a farmstead, abandoned in the blowing dust. Hoofs and wheels, drums and chanting grew louder again. Brak gave a tight nod, turned and began to clamber up the hillside.

He moved cautiously, with the craft of the steppe-born hunter. Twice he stopped still and cursed, as the damnable chains between his wrists clinked too loudly.

He turned once to see Captain Xeraph staring up at him with an absolutely terrified expression. Brak hardened his heart and continued his climb. Whatever lay on the other side of the ridge was not sacred to him. And in his travels toward Khurdisan's golden crescent in the far south, he had encountered many marvels and enchantments. He did not precisely fear the sight of an inept wizard.

At length he worked himself between two boulders,

his lips already dry and cracked from the heat. He looked out and down—

And blinked in astonishment.

As Xeraph had said, an immense, stone-lined channel lay below. It stretched east toward the mountains, west toward the city. The channel was filled with blowing dust.

Along a track on the far side, an imposing gold-chased chariot drawn by four white horses raced at furious speed. Brak counted five people in the oversized car, in addition to the driver.

Gripping the car's front rail, his voluminous robes flying behind him, stood Ool the magician, head thrown back. It was Ool uttering that weird, ululating chant.

Behind him, swaying and knocking against one another, was a quartet of boys with pudgy pink legs, ringleted hair, soft hands and generally feminine appearance. One had a pair of drums suspended on a strap around his neck. Another pounded the skin drumhead with padded beaters. A third picked up lengths of wood from the floor of the car and set them afire with a torch. The fourth threw the fresh-lit firebrands out of the car while Ool continued to chant.

Brak swore a foul oath. The whole expedition had been wasted. He had seen a similar ceremony in his youth in the wild lands of the north—and if this was all Ool could muster to open the heavens and relieve the drought, he was a poor wizard indeed.

The chariot continued to race along beside the channel, traveling a short way eastward before wheeling back again. Ool kept up his singsong chant. The drums pounded. The torches arched out of the car every which way—

Despairing, Brak watched only a few moments longer. Just as the chariot completed its course away on his left and turned back toward his vantage point, he prepared to rejoin Xeraph. The chariot swept along beside the channel—and a gust of wind caught the magician's gown, flattened his sleeves back against his forearms. Suddenly Brak's belly flip-flopped. He stared through the sweat running off his eyebrows. Stared and stared as the chariot raced nearer, boiling dust out behind—

Firebrands scattered sparks. The drums *thud-thudded*. Brak squinted against the sun-glare, watching Ool's hands gripping the rail of the car—

As the chariot swept past, a thin suspicion became an alarming possibility.

The chariot thundered on, the drum-throbs and hoof-rattles and wheel-creaks diminishing again. Brak scrambled up, avoiding Captain Xeraph's anxious gaze from the bottom of the ridge.

What should he do? Go instantly to Lord Magnus? No, he'd never be believed. He was an outlander with no status except the useless one of prisoner. Automatically, he would be counted a liar.

And if Ool heard of an accusation, he would probably move against the barbarian in some secret way. Have him slain before the time limit expired—

Yet Brak knew he had to act. Gazing into the dusty sunlight, he let his mind cast up images of the magician in the chariot. White cheeks. Jowls jiggling, soft and flabby. And the hands; the momentarily bared hands and forearms—those Brak saw most vividly of all.

Not a little frightened, he clambered down. Xeraph clutched his arm:

"What did you see?"

"Trumpery," Brak said with a curt wave, wanting no hint of his suspicion to show on his face. "Magic such as the pathetic shamans of my own land practiced in hopes of changing the weather—"

Briefly he described the sights he'd observed—except for Ool's revealed hands.

Captain Xeraph was baffled by the details Brak reported. He asked for further explanation.

"They beat drums and throw torches helter-skelter to simulate thunder and lightning. Along with that, Ool howls some spell or other. The idea is to summon storms by imitating them. I've never seen it work before and I venture it won't work now."

Because, whispered a cold little serpent voice in his mind, *it is not meant to work.*

"Captain Xeraph," he said, "we must immediately—"

He stopped. Would this plain soldier who dealt in simple, fundamental concepts such as marching formations and use of weapons understand what he did not fully understand himself? Certainly he could not prove so much as one jot of his suspicion—yet. An accusation now, even presented to one such as Xeraph who, Brak felt, half-trusted him, would only bring ridicule.

Brow furrowed, Xeraph stared at him. "Must what, outlander? Finish what you started to say."

At last Brak knew what he must do. *Tonight.* Tonight would provide the only hours of darkness left.

But as he realized what he had to do—and do alone —he felt dismayed. If he took the risk, followed out the sketchy plan already in mind, he might put Captain Xeraph's life in jeopardy. And while he would never be fond of any captor, Xeraph was at least more agreeable than most.

Still, his own life was in jeopardy too. That made the difference.

"We must immediately return to the city," Brak concluded, a hasty lie. He felt the shame of a betrayer, the dread of the night's work waiting. "I saw nothing but a eunuch doing child's magic."

Xeraph looked relieved. They crept away from the ridge. The drumming and chanting and chariot-clatter faded.

Cloaked again, they trudged west in the heat. Each was silent, but for different reasons.

6

A night and a day. Like some drunken balladeer's refrain, the words kept coming to Brak's thoughts as he lay tensely on his pallet, counting time. *A night and a day*—

Outside, steamy darkness; his final night was perhaps half gone already. On the morrow, he would have no more chance. The light of the simmering sky would make his desperate gamble impossible. *A night and a day to make it rain*—

No, he amended in the grim silence of his thoughts, *a night—this night—to discover why it does* not *rain.*

At last, the stertorous breathing of Captain Xeraph subsided in the adjoining room. Brak rolled over, raised himself on an elbow, then bunched his legs beneath him.

Slowly he rose to a standing position. His body was already slicked with perspiration. The fall of the sun had brought no relief, no coolness. Through the arch that led to the apartment's regular bedchamber, the sounds of Xeraph thrashing came again.

As he stole barefoot toward the peg where Xeraph's sword-scabbard hung, Brak tried to remember the position of the hilt—about half way up the wall, wasn't it? He kept moving, cautiously—

Another pace.

Another.

Three more to go.

Then two.

He froze.

Soldiers were crossing the courtyard below the balcony. Three or four of them, he couldn't be certain. They were singing an obscene barracks ditty.

At last a heavy door closed. Brak moved again, wondering that the men of Lord Magnus had the heart to sing while the red of last night's fires still flickered throughout one quarter of the sky. A vast tenement section had been set ablaze, Xeraph had reported after the evening meal. The flaming devastation had yet to be contained—

Well, perhaps the soldiers of Magnus drank heaviest and sang loudest when they were powerless against certain defeat.

He listened. The courtyard was silent.

He lifted his hand, groping for the hilt of the short-sword. But somehow, while his attention had been distracted by the noises below, he had lost his precise sense of distances in the dark. Reaching out, he felt the back of his right hand collide suddenly with the hilt while his fingers closed on empty air. The scabbard knocked the wall. Loudly—

For a moment he held absolutely still, breath sucked in. But the damage was done. Wakened by the noisy thump against the intervening wall, Xeraph muttered a questioning monosyllable.

Brak didn't debate with himself for long. There would be no arguing with Xeraph. The captain would forbid what he'd planned. He jerked the short-sword from the scabbard, heedless of the racket of his chain. He pivoted and plunged toward the balcony.

Behind him he heard Xeraph thrash, call out. Then Brak caught the *slap-slap* of running feet.

One thick, scarred leg hooked over the low balcony wall as Xeraph rushed from the darkened apartment. Both hands on the hilt, Brak whipped up the short-sword, turning the blade just so and hammering it down in what he hoped would be a felling but not wounding blow.

Again he cursed his bad luck. He could tell the blow was mis-aimed. Xeraph was moving too fast, cursing him as a damned trickster—

The sword-flat thwacked and slid away. Captain Xeraph let out a loud, hurt cry as he crumpled.

Brak listened again, hoping that the doorkeeper on the floor below was drowsing in his booth. But again luck eluded him. The distant rapping of boots signaled the doorkeeper climbing the inner stairs to investigate the cry.

Brak faced a terrible decision. Remain—and fail. Or go on, and leave Xeraph to be discovered. Minus his prisoner. The barbarian knew what Xeraph's punishment would be—

In the hot darkness, Brak's face hardened. He would try to complete his night errand swiftly. Come back to Xeraph in time.

But if he failed—

Well, better not to think of that.

Xeraph was a decent, kindly jailer. But something deeper and darker within the huge barbarian swept that consideration aside. Something deeper, darker—and as heavy as the chains between his wrists.

The doorkeeper hammered outside Xeraph's apartment. A querulous voice inquired whether something was amiss. Xeraph, a fallen lump, stirred. Groaned.

Brak's face was pitiless, a mask for his regret as he swung his other leg over and dropped toward the courtyard.

He would save Xeraph if he could. But above all, he would not live in chains.

7

Infuriated by the series of unlucky circumstances that had so far wrecked all but the basic thrust of his plan, Brak landed in a jarring crouch. He did his best to muffle the clinking links against his naked belly, at the same time maneuvering to keep from being cut by the sword.

He heard the doorkeeper knocking more insistently now. He bolted for the far side of the quadrangle, and a passage that would lead to a second, larger yard in the palace complex.

The knocking and shouting continued. Brak dodged into the passage just as a lamp was lit in another officer's apartment. The whole area would be awake soon. Damn and damn again!

Racing down the passage, he checked where the wall ended. He flattened his naked back against stone that still radiated heat. Behind him, more lamps bobbed. Shouts of genuine alarm were being raised.

He forced his concentration ahead. Saw a tired, limping soldier crossing the dark square on guard duty. The man walked with infernal slowness. Would he hear the commotion—?

Brak's breath hissed in and out of his lungs, a low, bestial sound. His eyes picked up some of the scarlet glare in the cloudless sky. Like a preying animal, he watched and counted time's destructive passage. If the soldier reacted to the distant noise from the officer's quarters—or if he about-faced to recross the square instead of proceeding on rounds elsewhere, Brak intended to kill him.

But the man did vanish inside a lantern-hung doorway. Perhaps he'd heard the racket and didn't care. Perhaps he wanted a drink of cool wine to break the night's sticky monotony. Whatever the reason, he was gone.

Whipping his head left and right, Brak checked for anyone else who might be observing him. He saw no one. He broke from cover, dashed toward the outer staircase of the two-story yellow building directly opposite.

On the second floor of that structure, he had learned via a casual inquiry to Xeraph, Ool the eunuch had his quarters. The floor below was occupied by the two dozen pink-lipped boys who served him. No one else was permitted to enter the building, Xeraph said. No other servants. Not even Lord Magnus.

Panting, Brak reached the exterior steps, crouched at the bottom, peering upward. He expected to see a guard posted on the terrace entrance to Ool's apartment. He saw no one.

Taking a tight grip on the sword's hilt, he began to climb, muffling the clinking chain as best he could. Time was running too fast for complete caution—

He still had no clear notion of what he expected to find, should he be lucky enough to penetrate Ool's private quarters. Evidence of treachery—but in what form? He couldn't predict.

Still, he was convinced his suspicions had some foundation. So he took the stairs three at a time.

By the time he neared the top, he wondered whether

Ool's position was so secure, and his powers so feared, that he needed no personal guards. Somehow, Brak couldn't believe that. Yet, conscious of Xeraph's peril, he didn't pause to ponder the question—

He reached the terrace, immediately turned right toward a doorless arch where thin hangings stirred slowly. Deep in the dark of the apartment beyond, he saw white light flicker. He heard a small, hollow rumbling, mysterious and inexplicable, that somehow made his spine crawl.

A slithering noise spun him around.

He sucked in a startled breath at the sight of one— no, two—gods, *three* of the plump-faced boys rising from the shadow of the terrace railing. Had they been squatted there all along? Because of his haste and the darkness, Brak had missed them.

Their peculiar bright eyes glistened with red reflections from the sky. One boy giggled, shuffled a sandaled foot forward. Pressed against him, his companions followed suit.

The three advanced another step with those gleeful, half-mad expressions on their faces. *Were they drugged assassins*—?

Wary, awaiting attack, Brak was in one way reassured. Ool's quarters were, in fact, guarded. Because he had something to conceal?

In a wet, lisping voice, one of the round-faced trio said, "No one may enter to disturb the slumber of the sexless one."

"I think this says otherwise," Brak growled, giving the short-sword a flourish.

From the apartment he heard that preternatural rumbling again. The white-fleshed boys interlocked their hands and laughed at him. High-pitched, feminine giggles—

They were not armed. *But they were laughing at him!*

He backed up a pace, dread grabbing at his bowels. The trio kept mincing toward him, hands clutching hands. The faces suddenly glowed paste-white, illuminated by that strange radiance flaring inside the apartment—

Somehow, Brak's eyes misted. He blinked. No, the trouble was not in his eyes. A fog seemed to be forming around the boys.

The middle boy opened his mouth to laugh again. And Brak's brain shrieked nameless terror as that mouth began to *grow*—

Began to stretch upward, downward, to both sides simultaneously, becoming a huge, spectral monstrosity with sharp, filed teeth that gleamed wet with spittle. *Teeth the size of Brak's own head*—

Suddenly there were three giant, slavering mouths, each swollen outward from the head of a boy. There was a mouth on his left, another on his right, one directly ahead—all three arching forward to bite his skull and crack it—

Enchantments! Brak's mind screamed. *Illusions! They need no weapons because Ool taught them to guard with spells*—

Yet his own terror was real. So was the horrendous *craack* as the gigantic, disembodied central mouth clashed its teeth together, almost taking off his left arm.

Brak could see nothing of the trio of boys now. Only the formless mist in which the distended mouths were the sole perverted reality. Huge pink-lipped maws, clicking and grimacing and coming closer, left and right and ahead, *closer*—

The left mouth clashed its teeth three times. Then

an immense, serpentine tongue shot from the maw and licked the lower lip in anticipation. A spittle-gob the size of fist dripped from the tongue's end—

Mesmerized with dread, Brak barely heard the noise on his right. He jerked his head around just in time to see the mouth arching over him, the gigantic teeth straining apart in preparation for the death-bite. Brak's brain howled his mortal fear. Yet something else within him still cried out:

Spells! Mind-dreams! You have seen them before! FIGHT THEM—

Both hands on the blade-hilt, he somehow found strength to hurl himself beneath the closing jaws— *CRAACK*—and stab into the mist as far as his chained arms would permit. Somewhere in that ghostly whorl of mind-smoke, the tip of his sword struck solid flesh—

A human shriek, bubbling and wild, roiled the smoke suddenly. The grinding mouth that had almost closed on him vanished.

The images of the other two began to shimmer and grow dim. Through the smoke he perceived a dying boy sprawled on the terrace flags, black-looking blood pouring out of his stabbed throat.

The mouth facing Brak flew at him, sharp-filed teeth wide open. But this time Brak fought his own hysteria more successfully, braced his legs and stabbed into the mist beneath the apparition—

And it too vanished, simultaneously with a cry of mortal hurt.

One phantom left—and that image was feeble. Through the vile, immense tongue, Brak glimpsed the reddened heavens of the city. He tossed his sword to his left hand, extended both arms as far as he could, and killed the unseen boy behind the snapping mouth—

Which shrank and puffed away, leaving three sad, suetlike bodies in a bloodied heap.

Gasping, Brak wiped sweat from his eyes. His heart pounded so heavily that it almost brought physical pain. Surely the cries of the boy-guards with their devilish mind projections had wakened the sleeper in the apartment. And others near the square—

Brak peered over the stone railing, saw the lone soldier pacing listlessly again. The only sounds the big barbarian heard were the drag of the soldier's boots and—behind him—that strange, hollow crashing that reverberated into stillness.

He leaned down, prodded one of the forlorn corpses. His fingers came away sticky with warm blood. No, the obscene mouths had not been real. But the briefly-invisible bodies that had tasted his iron had been real. That in itself was a reassurance of sanity, giving him the courage to turn, take three steps, raise his short-sword to touch the edge of one of the hangings and lift it—

Again that eerie white light flickered and danced deep in the apartment's gloom.

Brak tried to discern the light's source. It seemed to radiate from behind another drapery. But he couldn't be sure.

He listened again.

Silence. Where was Ool?

If Brak had somehow slain the evil boys without a sound, perhaps the wizard had not been awakened. Perhaps all the noises he'd heard during the struggle had been illusions too. The thought emboldened him to the point of taking one step past the hanging. From the concealment of the distant drapery, the hollow booming sounded once more.

Brak's backbone crawled as a sibilant voice spoke:

"Even in sleep, my mind is linked with those of my protectors. Their power comes from my thoughts, you see. When they died, I awakened. To give you a fitting reception, my curious outlander."

On the last word spoken by the unseen Ool, the short-sword in Brak's right hand burned. He screamed and let go.

The blade flew toward the ceiling, lighting the whole splendidly-furnished apartment for one bizarre instant. The sword turned molten, dripping. Dollops of glowing fire struck the apartment's tiles and burned smoking pits into them.

Brak dodged back from the fire-shower, seeing beyond it the hairless body of Ool standing beside his canopied bed, naked save for a loin-wrapping of linen that matched the whiteness of his flesh.

The last droplets of the destroyed sword struck the tiles and hissed out. But not before Brak had glimpsed the damning evidence again:

Ool's left wrist did bear the mark Brak thought he had seen when the wind blew back the wizard's sleeves in the chariot—

The mark was a scarred ridge of tissue circling the left wrist. Once, the man's flesh had been bound by a tight bracelet.

"You have come to perish, then," smiled Ool. "I shan't disappoint you—"

Immense, invisible hands created with no more than a blink of Ool's basilisk eyes lifted Brak and hurled him to the floor. His ears rang as he hit. His body went numb with pain.

Slowly, the pale wizard advanced toward the place where the big barbarian lay writhing, trying to regather his strength. With a little purse of his lips, Ool lifted one bare foot and placed it on Brak's sweating chest. With his right hand he made a quick mesmeric pass.

Instantly, Brak felt as though the weight of a building pressed down on him. He clenched his teeth, lashed his head from side to side, growled savagely—

But he could not move. He was held by the magical weight of Ool's soft, clammy foot.

From where he sprawled, Brak saw the magician's obscenely white shine in the glare from behind the far curtain. Ool the sexless one lifted his left forearm, displayed the scarred wrist almost mockingly.

"Is this what you came to see, outlander? Well—" An exquisite shrug. "Look your last."

8

Brak the barbarian lay helpless under that pasty white foot, his arms and legs and trunk tingling faintly. The pain of his hard fall was diminishing. But he was still unable to move. He was prisoned not by visible weight, but by the weight of Ool's arcane talents.

From what Brak could see of Ool, whenever the white light-source flared behind the distant curtain, the wizard continued to act amused. At length he gave voice to that amusement:

"You played boldly before my Lord Magnus, that I'll put to your credit. But you were foredoomed. Consider it an act of mercy on my part when I suggested you be allowed only two days and nights to work your nonexistent magic. No one can draw down the rain because I have gathered and held it. There."

A supple, almost boneless gesture with the left hand —toward the rumbling light-source.

"For the Children of the Smoke," Brak gasped out.

"Ultimately," Ool agreed. "But in chief, for myself. You see—" the whitish lips hardened into a cruel line, "—years ago, the Worldbreaker took something from me that represented irredeemable loss. Not by his own hand did he take it from me. But the hand which did the deed was his instrument. So I fled west to the lands of Shend, and for several years I discipled myself to their great wizards. I had some natural talent, I discovered—most humans do. Perhaps even you. But such talents lie dormant for lack of training and development. Had I not been so blessed, however, I would have sought another means of revenging myself. In any case, when my preparations were complete, I returned to his court as a different man. Unrecognized. My plan was to gain the confidence of Lord Magnus. Thus I served him well and faithfully for years—"

"Until the time when you were ready to strike against him."

Ool nodded. "You have a sharper wit than the few northlanders I've encountered. You have brains you put to use—guessing, puzzling out answers—yes, you're right. I waited. Always maintaining secret communication with the Children. Always urging *them* to wait until their numbers were great enough—and Lord Magnus was old, his powers failing. The hour came finally, as I knew it would," Ool said with another purse of the moist lips. "In a few weeks—a month or two—but soon, the Children will sweep out of the east. By then, the maddened people within these walls will have no more heart or strength to resist. Even the army will rise, I imagine. Such is the miraculous power of nature's rain—and the lack thereof."

"Was—" Brak thrashed again. But the supernatural weight seemed to restrain every part of him. "—was it you, then, who blacked the sky and filled the crystal idols with what looked like blood?"

"Of course." Ool smiled. "There will be additional—ah—demonstrations of that sort before I send my last signal to the Children. Alas, you spoiled that particular illusion. The blow from your chain, I think. Breaking the idol, it broke the projective trance. I was lying yonder—" he indicated the rumpled bedclothes that exuded a sweet but somehow foul perfume, "—arranging it all with my mind. Of a sudden, I was jolted awake. Much the same thing happened when you killed my dear little guards. But enough of that. Although you are the loser and I am the winner in this small contest—"

He smiled again, seeing the glare in Brak's eyes. Again the big barbarian tried to move; futile. The naked foot held him. He could do nothing but clench and unclench his fists.

"—I respect certain of your qualities. I would like to know this much. What brought you here? These rooms are forbidden, even to the lord. I made sure of that long ago, so I could pursue my—private ventures undisturbed."

"The sight of the scar brought me," Brak said. "And certain things repeated by Captain Xeraph—"

Ool's hairless brows quirked, the back and sides of his oval head illuminated by another glare from behind the drape. "But when did you see the scar, pray? In public, I keep my hands forever hid in full sleeves."

"I spied on your so-called spell-working at the water-channel yesterday. While you were in the chariot, the wind blew your gown aside as the car went by the rocks where I was watching."

Ool was genuinely amused.

"I don't doubt your own people cast you out, my friend. No spell-worker of small talent could abide a man of your perceptions observing his mummery."

"But the holding back of the rain is no mummery—"

"I told you, I have not held it back," Ool corrected, crooking one pudgy finger in an almost schoolmasterish way. "I have imprisoned it. That, too, I learned in Shend, and thought it an excellent major weapon at the proper time. That time, mercifully, has come."

"Will—" Again Brak forced out each word. "Will you rule the Children when they take over the World-breaker's kingdom?"

After a thoughtful pause, Ool replied, "I think not. I'll advise them, no doubt. Influence them. But the real savor of this victory will come long before I find my-self in such a position." The white-oval face wrenched. "My only desire is to bring down that swilling, postur-ing little war-cock!"

"At least—" Brak struggled to breathe. "—at least he'll die a man. Which is more than you can ever claim."

Ool's pale face contorted. He shrilled an almost feminine scream, leaning over. One wrathful hand slapped Brak's face. The blow was sharp, vicious. But the big barbarian hardly felt it; he felt something more important. Something for which he'd hoped and gambled with the gasped insult—

He felt the shift in weight on his chest. The pressure lessened ever so little. Still bent over, Ool was prey now. If he could strike fast enough—

Brak's chained hands came up. An inch. Another. Faster, rising—

By leaning to strike Brak's face, Ool had somehow weakened the occult weight. Brak could shift his trunk a little, raise one shoulder up in the same instant he seized Ool's left ankle with both hands, and wrenched.

Heaving against the phantom power holding him

down, Brak managed to hurl the wizard off balance. Ool toppled backwards, linen wrap flying.

The wizard reeled into a taboret, collapsed it as he fell, floundering and shrieking. Brak struggled to his feet, his huge, rope-muscled body washed by the white glare from behind the drapery. The hollow boom rolled through the chamber as Brak drove himself toward that curtain and the secret it concealed—

Behind him, Ool squealed and gibbered in rage. At any moment Brak expected some ensorcelled bolt of fire to strike him, char the flesh off his bones, burn him dead. His leaping strides were long, fear-driven—

Ool still flopped about on hands and knees, not yet fully recovered from his upsetting. Brak's hands closed on the white-shimmering drapery, coarse stuff. He tugged. Rings clattered. Fabric tore—

With a cry of terror, Brak flung up an arm to shield his eyes.

On a low stone pedestal in an alcove stood a flask of strangely opalescent glass. The flask, stoppered, was no more than four hands high. Inside—*inside*—

Brak's skin crawled. His mouth tasted the bile of nauseous terror as he watched miniature stormclouds whirl and tumble within the flask.

The clouds moved with incredible speed, smashing the side of the glass prison, turning under and smashing again. Tiny lightning bolts sizzled and spat within the flask, spending themselves against the sides in unearthly fire-showers—

As Ool had said: the storms of heaven, magically imprisoned.

Noise behind him. The wizard scrambling up—

Terrified almost witless, Brak grabbed at the awful flask, heard Ool shriek:

"Do not touch it—!"

The flask vibrated in Brak's hand, shooting off its white glare of prisoned lightnings, booming the sound of captured thunder. The flask cast a sickly white aura between the barbarian and the sorcerer, who was framed against the terrace where his dead guardians lay. Ool's supple white hands rose in the beginning of what Brak knew would be a last, death-bringing spell-cast—

He hurled the flask with all his strength.

Ool saw it flying at him, white and thundering. The motions of his spell dissolved into frantic, fending gestures. He managed to hit the flask, deflect it. But when he saw the direction, he screamed and screamed—

The flask fell toward the floor.

Struck the tiles.

Shattered—

A cataclysm of lightbursts and thunderclaps smote Brak's brain and body. Unleashed winds picked him up, tossed him toward the splitting ceiling, tumbled him and bounced him off a wall while noise drummed, glare burned, shrieking gale-winds funneled skyward—

The whirlwind dropped Brak through white-glaring darkness, smashing the sense out of him an instant after he heard Ool's final scream drowned in the roar of furious, downpouring rain.

9

Bloodied, only half in possession of his senses, wracked with pain yet forcing himself to drag the flaccid white corpse by its ankle, Brak the barbarian sought the hall of Lord Magnus the Worldbreaker.

It was not hard to find. Drums hammered. Pipes skirled. Joyous, almost hysterical voices whooped and sang as he came limping up a long, empty corridor where torches blew and sheeting rain gusted in through high slot windows.

Staggering, Brak dropped to one knee. He released Ool's ankle, held both palms against his eyelids, fighting back the pain.

He had wakened in the apartment, finding half the ceiling caved away. The snapped end of a beam had crushed Ool's skull. Behind him along the ghostly corridor, Brak could see a trail of red and gray paste where Ool's head had dragged.

For his part, Brak had been prisoned beneath a rubble-heap, badly knocked and gashed, but with no detectable damage besides general pain and a sharper one that might indicate a shattered bone somewhere in his left leg. He could barely support himself on that side.

Some of Ool's boy guardians had come creeping upstairs fearfully. At the sight of their dead master, they fled into the night. Brak had pulled himself up and out of the ruins of the ceiling from which the prisoned storm-forces had escaped to spread and deluge the land with the rain; rain that even now rivered loudly off the palace rooftop. He'd hauled Ool's shattered body through empty squares and courtyards while his pain-dulled mind perceived cries of jubilation from streets and palace buildings alike.

Now he gained his feet again. He saw a turning in the corridor just ahead. He clutched Ool's ankle, shambled on, drenched by a gust of rain through a window he passed. Cold, clean rain pouring down on the kingdom of Lord Magnus the Worldbreaker—

Weaving on his feet, struggling against the agony that seared his whole left side, Brak limped to the entrance of the huge hall, and waited.

A thousand people thronged there, it seemed, reveling. They axed open wine casks, lay beneath the pouring red streams, bathing in them. Others whooped and danced impromptu steps: soldiers and courtiers, ladies and serving-maids alike——

One wine-drenched bawd saw Brak slouched in the great doorway and screamed.

The merrymaking ended. Heads turned. Mouths gaped.

Like some great wounded animal, Brak the barbarian dragged his victim on, up through a long, quickly-opened aisle of faces to the foot of the beast-throne where Magnus the Worldbreaker sat, wine cup in hand.

The rain drummed and hammered in the dark night outside. Magnus's lined face bore a disbelieving look as he stared down at the grim, bloodied hulk of a man who, with his good right foot, rolled the wizard's corpse to the base of the throne stairs and then simply stared upward.

"Was it you who brought the rain—at the price of my wizard's life?" Magnus asked, as if he couldn't quite countenance it. Ripples of amazement noised through the crowd, stilled suddenly by the lord's upraised hand.

At first Brak could manage no more than a single, pain-wracked shake of his head. Then he said:

"I only freed what your treacherous magician prisoned inside a flask with a powerful spell—to bring this kingdom down. Many——"

Brak saw three lords seated on the throne. Then two. He rubbed his eyes; fought the hurt spearing up his left side; stiffened his injured leg so he wouldn't totter and fall.

"——many years ago, I was told, a soldier ravished your wife, and escaped. But not before a spear gave him a wound. Look at the wizard's arm, which he has kept concealed from you—from everyone—since the first day he came to your court. Once he wore your bracelet. Pull away his waist linen—" This Brak had already done, back in the apartment, to verify his suspicion. "A spear that struck in darkness robbed him of what a man can afford to lose least of all—"

He swayed, dizzy, as soldiers and courtiers ran forward to strip the corpse and expose the sexless, scarred ruin at the joining of Ool's pale legs.

A woman fainted. The linen was hastily replaced.

Lord Magnus gazed down in wonder and loathing. Brak forced out more hoarse words:

"He escaped to the land of Shend, and there learned sorceries. He returned and gained your favor under the name by which you knew him. For years he conspired with the Children of the Smoke, until the arrival of the hour he deemed opportune to—" A wracking cough that started deep in his belly nearly spilled Brak over. "—to bring you down. All this I will repeat in detail at—some better time." Glowering, he swung his head left and right. He missed the one face he sought: "Where is Captain Xeraph?"

"In the dungeons, being drawn on the wheel for permitting your escape."

"I struck him by surprise. He had no chance—let him go."

Silence.

"I said let him go!"

Lord Magnus signaled. Two senior officers dashed for a portal as Brak went on:

"Before I make my departure, I will explain fully how I destroyed the man who would have destroyed you, lord. But I want your leave—" Again a terrible, sick spell of dizziness swept him. The pain climbed through his left leg and his torso to eat at his brain. He braced his gashed left leg, dug horny nails into his palms: fresh pain, to sting his senses alive again.

"—to claim what you promised me if the rain came down in two days and two nights. That I will be free of your bondage."

Suddenly, horrifyingly, in the small, scarred face of Lord Magnus the Worldbreaker whose booted feet did not reach the floor in front of his throne, there was both cheerfulness and cunning. In the rain-hissing silence, the lord said:

"Barbarian, you heard me amiss. I spoke exactly this. *You will not die. You will not wear chains.* I never said you would go free. In fact I never intended that at all— and chose my words accordingly. I am ever in need of stout, quick-witted fighters—and will number you among such from this day forward. Instead of chains, you will only wear the bronze bracelet of my army."

10

From somewhere deep in his hurt body, Brak's cry of betrayal bellowed out:

"The gods damn you for deception—*I will escape!*"

Looking down on his new thrall with scarcely-concealed admiration, Lord Magnus gave a tired, pleased nod.

"Accepted. I will prevent it, if I can."

It made no difference to Brak the barbarian that he knew why Lord Magnus had deceived him, and would impress him into service. In his terrible pain, he felt only hatred. Faces, forms, firelight from socketed torches swam together and melted into darkness as he threw his head back and let out one long, baying howl of animal rage.

Lunging, he tried to climb the throne stairs to his captor. But he was too weak. He fell back, sprawling over the corpse of Ool. His mind darkened swiftly—

There was sudden stillness except for the hammer of the rain. The unconscious barbarian's right arm slipped off the dead magician's shoulder where it had rested, and struck the floor with a last faint clattering of chain.

SWORDS AGAINST
THE MARLUK

Katherine Kurtz

KATHERINE KURTZ

One of our newest members, Katherine is a young woman who was born in Coral Gables, Florida, and now makes her home in Los Angeles. She has worked in such diverse areas as oceanography, television, and law enforcement, and once held a job cataloging Chinese art.

Unlike her fellow SAGApersons, she's never published anything but fantasy and likes it that way. Her novels are meticulously believable tapestries of life in a Medieval version of Wales that never actually was, and her ability to bring this age to life is doubtless made easier by the fact that she took her master's degree in the history of Britain during the Middle Ages.

Her first novel, *Deryni Rising,* appeared as recently as 1970. Since then she has published *Deryni Checkmate* and *High Deryni,* and a fourth novel in the sequence will probably be in print by the time you read this.

When I asked her if she could give me a new story about the Deryni, she said, yes, she could: there was an important event which took place before the beginning of her first Deryni novel, and which has only been alluded to in her books, never described. It was the confrontation and magical duel between King Brion of Gwynedd and his powerful archfoe, the Marluk.

I said: *write it.* She did. Here it is.

L.C.

SWORDS AGAINST THE MARLUK

They had not anticipated trouble from the Marluk that summer. In those days, the name of Hogan Gwernach was little more than legend, a vague menace in far-off Tolan who might or might not ever materialize as a threat to Brion's throne. Though rumored to be a descendant of the last Deryni sorceror-king of Gwynedd, Gwernach's line had not set foot in Gwynedd for nearly three generations—not since Duchad Mor's ill-fated invasion in the reign of Jasher Haldane. Most people who knew of his existence at all believed that he had abandoned his claim to Gwynedd's crown.

And so, late spring found King Brion in Eastmarch to put down the rebellion of one of his own earls, with a young, half-Deryni squire named Alaric Morgan riding at his side. Rorik, the Earl of Eastmarch, had defied royal writ and begun to overrun neighboring Marley— a move he had been threatening for years—aided by his brash son-in-law, Rhydon, who was then only *suspected* of being Deryni. Arban Howell, one of the local barons whose lands lay along the line of Rorik's march, sent frantic word to the king of what was happening, then called up his own feudal levies to make a stand until help could arrive.

Only, by the time the royal armies did arrive, Brion's from the capital and an auxiliary force from Claibourne in the north, there was little left to do but assist Arban's knights in the mop-up operation. Miraculously, Arban had managed to defeat and capture Earl Rorik, scattering the remnants of the rebel forces and putting the impetuous Rhydon to flight. Only the formalities remained to be done by the time the king himself rode into Arban's camp.

Trial was held, the accused condemned, the royal sentence carried out. The traitorous Rorik, his lands and titles attainted, was hanged, drawn, and quartered before the officers of the combined armies, his head destined to be returned to his old capital and displayed as a deterrent to those contemplating similar indiscretions in the future. Rhydon, who had assisted his father-in-law's treason, was condemned in absentia and banished. Loyal Arban Howell became the new Earl of Eastmarch for his trouble, swearing fealty to King Brion before the same armies which had witnessed the execution of his predecessor only minutes before.

And so the rebellion ended in Eastmarch. Brion dismissed the Claibourne levies with thanks, wished his new earl godspeed, then turned over command of the royal army to his brother Nigel. Nigel and their uncle, Duke Richard, would see the royal levies back to Rhemuth. Brion, impatient with the blood and killing of the past week, set out for home along a different route, taking only his squire with him.

It was late afternoon when Brion and Alaric found a suitable campsite. Since their predawn rising, there had been little opportunity for rest; and accordingly, riders and horses both were tired and travel-worn when at last they stopped. The horses smelled the water up ahead and tugged at their bits as the riders drew rein.

"God's wounds, but I'm tired, Alaric!" the king

sighed, kicking clear of his stirrups and sliding gratefully from the saddle. "I sometimes think the aftermath
is almost worse than the battle. I must be getting old."

As Alaric grabbed at the royal reins to secure the
horses, Brion pulled off helmet and coif and let them
fall as he made his way to the edge of the nearby
stream. Letting himself fall face-down, he buried his
head in the cooling water. The long black hair floated
on the current, streaming down the royal back just past
his shoulders as he rolled over and sat up, obviously the
better for wear. Alaric, the horses tethered nearby,
picked up his master's helm and coif and laid them
beside the horses, then walked lightly toward the king.

"Your mail will rust if you insist upon bathing in it,
Sire," the boy smiled, kneeling beside the older man
and reaching to unbuckle the heavy swordbelt.

Brion leaned back on both elbows to facilitate the
disarming, shaking his head in appreciation as the boy
began removing vambraces and gauntlets.

"I don't think I shall ever understand how I came
to deserve you, Alaric." He raised a foot so the boy
could unbuckle greaves and spurs and dusty boots.
"You must think me benighted, to ride off alone like
this, without even an armed escort other than yourself,
just to be away from my army."

"My liege is a man of war and a leader of men," the
boy grinned, "but he is also a man unto himself, and
must have time away from the pursuits of kings. The
need for solitude is a familiar one to me."

"You understand, don't you?"

Alaric shrugged. "Who better than a Deryni, Sire?
Like Your Grace, we are also solitary men on most
occasions—though our solitude is not always by
choice."

Brion smiled agreement, trying to imagine what it must be like to be Deryni like Alaric, a member of that persecuted race so feared still by so many. He allowed the boy to pull the lion surcoat off over his head while he thought about it, then stood and shrugged out of his mail hauberk. Discarding padding and singlet as well, he stepped into the water and submerged himself with a sigh, letting the water melt away the grime and soothe the galls of combat and ill-fitting harness and too many hours in the saddle. Alaric joined him after a while, gliding eellike in the dappled shadows. When the light began to fail, the boy was on the bank without a reminder and pulling on clean clothes, packing away the battle-stained armor, laying out fresh garb for his master. Reluctantly, Brion came to ground on the sandy bottom and climbed to his feet, slicked back the long, black hair.

There was a small wood fire waiting when he had dressed, and wild rabbit spitted above the flames, and mulled wine in sturdy leather traveling cups. Wrapped in their cloaks against the growing night chill, king and squire feasted on rabbit and ripe cheese and biscuits only a little gone to mold after a week in the pack. The meal was finished and the camp secured by the time it was fully dark, and Brion fell asleep almost immediately, his head pillowed on his saddle by the banked fire. After a final check of the horses, Alaric slept, too.

It was sometime after moonrise when they were awakened by the sound of hoofbeats approaching from the way they had come. It was a lone horseman—that much Brion could determine, even through the fog of sleep he was shaking off as he sat and reached for his sword. But there was something else, too, and the boy Alaric sensed it. The lad was already on his feet, sword in hand, ready to defend his master if need be. But now he was frozen in the shadow of a tree, sword at rest, his head cocked in an attitude of more than listening.

"Prince Nigel," the boy murmured confidently, returning his sword to its sheath. Brion, used by now to relying on the boy's extraordinary powers, straightened and peered toward the moonlit road, throwing his cloak around him and groping for his boots in the darkness.

"A Haldane!" a young voice cried.

"Haldane, ho!" Brion shouted in response, stepping into the moonlight to hail the newcomer. The rider reined his lathered horse back on its haunches and half fell from the saddle, tossing the reins in Alaric's general direction as the boy came running to meet him.

"Brion, thank God I've found you!" Nigel cried, stumbling to embrace his older brother. "I feared you might have taken another route!"

The prince was foam-flecked and grimy from his breakneck ride, and his breath came in ragged gasps as he allowed Brion to help him to a seat by the fire. Collapsing against a tree trunk, he gulped the wine that Brion offered and tried to still his trembling hands. After a few minutes, and without attempting to speak, he pulled off one gauntlet with his teeth and reached into a fold of his surcoat. He took a deep breath as he withdrew a folded piece of parchment and gave it over to his brother.

"This was delivered several hours after you and Alaric left us. It's from Hogan Gwernach."

"The Marluk?" Brion murmured. His face went still and strange, the gray Haldane eyes flashing like polished agate, as he held the missive toward the firelight.

There was no seal on the outside of the letter—only a name, written in a fine, educated hand: *Brion Haldane, Pretender of Gwynedd.* Slowly, deliberately, Brion unfolded the parchment, let his eyes scan it as his brother plucked a brand from the fire and held it close for light. The boy Alaric listened silently as the king read.

"To Brion Haldane, Pretender of Gwynedd, from the Lord Hogan Gwernach of Tolan, Festillic Heir to the Thrones and Crowns of the Eleven Kingdoms. Know that We, Hogan, have determined to exercise that prerogative of birth which is the right of Our Festillic Ancestors, to reclaim the Thrones which are rightfully Ours. We therefore give notice to you, Brion Haldane, that your stewardship and usurpation of Gwynedd is at an end, your lands and Crown forfeit to the House of Festil. We charge you to present yourself and all members of your Haldane Line before Our Royal Presence at Cardosa, no later than the Feast of Saint Asaph, there to surrender yourself and the symbols of your sovereignty into Our Royal Hands. Sic dicto, Hoganus Rex Regnorum Undecim."

"King of the Eleven Kingdoms?" Alaric snorted, then remembered who and where he was. "Pardon, Sire, but he must be joking!"

Nigel shook his head. "I fear not, Alaric. This was delivered by Rhydon of Eastmarch under a flag of truce."

"The treasonous dog!" Brion whispered.

"Aye." Nigel nodded. "He said to tell you that if you wished to contest this," he tapped the parchment lightly with his fingernail, "the Marluk would meet you in combat tomorrow near the Rustan Cliffs. If you do not appear, he will sack and burn the town of Rustan, putting every man, woman, and child to the sword. If we leave by dawn, we can just make it."

"Our strength?" Brion asked.

"I have my vanguard of eighty. I sent sixty of them ahead to rendezvous with us at Rustan and the rest are probably a few hours behind me. I also sent a messenger ahead to Uncle Richard with the main army. With any luck at all, he'll receive word in time to turn back the Haldane levies to assist. Earl Ewan was too far north to call back, though I sent a rider anyway."

"Thank you. You've done well."

With a distracted nod, Brion laid a hand on his brother's shoulder and got slowly to his feet. As he stood gazing sightlessly into the fire, the light gleamed on a great ruby in his ear, on a wide bracelet of silver clasped to his right wrist. He folded his arms across his chest against the chill, bowing his head in thought. The boy Alaric, with a glance at Prince Nigel, moved to pull the king's cloak more closely around him, to fasten the lion brooch beneath his chin as the king spoke.

"The Marluk does not mean to fight a physical battle. You know that, Nigel," he said in a low voice. "Oh, there may be battle among our various troops in the beginning. But all of that is but prelude. Armed combat is not what Hogan Gwernach desires of me."

"Aye. He is Deryni," Nigel breathed. He watched Brion's slow nod in the firelight.

"But, Brion," Nigel began, after a long pause. "It's been two generations since a Haldane king has had to stand against Deryni magic. Can you do it?"

"I—don't know." Brion, his cloak drawn close about him, sank down beside his brother once again, his manner grave and thoughtful. "I'm sorry if I appear preoccupied, but I keep having this vague recollection that there is something I'm supposed to do now. I seem to remember that Father made some provision, some preparation against this possibility, but—"

He ran a hand through sable hair, the firelight winking again on the silver at his wrist, and the boy Alaric froze, head cocked in a strained listening attitude, eyes slightly glazed. As Nigel nudged his brother lightly in the ribs, the boy sank slowly to his knees. Both pairs of royal eyes stared at him fixedly.

"There is that which must be done," the boy whispered, "which was ordained many years ago, when I was but a babe and you were not yet king, Sire."

"My father?"

"Aye. The key is—the bracelet you wear upon your arm." Brion's eyes darted instinctively to the silver. "May I see it, Sire?"

Without a word, Brion removed the bracelet and laid it in the boy's left hand. Alaric stared at it for a long moment, his pupils dilating until they were pools of inky blackness. Then, taking a deep breath to steel himself for the rush of memories he knew must follow, he bowed his head and laid his right hand over the design incised in the silver. Abruptly he remembered the first time he had seen the bracelet.

He had been just four when it happened, and it was mid-autumn. He had been snuggled down in his bed, dreaming of some childhood fantasy which he would never remember now, when he became aware of someone standing by his couch—and *that* was *not* a dream.

He opened his eyes to see his mother staring down at him intently, golden hair spilling bright around her shoulders, a loose-fitting gown of green disguising the thickening of her body from the child she carried. There was a candle in her hand, and by its light he could see his father standing gravely at her side. He had never seen such a look of stern concentration upon his father's face before, and that almost frightened him.

He made an inquisitive noise in his throat and started to ask what was wrong, but his mother laid a finger against her lips and shook her head. Then his father was reaching down to pull the blankets back, gathering him sleepily into his arms. He watched as his mother followed them out of the room and across the great hall, toward his father's library. The hall was empty even of the hounds his father loved, and outside he could hear the sounds of horses stamping in the yard—perhaps as many as a score of them—and the low-voiced murmur of the soldiers talking their soldier-talk.

At first, he thought the library was empty. But then he noticed an old, gray-haired man sitting in the shadows of his father's favorite armchair by the fireplace, an ornately carved staff cradled in the crook of his arm. The man's garments were rich and costly, but stained with mud at the hem. Jewels winked dimly in the crown of his leather cap, and a great red stone gleamed in his right earlobe. His cloak of red leather was clasped with a massive enameled brooch bearing the figure of a golden lion.

"Good evening, Alaric," the old man said quietly, as the boy's father knelt before the man and turned his son to face the visitor.

His mother made a slight curtsy, awkward in her condition, then moved to stand at the man's right hand, leaning heavily against the side of his chair. Alaric thought it strange, even at that young age, that the man did not invite his mother to sit down—but perhaps the man was sick; he was certainly very old. Curiously, and still blinking the sleep from his eyes, he looked up at his mother. To his surprise, it was his father who spoke.

"Alaric, this is the king," his father said in a low voice. "Do you remember your duty to His Majesty?"

Alaric turned to regard his father gravely, then nodded and disengaged himself from his father's embrace, stood to attention, made a deep, correct bow from the waist. The king, who had watched the preceding without comment, smiled and held out his right hand to the child. A silver bracelet flashed in the firelight as the boy put his small hand into the king's great, scarred one.

"Come and sit beside me, boy," the king said, lifting Alaric to a position half in his lap and half supported by the carven chair arms. "I want to show you something."

Alaric squirmed a little as he settled down, for the royal lap was thin and bony, and the royal belt bristled with pouches and daggers and other grown-up accoutrements fascinating to a small child. He started to touch one careful, stubby finger to the jewel at the end of the king's great dagger, but before he could do it, his mother reached across and touched his forehead lightly with her hand. Instantly, the room took on a new brightness and clarity, became more silent, almost reverberated with expectation. He did not know what was going to happen, but his mother's signal warned him that it was in that realm of special things of which he was never to speak, and to which he must give his undivided attention. In awed expectation, he turned his wide child-eyes upon the king, watched attentively as the old man reached around him and removed the silver bracelet from his wrist.

"This is a very special bracelet, Alaric. Did you know that?"

The boy shook his head, his gray eyes flicking from the king's face to the flash of silver. The bracelet was a curved rectangle of metal as wide as a man's hand, its mirror-sheen broken only by the carved outline of a heraldic rose. But it was the inside which the king turned toward him now—the inner surface, also highly polished but bearing a series of three curiously carved symbols which the boy did not recognize—though at four, he could already read the scriptures and simple texts from which his mother taught him.

The king turned the bracelet so that the first sigil was visible and held his fingernail beneath it. With a piercing glance at the boy's mother, he murmured the word, *"One!"* The room spun, and Alaric had remembered nothing more of that night.

But the fourteen-year-old Alaric remembered now. Holding the bracelet in his hands, the old king's successor waiting expectantly beside him, Alaric suddenly knew that this was the key, that *he* was the key who could unlock the instructions left him by a dying man so many years before. He turned the bracelet in his hands and peered at the inside—he knew now that the symbols were runes, though he still could not read them—then raised gray eyes to meet those of his king.

"This is a time which your royal father anticipated, Sire. There are things which I must do, and you, and," he glanced uneasily at the bracelet before meeting Brion's eyes again, "and somehow he knew that I would be at your side when this time arrived."

"Yes, I can see that now," Brion said softly. " *'There will be a half-Deryni child called Morgan who will come to you in his youth,'* my father said. *'Him you may trust with your life and with all. He is the key who unlocks many doors.'* " He searched Alaric's eyes carefully. "He knew. Even your presence was by his design."

"And was the Marluk also his design?" Nigel whispered, his tone conveying resentment at the implied manipulation, though the matter was now rendered academic.

"Ancient mine enemy," Brion murmured. His face

assumed a gentle, faraway air. "No, he did not cause the Marluk to be, Nigel. But he knew there was a possibility, and he planned for *that*. It is said that the sister of the last Festillic king was with child when she was forced to flee Gwynedd. The child's name was—I forget—not that it matters. But his line grew strong in Tolan, and they were never forced to put aside their Deryni powers. The Marluk is said to be that child's descendant."

"And full Deryni, if what they say is true," Nigel replied, his face going sullen. "Brion, we aren't equipped to handle a confrontation with the Marluk. He's going to be waiting for us tomorrow with an army and his *full Deryni powers*. And us? We'll have eighty men of my vanguard, *maybe* we'll have the rest of the Haldane levies, *if* Uncle Richard gets back in time, and you'll have—what?—to stand against a full Deryni Lord who has good reason to want your throne!"

Brion wet his lips, avoiding his brother's eyes. "Alaric says that Father made provisions. We have no choice but to trust and see. Regardless of the outcome, we must try to save Rustan town tomorrow. Alaric, can you help us?"

"I—will try, Sire."

Disturbed by the near-clash between the two brothers, and sobered by the responsibility Brion had laid upon him, Alaric laid his right forefinger beneath the first rune, grubby fingernail underscoring the deeply carved sign. He could feel the Haldane eyes upon him as he whispered the word, *"One!"*

The word paralyzed him, and he was struck deaf and blind to all externals, oblivious to everything except the images flashing through his mind—the face of the old king seen through the eyes of a four-year-old boy—and the instructions, meaningless to the four-year-old, now reengraving themselves in the young man's mind as deeply as the runes inscribed on the silver in his hand.

A dozen heartbeats, a blink, and he was in the world again, turning his gray gaze on the waiting Brion. The king and Nigel stared at him with something approaching awe, their faces washed clean of whatever doubts had remained until that moment. In the moonlight, Alaric seemed to glow a little.

"We must find a level area facing east," the boy said. His young brow furrowed in concentration. "There must be a large rock in the center, living water at our backs, and—and we must gather wildflowers."

It was nearing first-light before they were ready. A suitable location had been found in a bend of the stream a little way below their camp, with water tumbling briskly along the northern as well as the western perimeter. To the east stretched an unobstructed view of the mountains from behind which the sun would shortly rise. A large, stream-smoothed chunk of granite half the height of a man had been dragged into the center of the clearing with the aid of the horses, and four lesser stones had been set up to mark the four cardinal compass points.

Now Alaric and Nigel were laying bunches of field flowers around each of the cornerstones, in a pattern which Alaric could not explain but which he knew must be maintained. Brion, silent and withdrawn beneath his crimson cloak, sat near the center stone with arms wrapped around his knees, sheathed sword lying beside him. A knot of blazing pine had been thrust into the ground at his right to provide light for what the others did, but Brion saw nothing, submerged in contemplation of what lay ahead. Alaric, with a glance at the brightening sky, set a small drinking vessel of water to the left of the center stone and dropped to one knee beside the king. An uneasy Nigel snuffed out the torch and drew back a few paces as Alaric took up the brace-let and laid his finger under the second rune.

"*Two!*"

There was a moment of profound silence in which none of the three moved, and then Alaric looked up and placed the bracelet in the king's hand once more.

"The dawn is nearly upon us, Sire," he said quietly. "I require the use of your sword."

"Eh?"

With a puzzled look, Brion glanced at the weapon and picked it up, wrapped the red leather belt more tidily around the scabbard, then scrambled to his feet. It had been his father's sword, and his grandfather's. It was also the sword with which he had been conse-crated king nearly ten years before. Since that day, no man had drawn it save himself.

But without further query, Brion drew the blade and formally extended it to Alaric across his left forearm, hilt first. Alaric made a profound bow as he took the weapon, appreciating the trust the act implied, then saluted the king and moved to the other side of the rock. Behind him, the eastern sky was ablaze with pink and coral.

"When the rim of the sun appears above the horizon, I must ward us with fire, my liege," he said. "Please do not be surprised or alarmed at anything which may happen."

Brion nodded, and as he and Nigel drew themselves to respectful attention, Alaric turned on his heel and strode to the eastern limit of the clearing. Raising the sword before him with both hands, he held the cross-hilt level with his eyes and gazed expectantly toward the eastern horizon. And then, as though the sun's movement had not been a gradual and natural thing, dawn was spilling from behind the mountains.

The first rays of sunlight on sword turned the steel to fire. Alaric let his gaze travel slowly up the blade, to the flame now blazing at its tip and shimmering down its length, then extended the sword in salute and brought it slowly to ground before him. Fire leaped up where blade touched sun-parched turf—a fire which burned but did not consume—and a ribbon of flame followed as he turned to the right and walked the confines of the wards.

When he had finished, he was back where he began, all three of them standing now within a hemisphere of golden light. The boy saluted sunward once again, with hands that shook only a little, then returned to the center of the circle. Grounding the now-normal blade, he extended it to Nigel with a bow, the hilt held crosswise before him. As the prince's fingers closed around the blade, Alaric turned back toward the center stone and bowed his head. Then he held his hands outstretched before him, fingers slightly cupped—gazed fixedly at the space between them.

Nothing appeared to happen for several minutes, though Alaric could feel the power building between his hands. King and prince and squire stared until their eyes watered, then blinked in astonishment as the space between Alaric's hands began to glow. Pulsating with the heartbeat of its creator, the glow coalesced in a sphere of cool, verdant light, swelling to head-size even as they watched. Slowly, almost reverently, Alaric lowered his hands toward the stream-smoothed surface of the center stone; watched as the sphere of light spread bright across the surface.

He did not dare to breathe, so tenuous was the balance he maintained. Drawing back the sleeve of his tunic, he swept his right hand and arm across the top of the stone like an adze, shearing away the granite as though it were softest sand. Another pass to level the surface even more, and then he was pressing out a gentle hollow with his hand, the stone melting beneath his touch like morning frost before the sun.

Then the fire was dead, and Alaric Morgan was no longer the master mage, tapping the energies of the earth's deepest forge, but only a boy of fourteen, staggering to his knees in exhaustion at the feet of his king and staring in wonder at what his hands had wrought. Already, he could not remember how he had done it.

Silence reigned for a long moment, finally broken by Brion's relieved sigh as he tore his gaze from the sheared-off stone. A taut, frightened Nigel was staring at him and Alaric, white-knuckled hands gripping the sword hilt as though it were his last remaining hold on reality. With a little smile of reassurance, Brion laid a hand on his brother's. He felt a little of the tension drain away as he turned back to the young man still kneeling at his feet.

"Alaric, are you all right?"

"Aye, m'lord."

With a weak nod, Alaric brought a hand to his forehead and closed his eyes, murmuring a brief spell to banish fatigue. Another deep breath and it was done. Smiling wanly, he climbed to his feet and took the bracelet from Brion's hands once more, bent it flat and laid it in the hollow he had made in the rock. The three runes, one yet unrevealed, shone in the sunlight as he stretched forth his right hand above the silver.

"'I form the light and create darkness,'" the boy

whispered. " '*I make peace and create evil: I the Lord do all these things.*' "

He did not physically move his hand, although muscles and tendons tensed beneath the tanned skin. Nonetheless, the silver began to curve away, to conform to the hollow of the stone as though another, invisible hand were pressing down between his hand and the metal. The bracelet collapsed on itself and grew molten then, though there was no heat given off. When Alaric removed his hand a few seconds later, the silver was bonded to the hollow like a shallow, silver bowl, all markings obliterated save the third and final rune. He laid his finger under the sign and spoke its name.

"Three!"

This time, there was but a fleeting outward hint of the reaction triggered: a blink, an interrupted breath immediately resumed. Then he was taking up the vessel of water and turning toward Brion, gesturing with his eyes for Brion to extend his hands. Water was poured over them, the edge of Alaric's cloak offered for a towel. When the king had dried his hands, Alaric handed him the rest of the water.

"Pour water in the silver to a finger's depth, Sire," he said softly.

Brion complied, setting the vessel on the ground when he had finished. Nigel, without being told, moved to the opposite side of the stone and knelt, holding the sword so that the long, cross-shadow of the hilt fell across rock and silver.

"Now," Alaric continued, "spread your hands flat above the water and repeat after me. Your hands are holy, consecrated with chrism at your coronation just as a priest's hands are consecrated. I am instructed that this is appropriate."

With a swallow, Brion obeyed, his eyes locking with Alaric's as the boy began speaking.

"I, Brion, the Lord's Anointed, . . ."

"I, Brion, the Lord's Anointed, . . ."

". . . bless and consecrate thee, O creature of water, . . ."

". . . bless and consecrate thee, O creature of water, . . . by the living God, by the true God, by the holy God, . . . by that God Who in the beginning separated thee by His word from the dry land, . . . and Whose Spirit moved upon thee."

"Amen," Alaric whispered.

"Amen," Brion echoed.

"Now, dip your fingers in the water," Alaric began, "and trace on the stone—"

"I *know* this part!" Brion interrupted, his hand already parting the water in the sign of a cross. He, too, was being caught up in that web of recall established so many years before by his royal father, and his every gesture, every nuance of phrasing and pronunciation, was correct and precise as he touched a moistened finger to the stone in front of the silver.

"Blessed be the Creator, yesterday and today, the Beginning and the End, the Alpha and the Omega."

A cross shone wetly on the stone, the Greek letters drawn haltingly but precisely at the east and west aspects.

"His are the seasons and the ages, to Him glory and dominion through all the ages of eternity. Blessed be the Lord. Blessed be His Holy Name."

The signs of the Elementals glistened where Brion had drawn them in the four quadrants cut by the cross —Air, Fire, Water, Earth—and Brion, as he recognized the alchemical signs, drew back his hand as though stung, stared aghast at Alaric.

"How—?" He swallowed. "How did I know that?"

Alaric permitted a wan smile, sharing Brion's discomfiture at being compelled to act upon memories and instructions which he could not consciously remember.

"You, too, have been schooled for this day, Sire," he said. "Now, you have but to carry out the rest of your father's instructions, and take up the power which is rightfully yours."

Brion bowed his head, sleek, raven hair catching the strengthening sunlight. "I—am not certain I know how. From what we have seen and done so far, there must be other triggers, other clues to aid me, but—" He glanced up at the boy. "You must give me guidance, Alaric. You are the master here—not I."

"No, you are the master, Sire," the boy said, touching one finger to the water and bringing a shimmering drop toward Brion's face.

The king's eyes tracked on the fingertip automatically, and as the droplet touched his forehead, the eyes closed. A shudder passed through the royal body and Brion blinked. Then in a daze, he reached to his throat and unfastened the great lion brooch which held his cloak in place. He hefted the piece in his hand as the cloak fell in a heap at his feet and the words came.

"Three drops of royal blood on water bright,
To gather flame within a bowl of light.
With consecrated hands, receive the Sight
Of Haldane—'tis thy sacred, royal Right."

The king glanced at Alaric unseeing, at Nigel, at the red enameled brooch heavy in his hand. Then he turned the brooch over and freed the golden clasp-pin from its catch, held out a left hand which did not waver.

"Three drops of royal blood on water bright," he re-

peated. He brought the clasp against his thumb in a swift, sharp jab.

Blood welled from the wound and fell thrice upon the water, rippling scarlet, concentric circles across the silver surface. A touch of tongue to wounded thumb, and then he was putting the brooch aside and spreading his hands above the water, the shadow of the cross bold upon his hands. He closed his eyes.

Stillness. A crystalline anticipation as Brion began to concentrate. And then, as Alaric extended his right hand above Brion's and added his strength to the spell, a deep, musical reverberation, more felt than heard, throbbing through their minds. As the sunlight brightened, so also brightened the space beneath Brion's hands, until finally could be seen the ghostly beginnings of crimson fire flickering on the water. Brion's emotionless expression did not change as Alaric withdrew his hand and knelt.

"Fear not, for I have redeemed thee," Alaric whispered, calling the words from memories not his own. *"I have called thee by name, and thou art mine. When thou walkest through the fire, thou shalt not be burned: neither shall the flame kindle upon thee."*

Brion did not open his eyes. But as Alaric's words ended, the king took a deep breath and slowly, deliberately, brought his hands to rest flat on the silver of the bowl. There was a gasp from Nigel as his brother's hands entered the flames, but no word or sound escaped Brion's lips to indicate the ordeal he was enduring. Head thrown back and eyes closed, he stood unflinching as the crimson fire climbed his arms and spread over his entire body. When the flames died away, Brion opened his eyes upon a world which would never appear precisely the same again, and in which he could never again be merely mortal.

He leaned heavily on the altar-stone for just a moment, letting the fatigue drain away. But when he lifted his hands from the stone, his brother stifled an oath. Where the royal hands had lain, the silver had been burned away. Only the blackened silhouettes remained, etched indelibly in the hollowed surface of the rock. Brion blanched a little when he saw what he had done, and Nigel crossed himself. But Alaric paid no heed—stood, instead, and turned to face the east once more, extending his arms in a banishing spell. The canopy of fire dissipated in the air.

They were no longer alone, however. While they had worked their magic, some of the men of Nigel's vanguard had found the royal campsite—an even dozen of his crack commanders and tacticians—and they were gathered now by the horses in as uneasy a band as Alaric had ever seen. Brion did not notice them immediately, his mind occupied still with sorting out his recent experience, but Alaric saw them and touched Brion's elbow in warning. As Brion turned toward them in surprise, they went to their knees as one man, several crossing themselves furtively. Brion's brow furrowed in momentary annoyance.

"Did they see?" he murmured, almost under his breath.

Alaric gave a careful nod. "So it would appear, Sire. I suggest you go to them immediately and reassure them. Otherwise, the more timid among them are apt to bolt and run."

"From me, their king?"

"You are more than just a man now, Sire," Alaric returned uncomfortably. "They have seen that with their own eyes. Go to them, and quickly."

With a sigh, Brion tugged his tunic into place and strode across the clearing toward the men, automati-

cally pulling his gauntlets from his belt and beginning
to draw them on. The men watched his movements
furtively as he came to a halt perhaps a half-dozen steps
from the nearest of them. Noting their scrutiny, Brion
froze in the act of pulling on the right glove; then, with
a smile, he removed it and held his hand toward them,
the palm exposed. There was no mark upon the lightly
calloused skin.

"You are entitled to an explanation," he said simply,
as all eyes fastened on the hand. "As you can see, I am
unharmed. I am sorry if my actions caused you some
concern. Please rise."

The men got to their feet, only the chinking of their
harness breaking the sudden stillness which had befallen
the glade. Behind the king, Nigel and Alaric moved to
back him, Nigel bearing the royal sword and Alaric the
crimson cloak with its lion brooch. The men were
silent, a few shifting uneasily, until one of the bolder
ones cleared his throat and took a half-step nearer.

"Sire."

"Lord Ralson?"

"Sire," the man shifted from one foot to the other
and glanced at his comrades. "Sire, it appears to us
that there was magic afoot," he said carefully. "We
question the wisdom of allowing a Deryni to influence
you so. When we saw—"

"What *did* you see, Gerard?" Brion asked softly.

Gerard Ralson cleared his throat. "Well, I—we—
when we arrived, Sire, you were holding that brooch
in your hand," he gestured toward the lion brooch
which Alaric held, "and then we saw you prick your
thumb with it." He paused. "You looked—not yourself, Sire, as though—something else was commanding
you." He glanced at Alaric meaningfully, and several

other of the men moved a little closer behind him, hands creeping to rest on the hilts of their weapons.

"I see," Brion said. "And you think that it was Alaric who commanded me, don't you?"

"It appeared so to us, Majesty," another man rumbled, his beard jutting defiantly.

Brion nodded. "And then you watched me hold my hands above the stone, and Alaric hold his above my own. And then you saw me engulfed in flame, and that frightened you most of all."

The speaker nodded tentatively, and his movement was echoed by nearly every head there. Brion sighed and glanced at the ground, looked up at them again.

"My Lords, I will not lie to you. You were witness to very powerful magic. And I will not deny, nor will Alaric, that his assistance was used in what you saw. And Alaric is, most definitely, Deryni."

The men said nothing, though glances were exchanged.

"But there is more that I would have you know," Brion continued, fixing them all with his Haldane stare. "Each of you has heard the legends of my House —how we returned to the throne of Gwynedd when the Deryni Imre was deposed. But if you consider, you will realize that the Haldanes could not have ousted Deryni Lords without some power of their own."

"Are you Deryni, then, Sire?" asked one bold soul from the rear ranks.

Brion smiled and shook his head. "No—or at least, I don't believe I am. But the Haldanes have very special gifts and abilities, nonetheless, handed down from father to son—or sometimes from brother to brother." He glanced at Nigel before continuing. "You know that we can Truth-Read, that we have great physical stamina. But we also have other powers, when they are needed, which enable us to function almost as though we were, ourselves, Deryni. My father, King Blaine, entrusted a few of these abilities to me before his death, but there were others whose very existence he kept secret, for which he left certain instructions with Alaric Morgan *unknown even to him*—and which were triggered by the threat of Hogan Gwernach's challenge which we received last night. Alaric was a child of four when he was instructed by my father—so that even *he* would not remember his instructions until it was necessary—and apparently I was also instructed.

"The result, in part, was what you saw. If there was a commanding force, another influence present within the fiery circle, it was my father's. The rite is now fulfilled, and I am my father's successor *in every way,* with all his powers and abilities."

"Your late *father* provided for all of this?" one of the men whispered.

Brion nodded. "There is no evil in it, Alwyne. You knew my father well. You know he would not draw down evil."

"Aye, he would not," the man replied, glancing at Alaric almost involuntarily. "But what of the Deryni lad?"

"Our fathers made a pact, that Alaric Morgan should come to Court to serve me when he reached the proper age. That bargain has been kept. Alaric Morgan serves me and the realm of Gwynedd."

"But, he is Deryni, Sire! What if he is in league with—"

"He is in league with *me!*" Brion snapped. "He is my liege man, just as all of you, sworn to my service since the age of nine. In that time, he has scarcely left my side. Given the compulsions which my father placed upon him, do you really believe that he could betray me?"

Ralson cleared his throat, stepping forward and making a bow before the king could continue.

"Sire, it is best we do not discuss the boy. None of us here, Your Majesty included, can truly know what is in his heart. You are the issue now. If you were to reassure us, in some way, that you harbor no ill intent, that you have not allied yourself with the Dark Powers,—"

"You wish my oath to that effect?" Brion asked. The stillness of his response was, itself, suddenly threatening. "You would be that bold?"

Ralson nodded carefully, not daring to respond by words, and his movement was again echoed by the men standing at his back. After a frozen moment, Brion made a curt gesture for his brother to kneel with the royal sword. As Nigel held up the cross hilt, Brion laid his bare right hand upon it and faced his waiting knights.

"Before all of you and before God, and upon this holy sword, I swear that I am innocent of your suspicions, that I have made no dark pact with any evil power, that the rite which you observed was benevolent and legitimate. I further swear that I have never been, nor am I now, commanded by Alaric Morgan or any other man, human or Deryni; that he is as innocent as I of any evil intent toward the people and Crown of Gwynedd. This is the word of Brion Haldane. If I be forsworn, may this sword break in my hour of need, may all succor desert me, and may the name of Haldane vanish from the earth."

With that, he crossed himself slowly, deliberately—a

motion which was echoed by Alaric, Nigel, and then
the rest of the men who had witnessed the oath. Preparations to leave for Rustan were made in total silence.

They met the Marluk while still an hour's ride
from Rustan and rendezvous with the rest of Nigel's
vanguard. All morning, they had been following the
rugged Llegoddin Canyon Trace—a winding trail
treacherous with stream-slicked stones which rolled and
shifted beneath their horses' hooves. The stream re-
sponsible for their footing ran shallow along their right,
had crossed their path several times in slimy, fast-flow-
ing fords that made the horses lace back their ears.
Even the canyon walls had closed in along the last
mile, until the riders were forced to go two abreast. It
was a perfect place for an ambush; but Alaric's usually
reliable knack for sensing danger gave them almost no
warning.

It was cool in the little canyon, the shade deep and
refreshing after the heat of the noonday sun, and the
echo of steel-shod hooves announced their progress
long before they actually reached the end of the narrows. There the track made a sharp turn through the
stream again, before widening out to an area of several
acres. In the center waited a line of armed horsemen,
nearly twice the number of Brion's forces.

They were mailed and helmed with steel, these fighting men of Tolan, and their lances and war axes
gleamed in the silent sunlight. Their white-clad leader
sat a heavy sorrel destrier before them, lance in hand
and banner bright at his back. The blazon left little
doubt as to his identity—Hogan Gwernach, called the
Marluk. He had quartered his arms with those of Royal
Gwynedd.

But there was no time for more than first impressions. Even as Alaric's lips moved in warning, and before more than a handful of Brion's men could clear the stream and canyon narrows, the Marluk lowered his lance and signaled the attack. As the great-horses thundered toward the stunned royal party, picking up momentum as they came, Brion couched his own lance and set spurs to his horse's sides. His men, overcoming their initial dismay with commendable speed, galloped after him in near-order, readying shields and weapons even as they rode.

The earth shook with the force of the charge, echoed with the jingle of harness and mail, the creak of leather, the snorting and labored breathing of the heavy war horses. Just before the two forces met, one of Brion's men shouted, *"A Haldane!"*—a cry which was picked up and echoed instantly by most of his comrades in arms. Then all were swept into the melee, and men were falling and horses screaming riderless and wounded as lances splintered on shield and mail and bone.

Steel clanged on steel as the fighting closed hand-to-hand, cries of the wounded and dying punctuating the butcher sounds of sword and ax on flesh. Alaric, emerging unscathed from the initial encounter, found himself locked shield to shield with a man twice his age and size, the man pressing him hard and trying to crush his helm with a mace. Alaric countered by ducking under his shield and wheeling to the right, hoping to come at his opponent from the other side, but the man was already anticipating his move and swinging in counterattack. At the last possible moment, Alaric deflected the blow with his shield, reeling in the saddle as he tried to recover his balance and strike at the same time. But his aim has been shaken, and instead of coming in from behind on the man's temporarily open right side, he only embedded his sword in the other's high cantle.

He recovered before the blade could be wrenched from his grasp, gripping hard with his knees as his charger lashed out and caught the man in the leg with a driving foreleg. Then, parrying a blow from a second attacker, he managed to cut the other's girth and wound his mount, off-handedly kicking out at yet a third man who was approaching from his shield side. The first knight hit the ground with a yelp as his horse went down, narrowly missing death by trampling as one of his own men thundered past in pursuit of one of Brion's wounded.

Another strike, low and deadly, and Alaric's would-be slayer was, himself, the slain. Drawing ragged breath, Alaric wheeled to scan the battle for Brion, and to defend himself from renewed attack by the two men on foot.

The king himself was in little better circumstances. Though still mounted and holding his own, Brion had been swept away from his mortal enemy in the initial clash, and had not yet been able to win free to engage with him. Nigel was fighting at his brother's side, the royal banner in his shield hand, but the banner only served to hamper Nigel and to tell the enemy where Gwynedd's monarch was. Just now, both royal brothers were sore beset, half a dozen of the Marluk's knights belaboring them from every side but skyward. The Marluk, meantime, was busily slaying a hundred yards away—content, thus far, to spend his time slaughtering some of Brion's lesser warriors, and shunning Brion's reputed superior skill. As Brion and Nigel beat back their attackers, the king glanced across the battlefield and saw his enemy, dispatched one of his harriers with a brutal thrust, raised his sword and shouted the enemy's name:

"Gwernach!"

The enemy turned in his direction and jerked his horse to a rear, circled his sword above his head. His helmet was gone, and pale hair blew wild from beneath his mail coif.

"The Haldane is mine!" the Marluk shouted, spurring toward Brion and cutting down another man in passing. "Stand and fight, usurper! Gwynedd is mine by right!"

The Marluk's men fell back from Brion as their master pounded across the field, and with a savage gesture, Brion waved his own men away and urged his horse toward the enemy. Now was the time both had been waiting for—the direct, personal combat of the two rival kings. Steel shivered against steel as the two men met and clashed in the center of the field, and the warriors of both sides drew back to watch, their own hostilities temporarily suspended.

For a time, the two seemed evenly matched. The Marluk took a chunk out of the top of Brion's shield, but Brion divested the Marluk of a stirrup, and nearly a foot. So they continued, neither man able to score a decisive blow, until finally Brion's sword found the throat of the Marluk's mount. The dying animal collapsed with a liquid scream, dumping its rider in a heap. Brion, pursuing his advantage, tried to ride down his enemy then and there.

But the Marluk rolled beneath his shield on the first pass and nearly tripped up Brion's horse, scrambling to his feet and bracing as Brion wheeled viciously to come at him again. The second pass cost Brion his mount, its belly ripped out by the Marluk's sword. As the horse went down, Brion leaped clear and whirled to face his opponent.

For a quarter hour the two battled with broadsword and shield, the Marluk with the advantage of weight and height, but Brion with youth and greater agility in his favor. Finally, when both men could barely lift their weapons for fatigue, they drew apart and leaned on heavy swords, breath coming in short, ragged gasps. After a moment, golden eyes met steely gray ones. The Marluk flashed a brief, sardonic grin at his opponent.

"You fight well, for a Haldane," the Marluk conceded, still breathing heavily. He gestured with his sword toward the waiting men. "We are well matched, at least in steel, and even were we to cast our men into the fray again, it would still come down to the same— you against me."

"Or my power against yours," Brion amended softly. "That is your eventual intention, is it not?"

The Marluk started to shrug, but Brion interrupted.

"No, you would have slain me by steel if you could," he said. "To win by magic exacts greater payment, and might not give you the sort of victory you seek if you would rule my human kingdom and not fear for your throne. The folk of Gwynedd would not take kindly to a Deryni king after your bloody ancestors."

The Marluk smiled. "By force, physical or arcane— it matters little in the long reckoning. It is the victory itself which will command the people after today. But you, Haldane, your position is far more precarious than mine, dynastically speaking. Do you see yon riders, and the slight one dressed in blue?"

He gestured with his sword toward the other opening of the clearing from which he and his men had come, where half a score of riders surrounded a pale, slight figure on a mouse-gray palfrey.

"Yonder is my daughter and heir, Haldane," the Marluk said smugly. "Regardless of the outcome here today, she rides free—you cannot stop her—to keep my name and memory until another time. But you —your brother and heir stands near, his life a certain forfeit if I win." He gestured toward Nigel, then rested the tip of his sword before him once more. "And the next and final Haldane is your Uncle Richard, a childless bachelor of fifty. After him, there are no others."

Brion's grip tightened on the hilt of his sword, and he glared across at his enemy with something approaching grudging respect. All that the Marluk had said was true. There *were* no other male Haldanes beyond his brother and his uncle, at least for now. Nor was there any way that he or his men could prevent the escape of the Marluk's heir. Even if he won today, the Marluk's daughter would remain a future menace. The centuries-long struggle for supremacy in Gwynedd would not end here—unless, of course, Brion lost.

The thought sobered him, cooled the hot blood racing through his veins and slowed his pounding heart. He must answer this usurper's challenge, and now, and with the only card he had left. They had fought with force of steel before, and all for nought. Now they must face one another with other weapons.

Displaying far more confidence than he felt, for he would never play for higher stakes than life and crown, Brion let fall his shield and helm and strode slowly across half the distance separating him from his mortal enemy. Carefully, decisively, he traced an equal-armed cross in the dust with the tip of his sword, the first arm pointing toward the Marluk.

"I, Brion, Anointed of the Lord, King of Gwynedd and Lord of the Purple March, call thee forth to combat mortal, Hogan Gwernach, for that thou hast raised

hostile hand against me and, through me, against my
people of Gwynedd. This I will defend upon my body
and my soul, to the death, so help me, God."

The Marluk's face had not changed expression during Brion's challenge, and now he, too, strode to the
figure scratched in the dust and laid his sword tip
along the same lines, retracing the cross.

"And I, Hogan Gwernach, descendant of the lawful
kings of Gwynedd in antiquity, do return thy challenge,
Brion Haldane, and charge that thou art base pretender
to the throne and crown thou holdest. And this I will
defend upon my body and my soul, to the death, so
help me, God."

With the last words, he began drawing another symbol in the earth beside the cross—a detailed, winding
interlace which caught and held Brion's concentration
with increasing power. Only just in time, Brion recognized the spell for what it was and, with an oath, dashed
aside the Marluk's sword with his own, erasing the
symbol with his boot. He glared at the enemy standing
but a sword's length away, keeping his anger in check
only with the greatest exertion of will.

If I let him get me angry, he thought, *I'm dead.*

Biting back his rage, he forced his sword-arm to relax.

The Marluk drew back a pace and shrugged almost
apologetically at that—he had not really expected his
diversion to work so well—then saluted with his sword
and backed off another dozen paces. Brion returned
the salute with a sharp, curt gesture and likewise withdrew the required distance. Then, without further pre-
liminaries, he extended his arms to either side and murmured the words of a warding spell. As answering fire
sprang up crimson at his back, the Marluk raised a

similar defense, blue fire joining crimson to complete
the protective circle. Beneath the canopy of light thus
formed, arcs of energy began to crackle sword to sword,
ebbing and flowing, as arcane battle was joined.

The circle brightened as they fought, containing
energies so immense that all around it would have
perished had the wards not held it in. The very air
within grew hazy, so that those without could no longer
see the principals who battled there. So it remained for
nearly half an hour, the warriors of both sides drawing
mistrustfully together to watch and wait. When, at last,
the fire began to flicker erratically and die down, nought
could be seen within the circle but two ghostly, fire-
edged figures in silhouette, one of them staggering
drunkenly.

They could not tell which was which. One of them
had fallen to his knees and remained there, sword upraised in a last, desperate, warding-off gesture. The
other stood poised to strike, but something seemed to
hold him back. The tableau remained frozen that way
for several heartbeats, the tension growing between the
two; but then the kneeling one reeled sidewards and let
fall his sword with a cry of anguish, collapsing forward
on his hands to bow his head in defeat. The victor's
sword descended as though in slow motion, severing
head from body in one blow and showering dust and
victor and vanquished with blood. The fire dimmed almost to nonexistence, and they could see that it was
Brion who lived.

Then went up a mighty cheer from the men of
Gwynedd. A few of the Marluk's men wheeled and
galloped away across the field toward the rest of their
party before anyone could stop them, but the rest cast
down their weapons and surrendered immediately. At

the mouth of the canyon beyond, a slender figure on a gray horse turned and rode away with her escort. There was no pursuit.

Brion could not have seen them through the haze, but he knew. Moving dazedly back to the center of the circle, he traced the dust-drawn cross a final time and mouthed the syllables of a banishing spell. Then, as the fiery circle died away, he gazed long at the now-empty canyon mouth before turning to stride slowly toward his men. They parted before him as he came, Gwynedd and Tolan men alike.

Perhaps a dozen men remained of Brion's force, a score or less of the Marluk's, and there was a taut, tense silence as he moved among them. He stopped and looked around him, at the men, at the wounded lying propped against their shields, at Nigel and Alaric still sitting upon their blood-bespattered war horses, at the bloody banner still in Nigel's hand. He stared at the banner for a long time, no one daring to break the strained silence. Then he let his gaze fall on each man in turn, catching and holding each man's attention in rapt, unshrinking thrall.

"We shall not speak of the details of this battle beyond this place," he said simply. The words crackled with authority, compulsion, and Alaric Morgan, of all who heard, knew the force behind that simple statement. Though most of them would never realize that fact, every man there had just been touched by the special Haldane magic.

Brion held them thus for several heartbeats, no sound or movement disturbing their rapt attention. Then Brion blinked and smiled and the otherworldliness was no more. Instantly, Nigel was springing from his horse to run and clasp his brother's arm. Alaric, in a more restrained movement, swung his leg over the saddle and slid to the ground, walked stiffly to greet his king.

"Well fought, Sire," he murmured, the words coming with great difficulty.

"My thanks for making that possible, Alaric," the king replied, "though the shedding of blood has never been my wish."

He handed his sword to Nigel and brushed a strand of hair from his eyes with a blood-streaked hand. Alaric swallowed and made a nervous bow.

"No thanks are necessary, Sire. I but gave my service as I must." He swallowed again and shifted uneasily, then abruptly dropped to his knees and bowed his head.

"Sire, may I crave a boon of you?"

"A boon? You know you have but to ask, Alaric. I pray you, stand not upon ceremony."

Alaric shook his head, brought his gaze to meet Brion's. "No, this I will and must do, Sire." He raised joined hands before him. "Sire, I would reaffirm my oath of fealty to you."

"Your oath?" Brion began. "But, you have already sworn to serve me, Alaric, and have given me your hand in friendship, which I value far more from you than any oath."

"And I, Sire," Alaric nodded slightly. "But the fealty I gave you before was such as any liegeman might give his Lord and King. What I offer now is fealty for the powers which we share. I would give you my fealty as Deryni."

There was a murmuring around them, and Nigel glanced at his brother in alarm, but neither king nor kneeling squire heard. A slight pause, a wry smile, and then Brion was taking the boy's hands between his own blood-stained ones, gray eyes meeting gray as he heard the oath of the first man to swear Deryni fealty to a human king in nearly two centuries.

"I, Alaric Anthony, Lord Morgan, do become your liegeman of life and limb and earthy worship. And faith and truth I will bear unto you, *with all the powers at my command,* so long as there is breath within me. This I swear upon my life, my honor, and my faith and soul. If I be forsworn, may my powers desert me in my hour of need."

Brion swallowed, his eyes never leaving Alaric's. "And I for my part, pledge fealty to you, Alaric Anthony, Lord Morgan, to protect and defend you, and any who may depend upon you, *with all the powers at my command,* so long as there is breath within me. This I swear upon my life, my throne, and my honor as a man. And if I be forsworn, may dark destruction overcome me. This is the promise of Brion Donal Cinhil Urien Haldane, King of Gwynedd, Lord of the Purple March, and friend of Alaric Morgan."

With these final words, Brion smiled and pressed Alaric's hands a bit more closely between his own, then released them and turned quickly to take back his sword from Nigel. He glanced at the stained blade as he held it before him.

"I trust you will not mind the blood," he said with a little smile, "since it is through the shedding of this blood that I am able to do what I do now."

Slowly he brought the flat of the blade to touch the boy's right shoulder.

"Alaric Anthony Morgan," the sword rose and crossed to touch the other shoulder, "I create thee Duke of Corwyn, by right of thy mother," the blade touched the top of his head lightly and remained there. "And I confirm thee in this title, for thy life and for the surviving issue of thy body, for so long as there shall be Morgan seed upon the earth." The sword was raised and touched to the royal lips, then reversed and brought to ground. "So say I, Brion of Gwynedd. Arise, Duke Alaric."

THE
LANDS BEYOND
THE WORLD

Michael Moorcock

MICHAEL MOORCOCK

Our only British member, Mike is an immensely prolific and wildly talented Sword & Sorcery writer, with—by my count—*at least* sixteen novels to his credit in the Sacred Genre. If you compare this to Sprague's seven, John Jakes's seven, and my fifteen, it can be demonstrated that Moorcock has published more novels in the heroic fantasy field than any other author in history, alive or dead.

Dorian Hawkmoon and his other characters have their own cults of admirers, of course; but for me it is Elric of Melniboné who remains his greatest creation. The doomed albino princeling, delicately perverse and decadent, the hero-villain of his own dark legend, towers above the rest of the Moorcockish *oeuvre* as a searingly brilliant imaginative conception.

And here is his latest adventure. For those who like to know such things, Mike tells me that it fits in between "Voyage on a Dark Ship" and "The Jade Man's Eyes." Mike is revising the latter and setting it in a different period of Elric's career. These three stories, according to Moorcock, will go into the next Elric book which he intends to call *The Sailor on the Seas of Fate*.

L.C.

THE LANDS BEYOND THE WORLD

1

His bone-white, long-fingered hand upon a carved demon's head in black-brown hardwood (one of the few such decorations to be found anywhere about the vessel), the tall man stood alone in the ship's fo'csle and stared through large, slanting, crimson eyes at the mist into which they moved with a speed and sureness to make any mortal mariner marvel and become incredulous.

There were sounds in the distance, incongruent with the sounds of even this nameless, timeless sea: thin sounds, agonized and terrible, for all that they remained remote—yet the ship followed them, as if drawn by them; they grew louder—pain and despair were there, but terror was predominant.

Elric had heard such sounds echoing from his cousin Yyrkoon's sardonically named "Pleasure Chambers" in the days before he had fled the responsibilities of ruling all that remained of the old Melnibonéan Empire. These were the voices of men whose very souls were under siege; men to whom death meant not mere extinction, but a continuation of existence, forever in thrall to some cruel and supernatural master. He had heard men cry so when his salvation and his nemesis, his great black battle-blade Stormbringer, drank their souls.

He did not savor the sound: he hated it, turned his back away from the source and was about to descend the ladder to the main deck when he realized that Otto Blendker had come up behind him. Now that Corum had been borne off by friends with chariots which could ride upon the surface of the water, Blendker was the last of those comrades to have fought at Elric's side against the two alien sorcerers Gagak and Agak.

Blendker's black, scarred face was troubled. The ex-scholar, turned hireling sword, covered his ears with his huge palms.

"Ach! By the Twelve Symbols of Reason, Elric, who makes that din? It's as though we sail close to the shores of Hell itself!"

Prince Elric of Melniboné shrugged. "I'd be prepared to forego an answer and leave my curiosity unsatisfied, Master Blendker, if only our ship would change course. As it is, we sail closer and closer to the source."

Blendker grunted his agreement. "I've no wish to encounter whatever it is that causes those poor fellows to scream so! Perhaps we should inform the Captain."

"You think he does not know where his own ship sails?" Elric's smile had little humor.

The tall black man rubbed at the inverted V-shaped scar which ran from his forehead to his jawbones. "I wonder if he plans to put us into battle again?"

"I'll not fight another for him." Elric's hand moved from the carved rail to the pommel of his runesword. "I have business of my own to attend to, once I'm back on real land."

A wind came from nowhere. There was a sudden rent in the mist. Now Elric could see that the ship sailed through rust-colored water. Peculiar lights gleamed in that water, just below the surface. There was an impression of creatures moving ponderously in the depths of the ocean and, for a moment, Elric thought he glimpsed a white, bloated face not dissimilar to his own—a Melnibonéan face. Impulsively he whirled, back to the rail, looking past Blendker as he strove to control the nausea in his throat.

For the first time since he had come aboard the Dark Ship he was able clearly to see the length of the vessel. Here were the two great wheels, one beside him on the foredeck, one at the far end of the ship on the rear deck, tended now as always by the Steersman, the Captain's sighted twin. There was the great mast bearing the taut black sail, and fore and aft of this, the two deck cabins, one of which was entirely empty (its occupants having been killed during their last landfall) and one of which was occupied only by himself and Blendker. Elric's gaze was drawn back to the Steersman and not for the first time the albino wondered how much influence the Captain's twin had over the course of the Dark Ship. The man seemed tireless, rarely, to Elric's knowledge, going below to his quarters which occupied the stern deck as the Captain's occupied the foredeck. Once or twice Elric or Blendker had tried to involve the Steersman in conversation, but he appeared to be as dumb as his brother was blind.

The cryptographic, geometrical carvings covering all the ship's wood and most of its metal, from sternpost to figurehead, were picked out by the shreds of pale mist still clinging to them (and again Elric wondered if the ship actually generated the mist normally surrounding it) and, as he watched, the designs slowly turned to pale pink fire as the light from that red star, which forever followed them, permeated the overhead cloud.

A noise from below. The Captain, his long red-gold hair drifting in a breeze which Elric could not feel, emerged from his cabin. The Captain's circlet of blue jade, worn like a diadem, had turned to something of a violet shade in the pink light, and even his buff-colored hose and tunic reflected the hue—even the silver sandals with their silver lacing glittered with the rosy tint.

Again Elric looked upon that mysterious blind face, as unhuman, in the accepted sense, as his own, and puzzled upon the origin of the one who would allow himself to be called nothing but "Captain."

As if at the Captain's summons, the mist drew itself about the ship again, as a woman might draw a froth of furs about her body. The red star's light faded, but the distant screams continued.

Did the Captain notice the screams now for the first time, or was this a pantomime of surprise. His blind head tilted, a hand went to his ear. He murmured in a tone of satisfaction: "Aha!" The head lifted. "Elric?"

"Here," said the albino. "Above you."

"We are almost there, Elric."

The apparently fragile hand found the rail of the companionway. The Captain began to climb.

Elric faced him at the top of the ladder. "If it's a battle . . ."

The Captain's smile was enigmatic, bitter. "It was a fight—or shall be one."

". . . we'll have no part of it," concluded the albino firmly.

"It is not one of the battles in which my ship is directly involved," the blind man reassured him. "Those whom you can hear are the vanquished—lost in some future which, I think, you will experience close to the end of your present incarnation."

Elric waved a dismissive hand. "I'll be glad, Captain, if you would cease such vapid mystification. I'm weary of it."

"I'm sorry it offends you. I answer literally, according to my instincts."

The Captain, going past Elric and Otto Blendker so that he could stand at the rail, seemed to be apologizing. He said nothing for a while but listened to the disturbing and confused babble from the mist. Then he nodded, apparently satisfied.

"We'll sight land shortly. If you would disembark and seek your own world, I should advise you to do so now. This is the closest we shall ever come again to your plane."

Elric let his anger show. He cursed, invoking Arioch's name, and put a hand upon the blind man's shoulder. "What? You cannot return me directly to my own plane?"

"It is too late." The Captain's dismay was apparently genuine. "The ship sails on. We near the end of our long voyage."

"But how shall I find my world. I have no sorcery great enough to move me between the spheres! And demonic assistance is denied me here."

"There is one gateway to your world," the Captain told him. "That is why I suggest you disembark. Elsewhere there are none at all. Your sphere and this one intersect directly."

"But you say this lies in my future?"

"Be sure—you will return to your own time. Here you are timeless. It is why your memory is so poor. It is why you remember so little of what befalls you. Seek for the gateway—it is crimson and it emerges from the sea off the coast of the island."

"Which island?"

"The one we approach."

Elric hesitated. "And where shall you go, when I have landed?"

"To Tanelorn," said the Captain. "There is something I must do there. My brother and I must complete our destiny. We carry cargo as well as men. Many will try to stop us now, for they fear our cargo. We might perish, but yet we must do all we can to reach Tanelorn."

"Was that not, then, Tanelorn, where we fought Agak and Gagak?"

"That was nothing more than a broken dream of Tanelorn, Elric."

The Melnibonéan knew that he would receive no more information from the Captain.

"You offer me a poor choice—to sail with you into danger and never see my own world again, or to risk landing on yonder island inhabited, by the sound of it, by the damned and those which prey upon the damned!"

The Captain's blind eyes moved in Elric's direction. "I know," he said softly. "But it is the best I can offer you, nonetheless."

The screams, the imploring, terrified shouts, were closer now, but there were fewer of them. Glancing over the side Elric thought he saw a pair of armored hands rising from the water; there was foam, red-flecked and noxious, and there was yellowish scum in which pieces of frightful flotsam drifted; there were broken timbers, scraps of canvas, tatters of flags and clothing, fragments of weapons and, increasingly, there were floating corpses.

"But where was the battle?" Blendker whispered, fascinated and horrified by the sight.

"Not on this plane," the Captain told him. "You see

only the wreckage which has drifted over from one world to another."

"Then it was a supernatural battle?"

The Captain smiled again. "I am not omniscient. But, yes, I believe there were supernatural agencies involved. The warriors of half a world fought in the sea-battle—to decide the fate of the multiverse. It is—or will be—one of the decisive battles to determine the fate of Mankind, to fix Man's destiny for the coming Cycle."

"Who were the participants?" asked Elric, asking the question in spite of his resolve. "What were the issues as they understood them?"

"You will know in time, I think." The Captain's head faced the sea again.

Blendker sniffed the air. "Ach! It's foul!"

Elric, too, found the odor increasingly unpleasant. Here and there now the water was lit by guttering fires which revealed the faces of the drowning, some of whom still managed to cling to pieces of blackened driftwood. Not all the faces were human (though they had the appearance of having, once, been human): Things with the snouts of pigs and of bulls raised twisted hands to the Dark Ship and grunted plaintively for succor, but the Captain ignored them and the Steersman held his course.

Fires spluttered and water hissed; smoke mingled with the mist. Elric had his sleeve over his mouth and nose and was glad that the smoke and mist between them helped obscure the sights, for as the wreckage grew thicker not a few of the corpses he saw reminded him more of reptiles than of men, their pale, lizard bellies spilling something other than blood.

"If that is my future," Elric told the Captain, "I've a mind to remain on board, after all."

"You have a duty, as have I," said the Captain quietly. "The future must be served, as much as the past and the present."

Elric shook his head. "I fled the duties of an Empire because I sought freedom," the albino told him. "And freedom I must have."

"No," murmured the Captain. "There is no such thing. Not yet. Not for us. We must go through much more before we can even begin to guess what freedom is. The price for the knowledge alone is probably higher than any you would care to pay at this stage of your life. Indeed, life itself is often the price."

"I also sought release from metaphysics when I left Melniboné," said Elric. "I'll fetch the rest of my gear and take the land that's offered. With luck this Crimson Gate will be quickly found and I'll be back amongst dangers and torments which will, as least, be familiar."

"It is the only decision you could have made." The Captain's blind head turned towards Blendker. "And you, Otto Blendker? What shall you do?"

"Elric's world is not mine and I like not the sound of those screams. What can you promise me, sir, if I sail on with you?"

"Nothing but a good death." There was regret in the Captain's voice.

"Death is the promise we're all born with, sir. A good death is better than a poor one. I'll sail on with you."

"As you like. I think you're wise." The Captain sighed. "I'll say farewell to you, then, Elric of Melniboné. You fought well in my service and I thank you."

"Fought for what?" Elric asked.

"Oh, call it Mankind. Call it Fate. Call it a dream or an ideal, if you wish."

"Shall I never have a clearer answer?"

"Not from me. I do not think there is one."

"You allow a man little faith." Elric began to descend the companionway.

"There are two kinds of faith, Elric. Like freedom, there is a kind which is easily kept but proves not worth the keeping and there is a kind which is hard-won. I agree, I offer little of the former."

Elric strode towards his cabin. He laughed, feeling genuine affection for the blind man at that moment. "I thought I had a penchant for such ambiguities, but I have met my match in you, Captain."

He noticed that the Steersman had left his place at the wheel and was swinging out a boat on its davits, preparatory to lowering it.

"Is that for me?"

The Steersman nodded.

Elric ducked into his cabin. He was leaving the ship with nothing but that which he had brought aboard, only his clothing and his armor were in a poorer state of repair than they had been, and his mind was in a considerably greater state of confusion.

Without hesitation he gathered up his things, drawing his heavy cloak about him, pulling on his gauntlets, fastening buckles and thongs, then he left the cabin and returned to the deck. The Captain was pointing through the mist at the dark outlines of a coast. "Can you see land, Elric?"

"I can."

"You must go quickly, then."

"Willingly."

Elric swung himself over the rail and into the boat. The boat struck the side of the ship several times, so that the hull boomed like the beating of some huge funeral drum. Otherwise there was silence now upon the misty waters and no sign of wreckage.

Blendker saluted him. "I wish you luck, comrade."

"You, too, Master Blendker."

The boat began to sink towards the flat surface of the sea, the pulleys of the davits creaking. Elric clung to the rope, letting go as the boat hit the water. He stumbled and sat down heavily upon the seat, releasing the ropes so that the boat drifted at once away from the Dark Ship. He got out the oars and fitted them into their rowlocks.

As he pulled toward the shore he heard the Captain's voice calling to him, but the words were muffled by the mist and he would never know, now, if the blind man's last communication had been a warning or merely some formal pleasantry. He did not care. The boat moved smoothly through the water; the mist began to thin, but so, too, did the light fade.

Suddenly he was under a twilight sky, the sun already gone and stars appearing. Before he had reached the shore it was already completely dark, with the moon not yet risen, and it was with difficulty that he beached the boat on what seemed flat rocks, and stumbled inland until he judged himself safe enough from any inrushing tide.

Then, with a sigh, he lay down, thinking just to order his thoughts before moving on; but, almost instantly, he was asleep.

2

Elric dreamed.

He dreamed not merely of the end of his world but of the end of an entire cycle in the history of the cosmos. He dreamed that he was not only Elric of Melniboné but that he was other men, too—men who were pledged to some numinous cause which even they could not describe. And he dreamed that he had dreamed of the Dark Ship and Tanelorn and Agak and Gagak while he lay exhausted upon a beach somewhere beyond the borders of Pikarayd and when he woke up he was smiling sardonically, congratulating himself for the possession of a grandiose imagination. But he could not clear his head entirely of the impression left by that dream.

This shore was not the same, so plainly something had befallen him—perhaps he had been drugged by slavers, then later abandoned when they found him not what they expected? But, no, the explanation would not do. If he could discover his whereabouts, he might also recall the true facts.

It was dawn, for certain. He sat up and looked about him.

He was sprawled upon a dark, sea-washed limestone pavement, cracked in a hundred places, the cracks so deep that the small streams of foaming saltwater rushing through these many narrow channels made raucous what would otherwise have been a very still evening.

Elric climbed to his feet, using his scabbarded runesword to steady himself. His bone-white lids closed for a moment over his crimson eyes as he sought, again, to recollect the events which had brought him here.

He recalled his flight from Pikarayd, his panic, his falling into a coma of hopelessness, his dreams. And, because he was evidently neither dead nor a prisoner, he could at least conclude that his pursuers had, after all, given up the chase, for if they had found him they would have killed him.

Opening his eyes and casting about him, he remarked the peculiar blue quality of the light (doubtless a trick of the sun behind the gray clouds) which made the landscape ghastly and gave the sea a dull, metallic look.

The limestone terraces which rose from the sea and
stretched above him shone intermittently like polished
lead. On an impulse he held his hand to the light and
inspected it. The normally lusterless white of his skin
was now tinged with a faint, bluish luminosity. He
found it pleasing and smiled as a child might smile, in
innocent wonder.

He had expected to be tired, but he now realised that
he felt unusually refreshed, as if he had slept long
after a good meal, and, deciding not to question the
fact of this fortunate (and unlikely) gift, he determined
to climb the cliffs in the hope that he might get some
idea of his bearings before he decided which direction
he would take.

Limestone could be a little treacherous, but it made
easy climbing, for there was almost always somewhere
that one terrace met another.

He climbed carefully and steadily, finding many
footholds, and seemed to gain considerable height quite
quickly, yet it was noon before he had reached the top
and found himself standing at the edge of a broad,
rocky plateau which fell away sharply to form a close
horizon. Beyond the plateau was only the sky. Save for
sparse, brownish grass, little grew here and there were
no signs at all of human habitation. It was now, for the
first time, that Elric realized the absence of any form of
wildlife. Not a single seabird flew in the air, not an
insect crept through the grass. Instead, there was an
enormous silence hanging over the brown plain.

Elric was still remarkably untired, so he decided to
make the best use he could of his energy and reach
the edge of the plateau in the hope that, from there,
he would sight a town or a village. He pressed on, feeling no lack of food and water, and his stride was singu-
larly energetic, still, but he had misjudged his distance

and the sun had begun to set well before his journey to
the edge was completed. The sky on all sides turned a
deep, velvety blue and the few clouds that there were
in it were also tinged blue, and now, for the first time,
Elric realized that the sun itself was not its normal
shade, that it burned blackish purple, and he wondered
again if he still dreamed.

The ground began to rise sharply and it was with
some effort that he walked, but before the light had
completely faded he was on the steep flank of a hill,
descending towards a wide valley which, though bereft
of trees, contained a river which wound through rocks
and russet turf and bracken. After a short rest, Elric
decided to press on, although night had fallen, and see
if he could reach the river where he might, at least,
drink and, possibly, in the morning, find fish to eat.

Again, no moon appeared to aid his progress and
he walked for two or three hours in a darkness which
was almost total, stumbling occasionally into large
rocks, until the ground leveled and he felt sure he had
reached the floor of the valley.

He had developed a strong thirst by now and was
feeling somewhat hungry, but decided that it might be
best to wait until morning before seeking the river
when, rounding a particularly tall rock, he saw, with
some astonishment, the light of a camp fire.

Hopefully this would be the fire of a company of
merchants, a trading caravan on its way to some civilized country which would allow him to travel with it,
perhaps in return for his services as a mercenary swords-
man (it would not be the first time, since he had left
Melniboné, that he had earned his bread in such a
way).

Yet Elric's old instincts did not desert him: he approached the fire cautiously and let no one see him.

Beneath an overhang of rock, made shadowy by the
flame's light, he stood and observed the group of fifteen or sixteen men who sat or lay close to the fire,
playing some kind of game involving dice and slivers
of numbered ivory.

Gold, bronze, and silver gleamed in the firelight as
the men staked large sums on the fall of a die and the
turn of a slip of ivory.

Elric guessed that, if they had not been so intent
on their game, these men must certainly have detected
his approach, for they were not, after all, merchants.
By the evidence, they were warriors, wearing scarred
leather and dented metal, their weapons ready to hand,
yet they belonged to no army—unless it be an army of
bandits—for they were of all races and (oddly) seemed
to be from various periods in the history of the Young
Kingdoms.

It was as if they had looted some scholar's collection
of relics. An axman of the later Lormyrian Republic,
which had come to an end some two hundred years
ago, lay with his shoulder rubbing the elbow of a Chalalite bowman, from a period roughly contemporary with
Elric's own. Close to the Chalalite sat a short Ilmioran
infantryman of a century past. Next to him was a Filkharian in the barbaric dress of that nation's earliest
times. Tarkeshites, Shazarians, Vilmirians, all mingled
and the only thing they had in common, by the look of
them, was a villainous, hungry cast to their features.

In other circumstances Elric might have skirted this
encampment and moved on, but he was so glad to find
human beings of any sort that he ignored the disturbing incongruities of the group, but yet he remained content to watch them.

One of the men, less unwholesome than the others,
was a bulky, black-bearded, bald-headed sea warrior

clad in the casual leathers and silks of the people of the Purple Towns. It was when this man produced a large, gold Melnibonéan wheel—a coin not minted, as most coins, but carved by carftsmen to a design both ancient and intricate—that Elric's caution was fully conquered by his curiosity.

Very few of those coins existed in Melniboné and none, that Elric had heard of, outside; for the coins were not used for trade with the Young Kingdoms. They were prized, even by the nobility of Melniboné.

It seemed to Elric that the bald-headed man could only have acquired the coin from another Melnibonéan traveler—and Elric knew of no other Melnibonéans who shared his penchant for exploration. His wariness dismissed, he stepped into the circle.

If he had not been completely obsessed by the thought of the Melnibonéan wheel he might have taken some satisfaction in the sudden scuffle to arms which resulted. Within seconds, the majority of the men were on their feet, their weapons drawn.

For a moment, the gold wheel was forgotten. His hand upon his runesword's pommel, he presented the other in a placatory gesture.

"Forgive the interruption, gentlemen. I am but one tired fellow soldier who seeks to join you. I would beg some information and purchase some food, if you have it to spare."

On foot, the warriors had an even more ruffianly appearance. They grinned among themselves, entertained by Elric's courtesy but not impressed by it.

One, in the feathered helmet of a Pan Tangian sea-chief, with features to match—swarthy, sinister—pushed his head forward on its long neck and said banteringly:

"We've company enough, white-face. And few here

are overfond of the man-demons of Melniboné. You must be rich."

Elric recalled the animosity with which Melnibonéans were regarded in the Young Kingdoms, particularly by those from Pan Tang who envied the Dragon Isle her power and her wisdom and, of late, had begun crudely to imitate Melniboné.

Increasingly on his guard, he said evenly: "I have a little money."

"Then we'll take it, demon." The Pan Tangian presented a dirty palm just below Elric's nose as he growled: "Give it over and be on your way."

Elric's smile was polite and fastidious, as if he had been told a poor joke.

The Pan Tangian evidently thought the joke better than did Elric, for he laughed heartily and looked to his nearest fellows for approval.

Coarse laughter infected the night and only the bald-headed, black-bearded man did not join in the jest, but took a step or two backward, while all the others pressed forward.

The Pan Tangian's face was close to Elric's own; his breath was foul and Elric saw that his beard and hair were alive with lice, yet he kept his head, replying in the same equable tone:

"Give me some decent food—a flask of water—some wine, if you have it—and I'll gladly give you the money I have."

The laughter rose and fell again as Elric continued:

"But if you would take my money and leave me with naught—then I must defend myself. I have a good sword."

The Pan Tangian strove to imitate Elric's irony. "But you will note, Sir Demon, that we outnumber you. Considerably."

Softly the albino spoke: "I've noticed that fact, but I'm not disturbed by it," and he had drawn the black blade even as he finished speaking, for they had come at him with a rush.

And the Pan Tangian was the first to die, sliced through the side, his vertebrae sheered, and Stormbringer, having taken its first soul, began to sing.

A Chalalite died next, leaping with stabbing javeline poised, on the point of the runesword, and Stormbringer murmured with pleasure.

But it was not until it had sliced the head clean off a Filkharian pikemaster that the sword began to croon and come fully to life, black fire flickering up and down its length, its strange runes glowing.

Now the warriors knew they battled sorcery and became more cautious, yet they scarcely paused in their attack, and Elric, thrusting and parrying, hacking and slicing, needed all of the fresh, dark energy the sword passed on to him.

Lance, sword, ax, and dirk were blocked, wounds were given and received, but the dead had not yet outnumbered the living when Elric found himself with his back against the rock and nigh a dozen sharp weapons seeking his vitals.

It was at this point, when Elric had become somewhat less than confident that he could best so many, that the bald-headed warrior, ax in one gloved hand, sword in the other, came swiftly into the firelight and set upon those of his fellows closest to him.

"I thank you, sir!" Elric was able to shout, during the short respite this sudden turn produced. His morale improved, he resumed the attack.

The Lormyrian was cloven from hip to pelvis as he dodged a feint; a Filkharian, who should have been dead four hundred years before, fell with the blood

bubbling from lips and nostrils, and the corpses began
to pile one upon the other. Still Stormbringer sang its
sinister battle-song and still the runesword passed its
power to its master so that with every death Elric
found strength to slay more of the soldiers.

Those who remained now began to express their regret for their hasty attack. Where oaths and threats had
issued from their mouths, now came plaintive petitions
for mercy and those who had laughed with such bold
braggadocio now wept like young girls, but Elric, full
of his old battle-joy, spared none.

Meanwhile the man from the Purple Towns, unaided
by sorcery, put ax and sword to good work and dealt
with three more of his one-time comrades, exulting in
his work as if he had nursed a taste for it for some time.

"Yoi! But this is worthwhile slaughter!" cried the
black-bearded one.

And then that busy butchery was suddenly done and
Elric realized that none were left save himself and his
new ally who stood leaning on his ax, panting and
grinning like a hound at the kill, replacing a steel skull-
cap upon his pate from where it had fallen during the
fight, and wiping a bloody sleeve over the sweat glisten-
ing on his brow, and saying, in a deep, good-humored
tone:

"Well, now, it is we who are wealthy, of a sudden."

Elric sheathed a Stormbringer still reluctant to return to its scabbard. "You desire their gold. Is that why
you aided me?"

The black-bearded soldier laughed. "I owed them a
debt and had been biding my time, waiting to pay.
These rascals are all that were left of a pirate crew
which slew everyone aboard my own ship when we wandered into strange waters—they would have slain me
had I not told them I wished to join them. Now I am

revenged. Not that I am above taking the gold, since much of it belongs to me and my dead brothers. It will go to their wives and their children when I return to the Purple Towns."

"How did you convince them not to kill you, too?" Elric sought amongst the ruins of the fire for something to eat. He found some cheese and began to chew upon it.

"They had no captain or navigator, it seemed. None are real sailors at all, but coast-huggers, based upon this island. They were stranded here, you see, and had taken to piracy as a last resort, but were too terrified to risk the open sea. Besides, after the fight, they had no ship. We had managed to sink that as we fought. We sailed mine to this shore, but provisions were already low and they had no stomach for setting sail without full holds, so I pretended that I knew this coast (may the Gods take my soul if I ever see it again after this business) and offered to lead them inland to a village they might loot. They had heard of no such village, but believed me when I said it lay in a hidden valley. That way I prolonged my life while I waited for the opportunity to be revenged upon them. It was a foolish hope, I know. Yet," grinning, "as it happened, it was well founded, after all! Eh?"

The black-bearded man glanced a little warily at Elric, uncertain of what the albino might say, hoping, however, for comradeship, though it was well known how haughty Melnibonéans were. Elric could tell that all these thoughts went through his new acquaintance's mind; he had seen many others make similar calculations. So he smiled openly and slapped the man on the shoulder.

"You saved my life, also, my friend. We are both fortunate."

The man sighed in relief and slung his ax upon his back "Aye—lucky's the word. But shall our luck hold, I wonder?"

"You do not know the island at all?"

"Nor the waters, either. How we came to them I'll never guess. Enchanted waters, though, without question. You've seen the color of the sun?"

"I have."

"Well," the seaman bent to remove a pendant from around the Pan Tangian's throat, "you'd know more about enchantments and sorceries than I. How came you here, Sir Melnibonéan?"

"I know not. I fled from some who hunted me. I came to a shore and could flee no further. Then I dreamed a great deal. When next I awoke I was on the shore again, but of this island."

"Spirits of some sort—maybe friendly to you—took you to safety, away from your enemies."

"That's just possible," Elric agreed, "for we have many allies amongst the elementals. I am called Elric and I am self-exiled from Melniboné. I travel because I believe I have something to learn from the folk of the Young Kingdoms. I have no power, save what you see . . ."

The black-bearded man's eyes narrowed in appraisal as he pointed at himself with his thumb. "I'm Smiorgan Baldhead, once a sealord of the Purple Towns. I commanded a fleet of merchantmen. Perhaps I still do. I shall not know until I return—if I ever do return."

"Then let us pool our knowledge and our resources, Smiorgan Baldhead, and make plans to leave this island as soon as we can."

Elric walked back to where he saw traces of the abandoned game, trampled into the mud and the blood. From amongst the dice and the ivory slips, the silver and the bronze coins, he found the gold Melnibonéan wheel. He picked it up and held it in his outstretched palm. The wheel almost covered the whole palm. In the old days, it had been the currency of kings.

"This was yours, friend?" he asked Smiorgan.

Smiorgan Baldhead looked up from where he was still searching the Pan Tangian for his stolen possessions. He nodded.

"Aye. Would you keep it as part of your share?"

Elric shrugged. "I'd rather know from whence it came. Who gave it you?"

"It was not stolen. It's Melnibonéan, then?"

"Yes."

"I guessed it."

"From whom did you obtain it?"

Smiorgan straightened up, having completed his search. He scratched at a slight wound on his forearm. "It was used to buy passage on our ship—before we were lost—before the raiders attacked us."

"Passage? By a Melnibonéan?"

"Maybe," said Smiorgan. He seemed reluctant to speculate.

"Was he a warrior?"

Smiorgan smiled in his beard. "No. It was a woman gave that to me."

"How came she to take passage?"

Smiorgan began to pick up the rest of the money. "It's a long tale and, in part, a familiar one to most merchant sailors. We were seeking new markets for our goods and had equipped a good sized fleet, which I commanded, as the largest shareholder." He seated himself casually upon the big corpse of the Chalalite and began to count the money. "Would you hear the the tale or do I bore you already?"

"I'd be glad to listen."

Reaching behind him, Smiorgan pulled a wine flask from the belt of the corpse and offered it to Elric who accepted it and drank sparingly of a wine which was unusually good.

Smiorgan took the flask when Elric had finished. "That's part of our cargo," he said. "We were proud of it. A good vintage, eh?"

"Excellent. So you set off from the Purple Towns?"

"Aye. Going east towards the Unknown Kingdoms. We sailed due east for a couple of weeks, sighting some of the bleakest coasts I have ever seen, and then we saw no land at all for another week. That was when we entered a stretch of water we came to call the Roaring Rocks—like the Serpent's Teeth off Shazar's coast, but much greater in expanse, and larger, too. Huge volcanic cliffs which rose from the sea on every side and around which the waters heaved and boiled and howled with a fierceness I've rarely experienced. Well, in short, the fleet was dispersed and at least four ships were lost on those rocks. At last we were able to escape those waters and found ourselves becalmed and alone. We searched for our sister ships for a while and then decided to give ourselves another week before turning for home, for we had no liking to go back into the Roaring Rocks again. Low on provisions, we sighted land at last—grassy cliffs and hospitable beaches and, inland, some signs of cultivation, so we knew we had found civilization again. We put into a small fishing port and satisfied the natives—who spoke no tongue used in the Young Kingdoms—that we were friendly. And that was when the woman approached us."

"The Melnibonéan woman?"

"If Melnibonéan she was. She was a fine-looking woman, I'll say that. We were short of provisions, as I told you, and short of any means of purchasing them,

for the fishermen desired little of what we had to trade.
Having given up our original quest, we were content
to head westward again."

"The woman?"

"She wished to buy passage to the Young Kingdoms
—and was content to go with us as far as Menii, our
home port. For her passage she gave us two of those
wheels. One was used to buy provisions in the town—
Graghin, I think it was called—and after making re-
pairs we set off again."

"You never reached the Purple Towns?"

"There were more storms—strange storms. Our in-
struments were useless, our lodestones were of no help
to us at all. We became even more completely lost than
before. Some of my men argued that we had gone beyond our own world altogether. Some blamed the
woman, saying she was a sorceress who had no intention of going to Menii. But I believed her. Night fell
and seemed to last forever until we sailed into a calm
dawn beneath a blue sun. My men were close to panic—
and it takes much to make my men panic—when we
sighted the island. As we headed for it those pirates
attacked us in a ship which belonged to history—it
should have been on the bottom of the ocean, not on
the surface. I've seen pictures of such craft in murals
on a temple wall in Tarkesh. In ramming us, she stove
in half her port side and was sinking even when they
swarmed aboard. They were desperate, savage men, Elric—half-starved and blood-hungry. We were weary
after our voyage but fought well. During the fighting the
woman disappeared, killed herself, maybe, when she
saw the stamp of our conquerors. After a long fight
only myself and one other, who died soon after, were
left. That was when I became cunning and decided to
wait for revenge."

"The woman had a name?"

"None she would give. I have thought the matter over and suspect that, after all, we were used by her. Perhaps she did not seek Menii and the Young Kingdoms. Perhaps it was this world she sought, and, by sorcery, led us here."

"This world? You think it different to our own?"

"If only because of the sun's strange color. Do you not think so, too? You, with your Melnibonéan knowledge of such things, must believe it?"

"I have dreamed of such things," Elric admitted, but he would say no more.

"Most of the pirates thought as I—they were from all the ages of the Young Kingdoms. That much I discovered. Some were from the earliest years of the era, some from our own time—and some were from the future. Adventurers, most of them, who, at some stage in their lives, sought a legendary land of great riches which lay on the other side of an ancient gateway, rising from the middle of the ocean, but they found themselves trapped here, unable to sail back through this mysterious gate. Others had been involved in sea fights, thought themselves drowned and woken up on the shores of the island. Many, I suppose, had once had reasonable virtues, but there is little to support life on the island and they had become wolves, living off one another or any ship unfortunate enough to pass, inadvertently, through this gate of theirs."

Elric recalled part of his dream. "Did any call it the 'Crimson Gate'?"

"Several did, aye."

"And yet the theory is unlikely, if you'll forgive my skepticism," Elric said. "As one who has passed through the Shade Gate to Ameeron . . ."

"You know of other worlds, then?"

"I've never heard of this one. And I am versed in such matters. That is why I doubt the reasoning. And yet, there was the dream . . ."

"Dream?"

"Oh, it was nothing. I am used to such dreams and give them no significance."

"The theory cannot seem surprising to a Melnibonéan, Elric!" Smiorgan grinned again. "It's I who should be skeptical, not you."

And Elric replied, half to himself: "Perhaps I fear the implications more." He lifted his head and, with the shaft of a broken spear, began to poke at the fire. "Certain ancient sorcerers of Melniboné proposed that an infinite number of worlds coexist with our own. Indeed, my dreams, of late, have hinted as much!" He forced himself to smile. "But I cannot afford to believe such things. Thus, I reject them."

"Wait for the dawn," said Smiorgan Baldhead. "The color of the sun shall prove the theory."

"Perhaps it will prove only that we both dream," said Elric. The smell of death was strong in his nostrils. He pushed aside those corpses nearest to the fire and settled himself to sleep.

Smiorgan Baldhead had begun to sing a strong yet lilting song in his own dialect, which Elric could scarcely follow.

"Do you sing of your victory over your enemies?" the albino asked.

Smiorgan paused for a moment, half amused. "No, Sir Elric, I sing to keep the shades at bay. After all, these fellows' ghosts must still be lurking nearby, in the dark, so little time has passed since they died."

"Fear not," Elric told him. "Their souls are already eaten."

But Smiorgan sang on, and his voice was louder,

his song more intense, than ever it had been before.

Just before he fell asleep, Elric thought he heard a horse whinny, and he meant to ask Smiorgan if any of the pirates had been mounted, but he fell asleep before he could do so.

3

Recalling little of his voyage on the Dark Ship, Elric would never know how he came to reach the world in which he now found himself. In later years he would recall most of these experiences as dreams and, indeed, they seemed dreamlike even as they occurred.

He slept uneasily, and, in the morning, the clouds were heavier, shining with that strange, leaden light, though the sun itself was obscured. Smiorgan Baldhead of the Purple Towns was pointing upwards, already on his feet, speaking with quiet triumph:

"Will that evidence suffice to convince you, Elric of Melniboné?"

"I am convinced of a quality about the light—possibly about this terrain—which makes the sun appear blue," Elric replied. He glanced with distaste at the carnage around him. The corpses made a wretched sight and he was filled with a nebulous misery that was neither remorse nor pity.

Smiorgan's sigh was sardonic. "Well, Sir Skeptic, we had best retrace my steps and seek my ship. What say you?"

"I agree," the albino told him.

"How far had you marched from the coast when you found us?"

Elric told him.

Smiorgan smiled. "You arrived in the nick of time, then. I should have been most embarrassed by today if

the sea had been reached and I could show my pirate
friends no village! I shall not forget this favor you have
done me, Elric. I am a Count of the Purple Towns and
have much influence. If there is any service I can per-
form for you when we return, you must let me know."

"I thank you," Elric said gravely. "But first we must
discover a means of escape."

Smiorgan had gathered up a satchel of food, some
water and some wine. Elric had no stomach to make
his breakfast among the dead, so he slung the satchel
over his shoulder. "I'm ready," he said.

Smiorgan was satisfied. "Come—we go this way."

Elric began to follow the sealord over the dry,
crunching turf. The steep sides of the valley loomed
over them, tinged with a peculiar and unpleasant green-
ish hue, the result of the brown foliage being stained
by the blue light from above. When they reached the
river, which was narrow and ran rapidly through boulders giving easy means of crossing, they rested and ate.
Both men were stiff from the previous night's fighting;
both were glad to wash the dried blood and mud from
their bodies in the water.

Refreshed, the pair climbed over the boulders and
left the river behind, ascending the slopes, speaking
little so that their breath was saved for the exertion. It
was noon by the time they reached the top of the valley
and observed a plain not unlike the one which Elric
had first crossed. Elric now had a fair idea of the
island's geography: it resembled the top of a mountain,
with an indentation near the center which was the valley. Again he became sharply aware of the absence of
any wildlife and remarked on this to Count Smiorgan,
who agreed that he had seen nothing—no bird, fish nor
beast since he had arrived.

"It's a barren little world, friend Elric, and a misfortune for a mariner to be wrecked upon its shores."

They moved on, until the sea could be observed meeting the horizon in the far distance.

It was Elric who first heard the sound behind them, recognizing the steady thump of the hooves of a galloping horse, but when he looked back over his shoulder he could see no sign of a rider, nor anywhere that a rider could hide. He guessed that, in his tiredness, his ears were betraying him. It had been thunder that he had heard.

Smiorgan strode implacably onward, though he, too, must have heard the sound.

Again it came. Again, Elric turned. Again he saw nothing.

"Smiorgan? Did you hear a rider?"

Smiorgan continued to walk without looking back. "I heard," he grunted.

"You have heard it before?"

"Many times since I arrived. The pirates heard it, too, and some believed it their nemesis—an Angel of Death seeking them out for retribution."

"You don't know the source?"

Smiorgan paused, then stopped, and when he turned his face was grim. "Once or twice I have caught a glimpse of a horse, I think. A tall horse—white—richly dressed—but with no man upon his back. Ignore it, Elric, as I do. We have larger mysteries with which to occupy our minds!"

"You are afraid of it, Smiorgan?"

He accepted this. "Aye. I confess it. But neither fear nor speculation will rid us of it. Come!"

Elric was bound to see the sense of Smiorgan's statement and he accepted it, yet, when the sound came again, about an hour later, he could not resist turning. Then he thought he glimpsed the outline of a large stallion, caparisoned for riding, but that might have been nothing more than an idea Smiorgan had put in his mind.

The day grew colder and in the air was a peculiar, bitter odor. Elric remarked on the smell to Count Smiorgan and learned that this, too, was familiar.

"The smell comes and goes, but it is usually here in some strength."

"Like sulphur," said Elric.

Count Smiorgan's laugh had much irony in it, as if Elric made reference to some private joke of Smiorgan's own. "Oh, aye! Sulphur right enough!"

The drumming of hooves grew louder behind them as they neared the coast and at last Elric, and Smiorgan too, turned round again, to look.

And now a horse could be seen plainly—riderless, but saddled and bridled, its dark eyes intelligent, its beautiful white head held proudly.

"Are you still convinced of the absence of sorcery here, Sir Elric?" Count Smiorgan asked with some satisfaction. "The horse was invisible. Now it is visible." He shrugged the battle-ax on his shoulder into a better position. "Either that, or it moves from one world to another with ease, so that all we mainly hear are its hoofbeats."

"If so," said Elric sardonically, eyeing the stallion, "it might bear us back to our own world."

"You admit, then, that we are marooned in some Limbo?"

"Very well, yes. I admit the possibility."

"Have you no sorcery to trap the horse?"

"Sorcery does not come so easily to me, for I have no great liking for it," the albino told him.

As they spoke, they approached the horse, but it would let them get no closer. It snorted and moved backward, keeping the same distance between them and itself.

At last, Elric said: "We waste time, Count Smiorgan. Let's get to your ship with speed and forget blue suns and enchanted horses as quickly as we may. Once aboard the ship I can doubtless help you with a little incantation or two, for we'll need aid of some sort if we're to sail a large ship by ourselves."

They marched on, but the horse continued to follow them. They came to the edge of the cliffs, standing high above a narrow, rocky bay in which a battered ship lay at anchor. The ship had the high, fine lines of a Purple Towns merchantman, but its decks were piled with shreds of torn canvas, pieces of broken rope, shards of timber, torn-open bales of cloth, smashed wine-jars, and all manner of other refuse, while in several places her rails were smashed and two or three of her yards had splintered. It was evident that she had been through both storms and sea-fights and it was a wonder that she still floated.

"We'll have to tidy her up as best we can, using only the mains'l for motion," mused Smiorgan. "Hopefully we can salvage enough food to last us . . ."

"Look!" Elric pointed, sure that he had seen someone in the shadows near the afterdeck. "Did the pirates leave any of their company behind?"

"None."

"Did you see anyone on the ship, just then?"

"My eyes play filthy tricks on my mind," Smiorgan told him. "It is this damned blue light. There is a rat or two aboard, that's all. And that's what you saw."

"Possibly." Elric looked back. The horse appeared to be unaware of them as it cropped the brown grass. "Well, let's finish the journey."

They scrambled down the steeply sloping cliff-face

and were soon on the shore, wading through the shallows for the ship, clambering up the slippery ropes which still hung over the sides and, at last, setting their feet with some relief upon the deck.

"I feel more secure already," said Smiorgan. "This ship was my home for so long!" He searched through the scattered cargo until he found an unbroken wine-jar, carved off the seal and handed it to Elric. Elric lifted the heavy jar and let a little of the good wine flow into his mouth. As Count Smiorgan began to drink, Elric was sure he saw another movement near the after-deck, and he moved closer.

Now he was certain that he heard strained, rapid breathing—like the breathing of one who sought to stifle their need for air rather than be detected. They were slight sounds, but the albino's ears, unlike his eyes, were sharp. His hand ready to draw his sword, he stalked towards the source of the sound, Smiorgan now behind him.

She emerged from her hiding place before he reached her. Her hair hung in heavy, dirty coils about her pale face; her shoulders were slumped and her soft arms hung limply at her sides, while her dress was stained and ripped.

As Elric approached, she fell on her knees before him. "Take my life," she said humbly, "but I beg you —do not take me back to Saxif D'Aan, though I know you must be his servant or his kinsman."

"It's she!" cried Smiorgan in astonishment. "It's our passenger. She must have been in hiding all this time."

Elric stepped forward, lifting up the girl's chin so that he could study her face. There was a Melnibonéan cast about her features, but she was, to his mind, of the Young Kingdoms; she lacked the pride of a Melnibonéan woman, too. "What name was that you used,

girl?" he asked kindly. "Did you speak of Saxif D'Aan?
Earl Saxif D'Aan of Melniboné?"

"I did, my lord."

"Do not fear me as his servant," Elric told her. "And
as for being a kinsman, I suppose you could call me
that—on my mother's side—or rather my great-grand-
mother's side. He was an ancestor. He must have been
dead for two centuries, at least!"

"No," she said. "He lives, my lord."

"On this island?"

"This island is not his home, but it is in this plane
that he exists. I sought to escape him through the
Crimson Gate. I fled through the gate in a skiff,
reached the town where you found me, Count Smiorgan, but he drew me back once I was aboard your
ship. He drew me back and the ship with me. For that,
I have remorse—and for what befell your crew. Now
I know he seeks me. I can feel his presence growing
nearer."

"Is he invisible," Smiorgan asked suddenly. "Does
he ride a white horse?"

She gasped. "You see! He is near! Why else should
the horse appear on this island?"

"He rides it?" Elric asked.

"No, no! He fears the horse almost as much as I fear
him. The horse pursues him!"

Elric produced the Melnibonéan gold wheel from his
purse. "Did you take these from Earl Saxif D'Aan?"

"I did."

The albino frowned.

"Who is this man, Elric?" Count Smiorgan asked.
"You describe him as an ancestor—yet he lives in this
world. What do you know of him?"

Elric weighed the large gold wheel in his hand be-

fore replacing it in his pouch. "He was something of
a legend in Melniboné. His story is part of our literature. He was a great sorcerer—one of the greatest—
and he fell in love. It's rare enough for Melnibonéans
to fall in love, as others understand the emotion, but
rarer for one to have such feelings for a girl who was
not even of our own race. She was half-Melnibonéan,
so I heard, but from a land which was, in those days,
a Melnibonéan possession, a western province close to
Dharijor. She was bought by him in a batch of slaves
he planned to use for some sorcerous experiment, but
he singled her out, saving her from whatever fate it was
the others suffered. He lavished his attention upon her,
giving her everything. For her, he abandoned his
practices, retired to live quietly away from Imrryr, and
I think she showed him a certain affection, though she
did not seem to love him. There was another, you see,
called Carolak, as I recall, and also half-Melnibonéan,
who had become a mercenary in Shazar and risen in
the favor of the Shazarian court. She had been pledged
to this Carolak before her abduction . . ."

"She loved him?" Count Smiorgan asked.

"She was pledged to marry him, but let me finish my
story . . ." Elric continued: "Well, at length Carolak,
now a man of some substance, second only to the king
in Shazar, heard of her fate and swore to rescue her.
He came with raiders to Melniboné's shores and, aided
by sorcery, sought out Saxif D'Aan's palace. That
done, he sought the girl, finding her at last in the apart-
ments Saxif D'Aan had set aside for her use. He told
her that he had come to claim her as his bride, to rescue her from persecution. Oddly, the girl resisted, suggesting that she had been too long a slave in the Melnibonéan harem to readapt to the life of a princess in the

Shazarian court. Carolak scoffed at this and seized her. He managed to escape the castle and had the girl over the saddle of his horse and was about to rejoin his men on the coast when Saxif D'Aan detected them. Carolak, I think, was slain, or else a spell was put on him, but Saxif D'Aan, in his terrible jealousy and certain that the girl had planned the escape with a lover, ordered her to die upon the wheel of Chaos—a machine rather like that coin in design. Her limbs were broken slowly and Saxif D'Aan sat and watched, through long days, while she died. Her skin was peeled from her flesh, and Earl Saxif D'Aan observed every detail of her punishment. Soon it was evident that the drugs and sorcery used to sustain her life were failing and Saxif D'Aan ordered her taken from the Wheel of Chaos and laid upon a couch. 'Well,' he said, 'you have been punished for betraying me and I am glad. Now you may die.' And he saw that her lips, blood-caked and frightful, were moving, and he bent to hear her words."

"Those words? Revenge? An oath?" asked Smiorgan.

"Her last gesture was an attempt to embrace him. And the words were those she had never uttered to him before, much as he had hoped that she would. She said simply, over and over again, until the last breath left her: 'I love you. I love you. I love you.' And then she died."

Smiorgan rubbed at his beard. "Gods! What then? What did your ancestor do?"

"He knew remorse."

"Of course!"

"Not so, for a Melnibonéan. Remorse is a rare emotion with us. Few have ever experienced it. Torn by guilt, Earl Saxif D'Aan left Melniboné, never to return. It was assumed that he had died in some remote land, trying to make amends for what he had done to the only creature he had ever loved. But now, it seems, he sought the Crimson Gate, perhaps thinking it an opening into Hell."

"But why should he plague me!" the girl cried. "I am not she! My name is Vassliss. I am a merchant's daughter, from Jharkor. I was voyaging to visit my uncle in Vilmir when our ship was wrecked. A few of us escaped in an open boat. More storms seized us. I was flung from the boat and was drowning when . . ." she shuddered—"when *his* galley found me. I was grateful, then . . ."

"What happened?" Elric pushed the matted hair away from her face and offered her some of their wine. She drank gratefully.

"He took me to his palace and told me that he would marry me, that I should be his Empress forever and rule beside him. But I was frightened. There was such pain in him—and such cruelty, too. I thought he must devour me, destroy me. Soon after my capture, I took the money and the boat and fled for the gateway, which he had told me about . . ."

"You could find this gateway for us?" Elric asked.

"I think so. I have some knowledge of seamanship, learned from my father. But what would be the use, sir? He would find us again and drag us back. And he must be very near, even now."

"I have a little sorcery myself," Elric assured her, "and will pit it against Saxif D'Aan's, if I must." He turned to Count Smiorgan. "Can we get a sail aloft quickly?"

"Fairly quickly."

"Then let's hurry, Count Smiorgan Baldhead. I might have the means of getting us through this Crimson Gate and free from any further involvement in the dealings of the dead!"

4

While Count Smiorgan and Vassliss of Jharkor watched, Elric lowered himself to the deck, panting and pale. His first attempt to work sorcery in this world had failed and had exhausted him.

"I am further convinced," he told Smiorgan, "that we are in another plane of existence, for I should have worked my incantations with less effort."

"You have failed."

Elric rose with some difficulty. "I shall try again."

He turned his white face skyward; he closed his eyes; he stretched out his arms and his body tensed as he began the incantation again, his voice growing louder and louder, higher and higher, so that it resembled the shrieking of a gale.

He forgot where he was; he forgot his own identity; he forgot those who were with him as his whole mind concentrated upon the summoning. He sent his call out beyond the confines of the world, into that strange plane where the elementals dwelled—where the powerful creatures of the air could still be found—the *sylphs* of the breeze, and the *sharnahs,* who lived in the storms, and the most powerful of all, the *h'Haar-shanns,* creatures of the whirlwind.

And now at last some of them began to come at his summons, ready to serve him as, by virtue of an ancient pact, the elementals had served his forefathers. And slowly the sail of the ship began to fill, and the timbers creaked, and Smiorgan raised the anchor, and the ship was sailing away from the island, through the rocky gap of the harbor, and out into the open sea, still beneath a strange, blue sun.

Soon a huge wave was forming around them, lifting up the ship and carrying it across the ocean, so that Count Smiorgan and the girl marveled at the speed of their progress, while Elric, his crimson eyes open now, but blank and unseeing, continued to croon to his unseen allies.

Thus the ship progressed across the waters of the sea, and at last the island was out of sight and the girl, checking their position against the position of the sun, was able to give Count Smiorgan sufficient information for him to steer a course.

As soon as he could, Count Smiorgan went up to Elric, who still straddled the deck, still as stiff-limbed as before, and shook him.

"Elric! You will kill yourself with this effort. We need your friends no longer!"

At once the wind dropped and the wave dispersed and Elric, gasping, fell to the deck.

"It is harder here," he said. "It is so much harder here. It is as if I have to call across far greater gulfs than any I have known before."

And then Elric slept.

He lay in a warm bunk in a cool cabin. Through the porthole filtered diffused blue light. He sniffed. He caught the odor of hot food and, turning his head, saw that Vassliss stood there, a bowl of broth in her hands. "I was able to cook this," she said. "It will improve your health. As far as I can tell, we are nearing the Crimson Gate. The seas are always rough around the gate, so you will need your strength."

Elric thanked her pleasantly and began to eat the broth as she watched him.

"You are very like Saxif D'Aan," she said. "Yet harder in a way—and gentler, too. He is so remote. I know why that girl could never tell him that she loved him."

Elric smiled. "Oh, it's nothing more than a folktale, probably, the story I told you. This Saxif D'Aan could be another person altogether—or an imposter, even, who has taken his name—or a sorcerer. Some sorcerers take the names of other sorcerers, for they think it gives them more power."

There came a cry from above, but Elric could not make out the words.

The girl's expression became alarmed. Without a word to Elric, she hurried from the cabin.

Elric, rising unsteadily, followed her up the companionway.

Count Smiorgan Baldhead was at the wheel of his ship and he was pointing towards the horizon behind them. "What do you make of that, Elric?"

Elric peered at the horizon, but could see nothing. Often his eyes were weak, as now. But the girl said in a voice of quiet despair.

"It is a golden sail."

"You recognize it?" Elric asked her.

"Oh, indeed I do. It is the galleon of Earl Saxif D'Aan. He has found us. Perhaps he was lying in wait along our route, knowing we must come this way."

"How far are we from the Gate?"

"I am not sure."

At that moment, there came a terrible noise from below, as if something sought to stave in the timbers of the ship.

"It's in the forward hatches!" cried Smiorgan. "See what it is, friend Elric! But take care, man!"

Cautiously Elric prized back one of the hatch covers and peered into the murky fastness of the hold. The noise of stamping and thumping continued and, as his eyes adjusted to the light, he saw the source.

The white horse was there. It whinnied as it saw him, almost in greeting.

"How did it come aboard?" Elric asked. "I saw nothing. I heard nothing."

The girl was almost as white as Elric. She sank to her knees beside the hatch, burying her face in her arms.

"He has us! He has us!"

"There is still a chance we can reach the Crimson Gate in time," Elric reassured her. "And once in my own world, why I can work much stronger sorcery to protect us."

"No," she sobbed, "it is too late. Why else would the white horse be here. He knows that Saxif D'Aan must soon board us."

"He'll have to fight us before he shall have you," Elric promised her.

"You have not seen his men. Cutthroats all. Desperate and wolfish! They'll show you no mercy. You would be best advised to hand me over to Saxif D'Aan at once and save yourselves. You'll gain nothing from trying to protect me. But I'd ask you a favor."

"What's that?"

"Find me a small knife to carry, that I may kill myself as soon as I know you two are safe."

Elric laughed, dragging her to her feet. "I'll have no such melodramatics from you, lass! We stand together. Perhaps we can bargain with Saxif D'Aan."

"What have you to barter?"

"Very little. But he is not aware of that."

"He can read your thoughts, seemingly. He has great powers!"

"I am Elric of Melniboné. I am said to possess a certain facility in the sorcerous arts, myself."

"But you are not as single-minded as Saxif D'Aan," she said simply. "Only one thing obsesses him—the need to make me his consort."

"Many girls would be flattered by the attention—glad to be an Empress with a Melnibonéan Emperor for a husband." Elric was sardonic.

She ignored his tone. "That is why I fear him so," she said in a murmur. "If I lost my determination for a moment, I could love him. I should be destroyed! It is what *she* must have known!"

5

The gleaming galleon, sails and sides all gilded so that it seemed the sun itself pursued them, moved rapidly upon them while the girl and Count Smiorgan watched aghast and Elric desperately attempted to recall his elemental allies, without success.

Through the pale blue light the golden ship sailed relentlessly in their wake. Its proportions were monstrous, its sense of power vast, its gigantic prow sending up huge, foamy waves on both sides as it sped silently towards them.

With the look of a man preparing himself to meet death, Count Smiorgan Baldhead of the Purple Towns unslung his battle-ax and loosened his sword in its scabbard, setting his little metal cap upon his bald pate. The girl made no sound, no movement at all, but she wept.

Elric shook his head and his long, milk-white hair formed a halo around his face for a moment. His moody, crimson eyes began to focus on the world around him. He recognized the ship; it was of a pat-

tern with the golden battle-barges of Melniboné—
doubtless the ship in which Earl Saxif D'Aan had fled
his homeland, searching for the Crimson Gate. Now
Elric was convinced that this must be that same Saxif
D'Aan and he knew less fear than did his companions,
but considerably greater curiosity. Indeed, it was almost
with nostalgia that he noted the ball of fire, like a
natural comet, glowing with green light, come hissing
and spluttering towards them, flung by the ship's
forward catapult. He half expected to see a great dragon wheeling in the sky overhead, for it was with drag-
ons and gilded battlecraft like these that Melniboné
had once conquered the world.

The fireball fell into the sea a few inches from their
bow and was evidently placed there deliberately, as a
warning.

"Don't stop!" cried Vassliss. "Let the flames slay us!
It will be better!"

Smiorgan was looking upwards. "We have no choice.
Look! He has banished the wind, it seems."

They were becalmed. Elric smiled a grim smile. He
knew now what the folk of the Young Kingdoms must
have felt when his ancestors had used these identical
tactics against them.

"Elric?" Smiorgan turned to the albino. "Are these
your people? That ship's Melnibonéan without question!"

"So are the methods," Elric told him. "I am of the
blood royal of Melniboné. I could be Emperor, even
now, if I chose to claim my throne. There is some
small chance that Earl Saxif D'Aan, though an ancestor,
will recognize me and, therefore, recognize my authority. We are a conservative people, the folk of the
Dragon Isle."

The girl spoke through dry lips, hopelessly: "He

recognizes only the authority of the Lords of Chaos, who give him aid."

"All Melnibonéans recognize that authority," Elric told her with a certain humor.

From the forward hatch, the sound of the stallion's stamping and snorting increased.

"We're besieged by enchantments!" Count Smiorgan's normally ruddy features had paled. "Have you none of your own, Prince Elric, you can use to counter them?"

"None, it seems."

The golden ship loomed over them. Elric saw that the rails, high overhead, were crowded not with Imrryrian warriors but with cutthroats equally as desperate as those he had fought upon the island, and, apparently, drawn from the same variety of historical periods and nations. The galleon's long sweeps scraped the sides of the smaller vessel as they folded, like the legs of some water insect, to enable the grappling irons to be flung out. Iron claws bit into the timbers of the little ship and the brigandly crowd overhead cheered, grinning at them, menacing them with their weapons.

The girl began to run to the seaward side of the ship, but Elric caught her by the arm.

"Do not stop me, I beg you!" she cried. "Rather, jump with me and drown!"

"You think that death will save you from Saxif D'Aan?" Elric said. "If he has the power you say, death will only bring you more firmly into his grasp!"

"Oh!" The girl shuddered and then, as a voice called down to them from one of the tall decks of the gilded ship, she gave a moan and fainted into Elric's arms, so that, weakened as he was by his spell-working, it was all that he could do to stop himself falling with her to the deck.

The voice rose over the coarse shouts and guffaws of the crew. It was pure, lilting and sardonic. It was the voice of a Melnibonéan, though it spoke the common tongue of the Young Kingdoms, a corruption, in itself, of the speech of the Bright Empire.

"May I have the captain's permission to come aboard?"

Count Smiorgan growled back: "You have us firm, sir! Don't try to disguise an act of piracy with a polite speech!"

"I take it I have your permission then." The unseen speaker's tone remained exactly the same.

Elric watched as part of the rail was drawn back to allow a gangplank, studded with golden nails to give firmer footing, to be lowered from the galleon's deck to theirs.

A tall figure appeared at the top of the gangplank. He had the fine features of a Melnibonéan nobleman, was thin, proud in his bearing, clad in voluminous robes of cloth-of-gold, an elaborate helmet in gold and ebony upon his long, auburn locks. He had gray-blue eyes, pale, slightly flushed skin, and he carried, so far as Elric could see, no weapons of any kind.

With considerable dignity, Earl Saxif D'Aan began to descend, his rascals at his back. The contrast between this beautiful intellectual and those he commanded was remarkable. Where he walked with straight back, elegant and noble, they slouched, filthy, degenerate, unintelligent, grinning with pleasure at their easy victory. Not a man amongst them showed any sign of human dignity; each was overdressed in tattered and unclean finery, each had at least three weapons upon his person, and there was much evidence of looted jewelry, of noserings, earrings, bangles, necklaces, toe- and finger-rings, pendants, cloak-pins and the like.

"Gods!" murmured Smiorgan. "I've rarely seen such a collection of scum, and I thought I'd encountered most kinds in my voyages. How can such a man bear to be in their company?"

"Perhaps it suits his sense of irony," Elric suggested.

Earl Saxif D'Aan reached their deck and stood looking up at them to where they still positioned themselves, in the poop. He gave a slight bow. His features were controlled and only his eyes suggested something of the intensity of emotion dwelling within him, particularly as they fell upon the girl in Elric's arms.

"I am Earl Saxif D'Aan of Melniboné, now of the Islands Beyond the Crimson Gate. You have something with you which is mine. I would claim it from you."

"You mean the Lady Vassliss of Jharkor?" Elric said, his voice as steady as Saxif D'Aan's.

Saxif D'Aan seemed to note Elric for the first time. A slight frown crossed his brow and was quickly dismissed. "She is mine," he said. "You may be assured that she will come to no harm at my hands."

Elric, seeking some advantage, knew that he risked much when he next spoke, in the High Tongue of Melniboné, used between those of the blood royal. "Knowledge of your history does not reassure me, Saxif D'Aan."

Almost imperceptibly, the golden man stiffened and fire flared in his gray-blue eyes. "Who are you, to speak the Tongue of Kings? Who are you, who claims knowledge of my past?"

"I am Elric, son of Sadric, and I am the four-hundred-and-twenty-eighth Emperor of the folk of R'lin K'ren A'a, who landed upon the Dragon Isle ten thousand years ago. I am Elric, your Emperor, Earl Saxif D'Aan, and I demand your fealty." And Elric held up his right hand, upon which still gleamed a ring set with a single Actorios stone, the Ring of Kings.

Earl Saxif D'Aan now had firm control of himself again. He gave no sign that he was impressed. "Your sovereignty does not extend beyond your own world, noble emperor, though I greet you as a fellow monarch." He spread his arms so that his long sleeves rustled. "This world is mine. All that exists beneath the blue sun do I rule. You trespass, therefore, in my domain. I have every right to do as I please."

"Pirate pomp," muttered Count Smiorgan, who had understood nothing of the conversation but had gathered something of what passed by the tone. "Pirate braggadocio. What does he say, Elric?"

"He convinces me that he is not, in your sense, a pirate, Count Smiorgan. He claims that he is ruler of this plane. Since there is apparently no other, we must accept his claim."

"Gods! Then let him behave like a monarch and let us sail safely out of his waters!"

"We may—if we give him the girl."

Count Smiorgan shook his head. "I'll not do that. She's my passenger, in my charge. I must die rather than do that. It is the Code of the Sealords of the Purple Towns."

"You are famous for your adherence to that Code," Elric said. "As for myself, I have taken this girl into my protection and, as hereditary emperor of Melniboné, I cannot allow myself to be browbeaten."

They had conversed in a murmur, but, somehow, Earl Saxif D'Aan had heard them.

"I must let you know," he said evenly, in the common tongue, "that the girl is mine. You steal her from me. Is that the action of an Emperor?"

"She is not a slave," Elric said, "but the daughter of a free merchant in Jharkor. You have no rights upon her."

Earl Saxif D'Aan said: "Then I cannot open the Crimson Gate for you. You must remain in my world forever."

"You have closed the gate? Is it possible?"

"To me."

"Do you know that the girl would rather die than be captured by you, Earl Saxif D'Aan? Does it give you pleasure to instill such fear?"

The golden man looked directly into Elric's eyes as if he made some cryptic challenge. "The gift of pain has ever been a favorite gift amongst our folk, has it not? Yet it is another gift I offer her. She calls herself Vassliss of Jharkor, but she does not know herself. I know her. She is Gratyesha, Princess of Fwem-Omeyo, and I would make her my bride."

"How can it be that she does not know her own name?"

"She is reincarnated—soul and flesh are identical— that is how I know. And I have waited, Emperor of Melniboné, for many scores of years for her. Now I shall not be cheated of her."

"As you cheated yourself, two centuries past, in Melniboné?"

"You risk much with your directness of language, brother monarch!" There was a hint of a warning in Saxif D'Aan's tone, a warning much fiercer than any implied by the words.

"Well," Elric shrugged, "you have more power than we. My sorcery works poorly in your world. Your ruffians outnumber us. It should not be difficult for you to take her from us."

"You must give her to me. Then you may go free, back to your own world and your own time."

Elric smiled. "There is sorcery here. She is no reincarnation. You'd bring your lost love's spirit from the netherworld to inhabit this girl's body. Am I not right? That is why she must be given freely, or your sorcery will rebound upon you—or might—and you would not take the risk."

Earl Saxif D'Aan turned his head away so that Elric might not see his eyes. "She is the girl," he said, in the High Tongue. "I know that she is. I mean her soul no harm. I would merely give it back its memory."

"Then it is stalemate," said Elric.

"Have you no loyalty to a brother of the royal blood?" Saxif D'Aan murmured, still refusing to look at Elric.

"You claimed no such loyalty, as I recall, Earl Saxif D'Aan. If you accept me as your emperor, then you must accept my decisions. I keep the girl in my custody. Or you must take her by force."

"I am too proud."

"Such pride shall ever destroy love," said Elric, almost in sympathy. "What now, King of Limbo? What shall you do with us?"

Earl Saxif D'Aan lifted his noble head, about to reply, when from the hold the stamping and the snorting began again. His eyes widened. He looked questioningly at Elric, and there was something close to terror in his face.

"What's that? What have you in the hold?"

"A mount, my lord, that is all," said Elric equably.

"A horse? An ordinary horse?"

"A white one. A stallion, with bridle and saddle. It has no rider."

At once Saxif D'Aan's voice rose as he shouted orders for his men. "Take those three aboard our ship. This one shall be sunk directly. Hurry! Hurry!"

Elric and Smiorgan shook off the hands which sought to seize them and they moved towards the gangplank, carrying the girl between them, while Smiorgan muttered: "At least we are not slain, Elric. But what becomes of us now?"

Elric shook his head. "We must hope that we can continue to use Earl Saxif D'Aan's pride against him, to our advantage, though the gods alone know how we shall resolve the dilemma."

Earl Saxif D'Aan was already hurrying up the gangplank ahead of them.

"Quickly," he shouted. "Raise the plank!"

They stood upon the decks of the golden battle-barge and watched as the gangplank was drawn up, the length of rail replaced.

"Bring up the catapults," Saxif D'Aan commanded. "Use lead. Sink that vessel at once!"

The noise from the forward hold increased. The horse's voice echoed over ships and water. Hooves smashed at timber and then, suddenly, it came crashing through the hatch-covers, scrambling for purchase on the deck with its front hooves, and then standing there, pawing at the planks, its neck arching, its nostrils dilating and its eyes glaring, as if ready to do battle.

Now Saxif D'Aan made no attempt to hide the terror on his face. His voice rose to a scream as he threatened his rascals with every sort of horror if they did not obey him with utmost speed. The catapults were dragged up and huge globes of lead were lobbed onto the decks of Smiorgan's ship, smashing through the planks like arrows through parchment so that almost immediately the ship began to sink.

"Cut the grappling hooks!" cried Saxif D'Aan, wrenching a blade from the hand of one of his men and sawing at the nearest rope. "Cast loose—quickly!"

Even as Smiorgan's ship groaned and roared like a drowning beast, the ropes were cut. The ship keeled over at once, and the horse disappeared.

"Turn about!" shouted Saxif D'Aan. "Back to Fhaligarn and swiftly, or your souls shall feed my fiercest demons!"

There came a peculiar, high-pitched neighing from the foaming water, as Smiorgan's ship, stern uppermost, gasped and was swallowed. Elric caught a glimpse of the white stallion, swimming strongly.

"Go below!" Saxif D'Aan ordered, indicating a hatchway. "The horse can smell the girl and thus is doubly difficult to lose."

"Why do you fear it?" Elric asked. "It is only a horse. It cannot harm you."

Saxif D'Aan uttered a laugh of profound bitterness. "Can it not, brother monarch? Can it not?"

As they carried the girl below, Elric was frowning, remembering a little more of the legend of Saxif D'Aan, of the girl he had punished so cruelly, and of her lover, Prince Carolak. The last he heard of Saxif D'Aan was the sorcerer crying:

"More sail! More sail!"

And then the hatch had closed behind them and they found themselves in an opulent Melnibonéan day-cabin, full of rich hangings, precious metal, decorations of exquisite beauty and, to Count Smiorgan, disturbing decadence. But it was Elric, as he lowered the girl to a couch, who noticed the smell.

"Augh! It's the smell of a tomb—of damp and mold.

Yet nothing rots. It is passing peculiar, friend Smiorgan, is it not?"

"I scarcely noticed, Elric." Smiorgan's voice was hollow. "But I would agree with you on one thing. We are entombed. I doubt we'll live to escape this world now."

6

An hour had passed since they had been forced aboard. The door had been locked behind them and, it seemed, Saxif D'Aan was too preoccupied with escaping the white stallion to bother with them. Peering through the lattice of a porthole, Elric could look back to where their ship had been sunk. They were many leagues distant, already, yet he still thought, from time to time, that he saw the head and shoulders of the stallion above the waves.

Vassliss had recovered and sat pale and shivering upon the couch.

"What more do you know of that horse?" Elric asked her. "It would be helpful to me if you could recall anything you have heard."

She shook her head. "Saxif D'Aan spoke little of it, but I gather he fears the rider more than he does the horse."

"Ah!" Elric frowned. "I suspected it! Have you ever seen the rider?"

"Never. I think that Saxif D'Aan has never seen him, either. I think he believes himself doomed if that rider should ever sit upon the white stallion."

Elric smiled to himself.

"Why do you ask so much about the horse?" Smiorgan wished to know.

Elric shook his head. "I have an instinct, that is all. Half a memory. But I'll say nothing and think as little as I may, for there is no doubt Saxif D'Aan, as Vassliss suggests, has some power of reading the mind."

They heard a footfall above, descending to their door. A bolt was drawn and Saxif D'Aan, his composure fully restored, stood in the opening, his hands in his golden sleeves.

"You will forgive, I hope, the peremptory way in which I sent you here. There was danger which had to be averted at all costs. As a result, my manners were not all that they should have been."

"Danger to us?" Elric asked. "Or to you, Earl Saxif D'Aan."

"In the circumstances, to all of us, I assure you."

"Who rides the horse?" Smiorgan asked bluntly. "And why do you fear him?"

Earl Saxif D'Aan was master of himself again, so there was no sign of a reaction. "That is very much my private concern," he said softly. "Will you dine with me now?"

The girl made a noise in her throat and Earl Saxif D'Aan turned piercing eyes upon her. "Gratyesha, you will want to cleanse yourself and make yourself beautiful again. I will see that facilities are placed at your disposal."

"I am not Gratyesha," she said. "I am Vassliss, the merchant's daughter."

"You will remember," he said. "In time, you will remember." There was such certainty, such obsessive power in his voice that even Elric experienced a frisson of awe. "The things will be brought to you, and you may use this cabin as your own until we return to my palace on Fhaligarn. My lords . . ." he indicated that they should leave.

Elric said: "I'll not leave her, Saxif D'Aan. She is too afraid."

"She fears only the truth, brother."

"She fears you and your madness."

Saxif D'Aan shrugged insouciantly. "I shall leave first then. If you would accompany me, my lords . . ." He strode from the cabin and they followed.

Elric said, over his shoulder: "Vassliss, you may depend upon my protection." And he closed the cabin doors behind him.

Earl Saxif D'Aan was standing upon the deck, exposing his noble face to the spray which was flung up by the ship as it moved with supernatural speed through the sea.

"You called me mad, Prince Elric? Yet you must be versed in sorcery, yourself?"

"Of course. I am of the blood royal. I am reckoned knowledgeable in my own world."

"But here? How well does your sorcery work?"

"Poorly, I'll admit. The spaces between the planes seems greater."

"Exactly. But I have bridged them. I have had time to learn how to bridge them."

"You are saying that you are more powerful than am I?"

"It is a fact, is it not?"

"It is. But I did not think we were about to indulge in sorcerous battles, Earl Saxif D'Aan."

"Of course. Yet, if you were to think of besting me by sorcery, you would think twice, eh?"

"I should be foolish to contemplate such a thing at all. It could cost me my soul. My life, at least."

"True. You are a realist, I see."

"I suppose so."

"Then we can progress on simpler lines, to settle the dispute between us."

"You propose a duel?" Elric was surprised.

Earl Saxif D'Aan's laughter was light. "Of course not—against your sword? That has power in all worlds, though the magnitude varies."

"I am glad that you are aware of that," Elric said significantly.

"Besides," added Earl Saxif D'Aan, his golden robes rustling as he moved a little nearer to the rail, "you would not kill me—for only I have the means of your escaping this world."

"Perhaps we'd elect to remain," said Elric.

"Then you would be my subjects. But, no—you would not like it here. I am self-exiled. I could not return to my own world now, even if I wished to do so. It has cost me much, my knowledge. But I would found a dynasty here, beneath the blue sun. I must have my wife, Prince Elric. I must have Gratyesha."

"Her name is Vassliss," said Elric obstinately.

"She thinks it is."

"Then it is. I have sworn to protect her, as has Count Smiorgan. Protect her we shall. You will have to kill us all."

"Exactly," said Earl Saxif D'Aan with the air of a man who has been coaching a poor student towards the correct answer to a problem. "Exactly. I shall have to kill you all. You leave me with little alternative, Prince Elric."

"Would that benefit you?"

"It would. It would put a certain powerful demon at my service for a few hours."

"We should resist."

"I have many men. I do not value them. Eventually, they would overwhelm you. Would they not?"

Elric remained silent.

"My men would be aided by sorcery," added Saxif D'Aan. "Some would die, but not too many, I think."

Elric was looking beyond Saxif D'Aan, staring out to sea. He was sure that the horse still followed. He was sure that Saxif D'Aan knew, also.

"And if we gave up the girl?"

"I should open the Crimson Gate for you. You would be honored guests. I should see that you were borne safely through, even taken safely to some hospitable land in your own world, for even if you passed through the gate there would be danger. The storms."

Elric appeared to deliberate.

"You have only a little time to make your decision, Prince Elric. I had hoped to reach my palace, Fhaligarn, by now. I shall not allow you very much longer. Come, make your decision. You know I speak the truth."

"You know that I can work some sorcery in your world, do you not?"

"You summoned a few friendly elementals to your aid, I know. But at what cost? Would you challenge me directly?"

"It would be unwise of me," said Elric.

Smiorgan was tugging at his sleeve. "Stop this useless talk. He knows that we have given our word to the girl and that we *must* fight him!"

Earl Saxif D'Aan sighed. There seemed to be genuine sorrow in his voice. "If you are determined to lose your lives . . ." he began.

"I should like to know why you set such importance upon the speed with which we make up our minds," Elric said. "Why cannot we wait until we reach Fhaligarn?"

Earl Saxif D'Aan's expression was calculating, and again he looked full into Elric's crimson eyes. "I think you know," he said, almost inaudibly.

But Elric shook his head. "I think you give me too much credit for intelligence."

"Perhaps."

Elric knew that Saxif D'Aan was attempting to read his thoughts; he deliberately blanked his mind, and suspected that he sensed frustration in the sorcerer's demeanor.

And then the albino had sprung at his kinsman, his hand chopping at Saxif D'Aan's throat. The earl was taken completely off guard. He tried to call out, but his vocal chords were numbed. Another blow, and he fell to the deck, senseless.

"Quickly, Smiorgan," Elric shouted, and he had leapt into the rigging, climbing swiftly upwards to the top yards. Smiorgan, bewildered, followed, and Elric had drawn his sword, even as he reached the crow's nest, driving upwards through the rail so that the lookout was taken in the groin scarcely before he realized it.

Next, Elric was hacking at the ropes holding the mainsail to the yard. Already a number of Saxif D'Aan's ruffians were climbing after them.

The heavy golden sail came loose, falling to envelop the pirates and take several of them down with it.

Elric climbed into the crow's nest and pitched the dead man over the rail in the wake of his comrades. Then he had raised his sword over his head, holding it in his two hands, his eyes blank again, his head raised to the blue sun, and Smiorgan, clinging to the mast below, shuddered as he heard a peculiar crooning come from the albino's throat.

More of the cutthroats were ascending, and Smiorgan hacked at the rigging, having the satisfaction of seeing half a score go flying down to break their bones on the deck below, or be swallowed by the waves.

Earl Saxif D'Aan was beginning to recover, but he was still stunned.

"Fool!" he was crying. "Fool!" But it was not possible to tell if he referred to Elric or to himself.

Elric's voice became a wail, rhythmical and chilling, as he chanted his incantation, and the strength from the man he had killed flowed into him and sustained. His crimson eyes seemed to flicker with fires of another, nameless color, and his whole body shook as the strange runes shaped themselves in a throat which had never been made to speak such sounds.

His voice became a vibrant groan as the incantation continued, and Smiorgan, watching as more of the crew made efforts to climb the mainmast, felt an unearthly cold creep through him.

Earl Saxif D'Aan screamed from below:

"You would not dare!"

The sorcerer began to make passes in the air, his own incantation tumbling from his lips, and Smiorgan gasped as a creature made of smoke took shape only a few feet below him. The creature smacked its lips and grinned and stretched a paw, which became flesh even as it moved, towards Smiorgan. He hacked at the paw with his sword, whimpering.

"Elric!" cried Count Smiorgan, clambering higher so that he grasped the rail of the crow's nest. "Elric! He sends demons against us now!"

But Elric ignored him. His whole mind was in another world, a darker, bleaker world even than this one. Through gray mists, he saw a figure, and he cried a name. "Come!" he called in the ancient tongue of his ancestors. "Come!"

Count Smiorgan cursed as the demon became increasingly substantial. Red fangs clashed and green eyes glared at him. A claw stroked his boot and no matter how much he struck with his sword, the demon did not appear to notice the blows.

There was no room for Smiorgan in the crow's nest, but he stood on the outer rim, shouting with terror, desperate for aid. Still Elric continued to chant.

"Elric! I am doomed!"

The demon's paw grasped Smiorgan by his ankle.

"Elric!"

Thunder rolled out at sea; a ball of lightning appeared for a second and then was gone. From nowhere there came the sound of a horse's hooves pounding, and a human voice shouting in triumph.

Elric sank back against the rail, opening his eyes in time to see Smiorgan being dragged slowly downward. With the last of his strength he flung himself forward, leaning far out to stab downwards with Stormbringer. The runesword sank cleanly into the demon's right eye and it roared, letting go of Smiorgan, striking at the blade which drew its energy from it and, as that energy passed into the blade and thence to Elric, the albino grinned a frightful grin so that, for a second, Smiorgan became more frightened of his friend than he had been of the demon. The demon began to dematerialize, its only means of escape from the sword which drank its life force, but more of Saxif D'Aan's rogues were behind it, and their blades rattled as they sought the pair.

Elric swung himself back over the rail, balanced precariously on the yard as he slashed at their attackers, yelling the old battle-cries of his people. Smiorgan could do little but watch. He noted that Saxif D'Aan was no longer on deck and he shouted urgently to Elric:

"Elric! Saxif D'Aan. He seeks out the girl."

Elric now took the attack to the pirates, and they were more than anxious to avoid the moaning runesword, some even leaping into the sea rather than encounter it. Swiftly the two leapt from yard to yard until they were again upon the deck.

"What does he fear? Why does he not use more sorcery?" panted Count Smiorgan, as they ran towards the cabin.

"I have summoned the one who rides the horse," Elric told him. "I had so little time—and I could tell you nothing of it, knowing that Saxif D'Aan would read my intention in your mind, if he could not in mine!"

The cabin doors were firmly secured from the inside. Elric began to hack at them with the black sword.

But the door resisted as it should not have resisted. "Sealed by sorcery and I've no means of unsealing it," said the albino.

"Will he kill her?"

"I don't know. He might try to take her into some other plane. We must—"

Hooves clattered on the deck and the white stallion reared behind them, only now it had a rider, clad in bright purple and yellow armor. He was bareheaded and youthful, though there were several old scars upon his face. His hair was thick and curly and blond and his eyes were a deep blue.

He drew tightly upon his reins, steadying the horse. He looked piercingly at Elric. "Was it you, Melnibonéan, who opened the pathway for me?"

"It was."

"Then I thank you, though I cannot repay you."

"You have repaid me," Elric told him, then drew Smiorgan aside as the rider leaned forward and spurred his horse directly at the closed doors, smashing through as though they were rotted cotton.

There came a terrible cry from within and then

Earl Saxif D'Aan, hampered by his complicated robes of gold, rushed from the cabin, seizing a sword from the hand of the nearest corpse, darting Elric a look not so much of hatred but of bewildered agony, as he turned to face the blond rider.

The rider had dismounted now and came from the cabin, one arm around the shivering girl, Vassliss, one hand upon the reins of his horse, and he said, sorrowfully:

"You did me a great wrong, Earl Saxif D'Aan, but you did Gratyesha an infinitely more terrible one. Now you must pay."

Saxif D'Aan paused, drawing a deep breath, and when he looked up again, his eyes were steady, his dignity had returned.

"Must I pay in full?" he said.

"In full."

"It is all I deserve," said Saxif D'Aan. "I escaped my doom for many years, but I could not escape the knowledge of my crime. She loved me, you know. Not you."

"She loved us both, I think. But the love she gave you was her entire soul and I should not want that from any woman."

"You would be the loser, then."

"You never knew how much she loved you."

"Only—only afterwards . . ."

"I pity you, Earl Saxif D'Aan." The young man gave the reins of his horse to the girl, and he drew his sword. "We are strange rivals, are we not?"

"You have been all these years in Limbo, where I banished you—in that garden on Melniboné?"

"All these years. Only my horse could follow you. The horse of Tendric, my father, also of Melniboné, and also a sorcerer."

"If I had known that, then, I'd have slain you cleanly and sent the horse to Limbo."

"Jealousy weakened you, Earl Saxif D'Aan. But now we fight as we should have fought then—man to man, with steel, for the hand of the one who loves us both. It is more than you deserve."

"Much more," agreed the sorcerer. And he brought up his sword to lunge at the young man who, Smiorgan guessed, could only be Prince Carolak himself.

The fight was predetermined. Saxif D'Aan knew that, if Carolak did not. Saxif D'Aan's skill in arms was up to the standard of any Melnibonéan nobleman, but it could not match the skill of a professional soldier, who had fought for his life time after time.

Back and forth across the deck, while Saxif D'Aan's rascals looked on in open-mouthed astonishment, the rivals fought a duel which should have been fought and resolved two centuries before, while the girl they both plainly thought was the reincarnation of Gratyesha watched them with as much concern as might her original have watched when Saxif D'Aan first encountered Prince Carolak in the gardens of his palace, so long ago.

Saxif D'Aan fought well, and Carolak fought nobly, for on many occasions he avoided an obvious advantage, but at length Saxif D'Aan threw away his sword, crying: "Enough. I'll give you your vengeance, Prince Carolak. I'll let you take the girl. But you'll not give me your damned mercy—you'll not take my pride."

And Carolak nodded, stepped forward, and struck straight for Saxif D'Aan's heart.

The blade entered clean and Earl Saxif D'Aan should have died, but he did not. He crawled along the deck until he reached the base of the mast, and he rested his back against it, while the blood pumped from the wounded heart. And he smiled.

"It appears," he said faintly, "that I cannot die, so long have I sustained my life by sorcery. I am no longer a man."

He did not seem pleased by this thought, but Prince Carolak, stepping forward and leaning over him, reassured him. "You will die," he promised, "soon."

"What will you do with her—with Gratyesha."

"Her name is Vassliss," said Count Smiorgan insistently. "She is a merchant's daughter, from Jharkor."

"She must make up her own mind," Carolak said, ignoring Smiorgan.

Earl Saxif D'Aan turned glazed eyes on Elric. "I must thank you," he said. "You brought me the one who could bring me peace, though I feared him."

"Is that why, I wonder, your sorcery was so weak against me," Elric said. "Because you wished Carolak to come and release you from your guilt."

"Possibly, Elric. You are wiser in some matters, it seems, than am I."

"What of the Crimson Gate?" Smiorgan growled. "Can that be opened? Have you still the power, Earl Saxif D'Aan?"

"I think so." From the folds of his bloodstained garments of gold, the sorcerer produced a large crystal which shone with the deep colors of a ruby. "This will not only lead you to the gate, it will enable you to pass through, only I must warn you . . ." Saxif D'Aan began to cough. "The ship—" he gasped, "the ship—like my body—has been sustained by means of sorcery—therefore . . ." His head slumped forward. He raised it with a huge effort and stared beyond them at the girl who still held the reins of the white stallion.

"Farewell, Gratyesha, Princess of Fwem-Omeyo. I loved you." The eyes remained fixed upon her, but they were dead eyes now.

Carolak turned back to look at the girl. "How do you call yourself, Gratyesha?"

"They call me Vassliss," she told him. She smiled up into his youthful, battle-scarred face. "That is what they call me, Prince Carolak."

"You know who I am?"

"I know you now."

"Will you come with me, Gratyesha? Will you be my bride, at last, in the strange new lands I have found, beyond the world?"

"I will come," she said.

He helped her up into the saddle of his white stallion and climbed so that he sat behind her. He bowed to Elric of Melniboné. "I thank you again, Sir Sorcerer, though I never thought to be helped by one of the royal blood of Melniboné."

Elric's expression was not without humor. "In Melniboné," he said, "I'm told it's tainted blood."

"Tainted with mercy, perhaps."

"Perhaps."

Prince Carolak saluted them. "I hope you find peace, Prince Elric, as I have found it."

"I fear my peace will more resemble that which Saxif D'Aan found," Elric said grimly. "Nonetheless, I thank you for your good words, Prince Carolak."

Then Carolak, laughing, had ridden his horse for the rail, leapt it, and vanished.

There was a silence upon the ship. The remaining ruffians looked uncertainly, one to the other. Elric addressed them:

"Know you this—I have the key to the Crimson Gate—and only I have the knowledge to use it. Help me sail the ship, and you'll have freedom from this world! What say you?"

"Give us our orders, captain," said a toothless individual, and he cackled with mirth. "It's the best offer we've had in a hundred years or more!"

7

It was Smiorgan who first saw the Crimson Gate. He held the great red gem in his hand and pointed ahead.

"There! There, Elric! Saxif D'Aan has not betrayed us!"

The sea had begun to heave with huge, turbulent waves and, with the mainsail still tangled upon the deck, it was all that the crew could do to control the ship, but the chance of escape from the world of the blue sun made them work with every ounce of energy and, slowly, the golden battle-barge neared the towering crimson pillars.

The pillars rose from the gray, roaring water, casting a peculiar light upon the crests of the waves. They appeared to have little substance, and yet stood firm against the battering of the tons of water lashing around them.

"Let us hope they are wider apart than they look," said Elric. "It would be a hard enough task steering through them in calm waters, let alone this kind of sea."

"I'd best take the wheel, I think," said Count Smiorgan, handing Elric the gem, and he strode back up the tilting deck, climbing to the covered wheelhouse and relieving the frightened man who stood there.

There was nothing Elric could do but watch as Smiorgan turned the huge vessel into the waves, riding the tops as best he could, but sometimes descending with a rush which made Elric's heart rise to his mouth. All around them, then, the cliffs of water threatened, but the ship was taking another wave before the main force of water could crash onto her decks. For all this, Elric was quickly soaked through and, though sense told him he would be best below, he clung to the rail, watching as Smiorgan steered the ship with uncanny sureness towards the Crimson Gate.

And then the deck was flooded with red light and Elric was half blinded. Gray water flew everywhere; there came a dreadful scraping sound, then a snapping as oars broke against the pillars. The ship shuddered and began to turn, sideways to the wind, but Smiorgan forced her round and suddenly the quality of the light changed subtly, though the sea remained as turbulent as ever and Elric knew, deep within him, that overhead, beyond the heavy clouds, a yellow sun was burning again.

But now there came a creaking and a crashing from within the bowels of the battle-barge. The smell of mold, which Elric had noted earlier, became stronger, almost overpowering.

Smiorgan came hurrying back, having handed over the wheel. His face was pale again. "She's breaking up, Elric," he called out, over the noise of the wind and the waves. He staggered as a huge wall of water struck the ship and snatched away several planks from the deck. "She's falling apart, man!"

"Saxif D'Aan tried to warn us of this!" Elric shouted back. "As he was kept alive by sorcery, so was his ship. She was old before he sailed her to that world. While there, the sorcery which sustained her remained strong—but on this plane it has no power at all. Look!" And he pulled at a piece of the rail, crumbling the rot-

ten wood with his fingers. "We must find a length of
timber which is still good."

At that moment a yard came crashing from the mast
and struck the deck, bouncing, then rolling towards
them.

Elric crawled up the sloping deck until he could
grasp the spar and test it. "This one's still good. Use
your belt or whatever else you can and tie yourself to
it!"

The wind wailed through the disintegrating rigging
of the ship; the sea smashed at the sides, driving great
holes below the waterline.

The ruffians who had crewed her were in a state of
complete panic, some trying to unship small boats
which crumbled even as they swung them out, others
lying flat against the rotted decks and praying to whatever gods they still worshipped.

Elric strapped himself to the broken yard as firmly
as he could and Smiorgan followed his example. The
next wave to hit the ship full-on lifted them with it,
cleanly over what remained of the rail and into the
chilling, shouting waters of that terrible sea.

Elric kept his mouth tight shut against swallowing
too much water and reflected on the irony of his situation. It seemed that, having escaped so much, he was
to die a very ordinary death, by drowning.

It was not long before his senses left him and he
gave himself up to the swirling and somehow friendly
waters of the ocean.

He awoke, struggling.

There were hands upon him. He strove to fight them
off, but he was too weak. Someone laughed, a rough,
good-humored sound.

The water no longer roared and crashed around him.

The wind no longer howled. Instead there was a gentler movement. He heard waves lapping against timber. He was aboard another ship.

He opened his eyes, blinking in warm, yellow sunlight. Red-cheeked Vilmirian sailors grinned down at him. "You're a lucky man—if man you be!" said one.

"My friend?" Elric sought for Smiorgan.

"He was in better shape than were you. He's down in Duke Avan's cabin now."

"Duke Avan?" Elric knew the name but, in his dazed condition, could remember nothing to help him place the man. "You saved us?"

"Aye. We found you both drifting, tied to a broken yard carved with the strangest designs I've ever seen. A Melnibonéan craft, was she?"

"Yes, but rather old."

And with a smile, more tranquil than most, he fell back into his slumbers.